A Vampire Story

Susan Shepherd

ISBN-10:0692441697
ISBN-13:9780692441695

PART ONE

One

Nikolai Larobya Vasilyevich stood under the sallow glow of a lone street lamp in the fog-shrouded moonlight, his colossal shoulders resting indifferently against the fissured bark of a diseased maple. It was his habit to lean his massive form against any object large enough to bear the weight of a man his size, although he weighed almost nothing. On occasion, just for effect, he would forgo this rule and allow himself to teeter eerily against a less substantial thing. He liked to tease his victims when he could, and he never grew tired of a good joke. He had, he believed, a superior sense of humor.

Nikolai Larobya was not, nevertheless, in good humor this evening. Under the awning of a pair of jet brows, his vermilion eyes glittered with devilment. He had come a great distance, and though not fatigued by his journey, he was restless to get on with

1

his purpose. He had waited long for this moment, for the day this victim needed him, and his patience was at an end.

He was standing now at the head of a narrow bluestone drive, at the far end of which sat a tiny, coffee-colored cottage. The little bungalow's asphalt shingles caught the moonlight and shimmered, and from the tops of the neatly trimmed shrubbery at its foundation, pointed shadows extended across the front lawn toward him. On the open front porch a white wicker rocker creaked in the May breeze, as if expecting company. Nikolai Larobya caught the cool night mist up into his dead lungs and exhaled an even cooler dew. Across the lawn a rabbit scooted over the silver grass, leaving tracks that for Nikolai, seemed to glow with the heat of its pass. A Siamese slipped from beneath the shrubbery to pursue it at an uncertain trot.

HERE KITTY, thought the vampire, and the cat turned its cobalt eyes at him and flicked its ears. COME KITTY, KITTY. "Come to papa," he said, speaking this last. He stooped to pick the animal up, then stroked its white bib gently until it purred.

"Nice kitty," he murmured, nuzzling the short fur between the little beast's ears with the tip of his nose. The cat purred aloud.

With a single, uninterrupted motion he palmed the cat's head and snatched its throat into his fangs. The cat squirmed, gyrating like a toy as the vampire fed, his brilliant eyes now vacant and unseeing.

When he was finished he tossed the limp little body into a neighboring yard and wiped his lips. "Pah," he said, pulling a tuft of tawny fur from his tongue. Brushing the lapels of his greatcoat he smoothed his black mane of hair back from his noble forehead and started for the house.

Inside the little cottage, Valarie Rossetti awoke with a start.

"Timmons," she said, and she rolled over to reach for the Chinese lamp on her nightstand. Moonlight poured into her bedroom from her eastern window, and the orange glow of the little lamp could not compete with it. She turned it off and sat up, raking her fingers through her hair as she listened to the stillness.

"Pssst. Timmy. Here Tim." She spoke softly into the dark, a habit formed during the short months of her marriage to a light sleeper. It was yet another habit she hadn't bothered to break in five years of widowhood.

"Damn. I must have forgotten to let you in last night, Timmy."

She lifted her digital alarm from the nightstand and examined the glowing red display. It was 3:33 a.m. She was all alone in the dark at the creepiest hour of the night, and the house was as silent as a corpse and Timmons was outside dodging drunk drivers, or maybe smattered on the road already in front of Edna's house. She hated the dark. Hated sleeping alone. Hated having to get out from under her sheets to wander around the house opening doors for the cat. Someone might be waiting outside for just that, some deranged criminal, lurking on her porch, Timmons under his arm, waiting for her to realize her cat was missing and open the front door. Or maybe she'd bump into a ghost. She knew they were here. She was sure her grandmother's ghost was standing in the hall even now, all 4'8' of her, her hands on her hips, her mouth pursed in a permanent frown of consternation.

Valarie sighed. She needed to get up and go find the cat, but without Claude beside her, she couldn't even muster the courage to get out from under the covers.

Claude.

At 22, before she knew her own course in life, Valarie Lorraine had married a West Point graduate with his eye on a long and successful military career. Within the space of a year she was widowed. Her husband was not honored by a hero's death. Neither on foreign soil nor dressed for battle, he had been a victim of a drunk driver in a stolen Karmann Ghia.

From the moment they had met Valarie had loved Claude Lafayette Rossetti III in a way only those destined for tragedy love. He was her Galahad, her Robin Hood; a noble and pure spirit whose fondest desire was to die in the service of others. His grandfather, a retired colonel and veteran of two world wars, had instilled in him a rare sense of duty to country that was, by Claude's day, understood by few and regarded with suspicion by most. A French immigrant who had come to the United States

4

during World War I to escape starvation, the first Claude Lafayette Rossetti had enlisted into the U.S. Army at the age of seventeen under an assumed name. It was not until he earned a Distinguished Service Cross that the error was duly noted and corrected. Claude II was less enthusiastic about war. He served in Korea and Vietnam, after which he studiously encouraged his son to be a doctor, an engineer, even a tradesman. But Claude had his grandfather's idealism. He chose instead, West Point.

Claude loved his country in a time when doing so was deviant, and had planned to devote his life to its safety. Instead, he lost his life in a moment of utter banality.

After the funeral, Valarie continued to live in the little cottage her grandmother had willed to her, the house she and Claude shared during their single year of marriage. But the house was full of ghosts for Valarie, and of apparitions of lovemaking in an undersized bed with the boy who had, so full of life and spirit, shaken her soul. A boy whose body now lay decaying in a military cemetery somewhere in Calverton.

Shuddering now in the empty bed, Valarie pulled her knees up to her chest and wrapped her sheets around them, cocooning herself in bedclothes. A noise, quick and fairy-light, rattled against her parlor window, like a dry leaf scuttling across macadam. It was not the cat, she was sure of it. It was the tap of fingernails against the parlor window. Someone was on her porch at 3:33 in the morning, and that someone expected to be invited in.

5

She chased an image of her Vice Principal, Gary Reynolds, from her mind. Gary had been hounding her for a date since she started subbing at the Old Inlet Middle School in January.

"Oh, man," she moaned aloud. "Who the hell is this?"

She pushed herself out of her cocoon and stumbled toward the front of the house. Under the hallway arch she stopped, straining to make out the silhouette that filled her parlor window, blocking the moonlight and darkening the shade.

"Go away," she grumbled, but the shadow on her porch remained, even bent to peer through the slice of darkness between the window frame and the shade, a preternatural glow emanating from its eye and piercing the dark room to probe the interior.

Valarie blinked. "What the devil is that?"

The glow sharpened to form a beam of greenish light that danced across the far wall, zigzagging along the wallpaper to the picture of Christ with Thorns above the mantelpiece.

"Who is it!" she demanded, moving across the room toward the kitchen and the telephone.

The compulsion came upon her like nausea, searing through her body, pulling her forward across the carpet to the front door, drawing her toward the thing that lurked behind it. She felt herself hurled against the frame, her body puppeteered by another's will. She watched, helpless, as her own hand turn the dead bolt and open the door.

6

He sailed into her parlor like a great black ship, his leather duster slapping his long legs, his hair, caught up in a braid, swinging against the black leather of his coat like a monkey's tail. In the dim moonlight his face was alabaster, his eyes, two jade lamps in the window of his face.

"Jesus Christ. Who are you?" Valarie choked, looking up into a face of long, flat planes and tip-tilted eyes, a handsome, otherworldly face that smiled indulgently at her question.

"I am Nikolai Larobya-" he began.

"Larob-y--, what?"

The intruder's dark brows lifted. He tilted his head and chuckled.

"Very well!" he agreed. "Laroby." He made a little bow. "At your service."

Valarie shrank back. A chill rose off his body like mist over an open grave.

"You have called me to you, my dear," he explained, looking about the tidy little room. "And I am here."

"Get out of my house! I didn't--"

"Mais oui, madamoiselle," he said, turning back to her. "You have."

He lifted a resin miniature of The Pieta off the mantelpiece and turned it in his hand. "I never enter uninvited."

"I called the cat," she murmured.

He shrugged. "Think what you like." He set the little statue down precisely where he'd found it. "I am yours."

"No..." She shook her head, less certain. "No, I don't want you..."

But he only laughed, fully attentive of her now, and stroked his chin. "What do you think I am?" he asked her, turning from the fireplace and leaning on his elbow in mid-air.

"Jesus!" she screamed, backing into a wall.

"Hardly."

"I'm dreaming, aren't I. I'm having another one. At least it's not the graveyard dream again. Even this is better than the graveyard dream. Shit, I wish I could wake myself up when this happens."

This he considered.

"Well?" she repeated. "Are you a dream?"

"Dream or devil, eh?" he asked, and he stroked his lips with the tip of his finger, thoughtfully.

"My dear," he said after some deliberation, "This might be more interesting for me if you were less of a little hypocrite. But as it is, perhaps if I were to explain a few basics to you, I might not die of boredom before you die of me."

He paced to the far side of the room and stopped, settling himself, impossibly, on the edge of a long legged antique under the parlor window. To Valarie's amazement the legs of the Martha

Washington neither splintered nor toppled under his weight, but supported him as if he were made of straw.

"I am a vampire," said Laroby. "I have come to steal your soul. To take your life, to empty your veins," he counted out the list on his fingers," to fill myself on your blood. In return," he stood and slipped his huge white hands into the pockets of his duster, "I bring you--" and he lifted his eyebrows and looked about the room for words he wanted, "eternity? Eternity. An eternity without human pains, human weaknesses, human..." he stepped toward her and leaned into her face, "nightmares?"

"You," she reminded him, "are a nightmare."

"You have no idea," he agreed. "Think of the benefits," he went on. "Think of the possibilities. What difference the logistics of the thing. 'Exitus acta probat.'"

He lifted his arms from his sides invitingly.

"What else?" asked Valarie.

"Pardon?" he said.

"What else is there? What about my soul? What happens to me when I die, do I go to Hell?"

"Hell is what you make of it, don't you think?" he quipped.

"What if I resist you?"

He lowered his arms.

"Well," he countered, "that may do for tonight, yes, but," he caught her wrist, turned it, kissed the veins at the base of her palm, "you will not always resist," he said, and disappeared.

9

Two

The digital display on her alarm clock was flashing a steady, uninformed "12:00 a.m." when Valarie opened her eyes to the brilliant daylight four hours later.

She jack-knifed to attention in bed, combing a long lock of chestnut hair back from her forehead as she attempted to comprehend her situation.

She had had another nightmare. That was for certain. Not the usual. Not the night-in-the-graveyard nightmare, the one that had been recurring since Claude's death. In that one she spent the entire night walking the loose stone paths between the old, family plots at the Community Cemetery. All alone, always in the dead of night, she wandered through the graves, desperately trying to recall the way out but never reaching it. The pervasive sense of decay would be all around her, the smell of mould and rot. Sometimes she would see herself, wrapped in a gauzy thing, like a shroud, sometimes she would just move about like the lens of a Steadycam, bodiless. But it was always the same dream. And she couldn't get out, she couldn't leave the dead. It was as if she were attached by some invisible cord or trapped within a wall of confusion that separated her from the living.

But last night was different. Last night she dreamed of an invader, a great, wicked man with a terrible, dead-white face and luminous vermillion eyes. A man who threatened to steal her soul.

She looked back at the blinking red display on the digital. Something else had happened last night, something far more common and explicable. Sometime during the night LILCO had played their little power-cut game, stealing a few seconds of service in the interests of saving "the public" a sum of money only LILCO knew the particulars of and only LILCO would ever spend.

She untangled herself from her sheets and stumbled into the kitchen to check the oven-timer clock, the only timepiece in the house that wouldn't lie to her this morning. It read 7:42 a.m.

The first period study hall she was covering for Mr. Roberge would be in full swing by now, unsupervised. Danny Albrecht would be opening the emergency window or setting off the fire alarm across the hall, or making a fire of his own under Roberge's desk.

Peter Miller would be starting a fight in the boy's room, and Larry Eleazer would be pitching in to help, hoping for a riot.

Her life was over. She'd never sub at the Old Inlet Middle again. The parents of injured children would sue. She'd lose the house. She might even end up in jail for endangering the welfare of children.

The electronic beep of the cordless interrupted her plunge into despair.

"Hey, Rossetti." Paul Brechard sounded winded but amicable. Paul taught Advanced English Lit across the hall from Roberge's study hall, and had been Valarie's Cooperating Teacher during her internship that fall. She sighed with relief.

"You've got it covered, Paul? Give me fifteen minutes,--"

"Make it ten. I'm in the middle of Hamlet, here. My cream-puffs are going to mutiny."

"Ten. I swear. I owe you big time, Brechard."

"I'll take that in trade, shweetheart," Brechard gave her his best Bogart and rang off.

That night Valarie arose at 3:33.a.m.. She walked through the dark house and out onto the front porch, and called for the cat. Then she curled up on the wicker rocker to wait.

When Laroby arrived, it was she who spoke first.

"Timmons has disappeared," she said to him straight away. "And you took him."

Laroby stood at the foot of the steps. Even so, he was eye level with her, making up the difference of the height of the porch with his peculiar stature.

"And what, may I ask, is a timmons?" he responded as he ascended and seated himself across from her on a bench.

"Timmons. My cat. Claude's cat. He's gone. What have you done with him?" she repeated.

Laroby paused, frowning. He looked down at his lap, examined his nails. He lifted his cape into little pleats and arranged them on his knees.

"Cats," he said at last, "irritate me. They see what they shouldn't, and miss what they should. Not unlike you, my dear. Swallowing camels and straining at gnats."

"How dare you use His words," she said.

He looked up from his fussing, raised an eyebrow. "Pah." He made a little wave with his hand.

"He's my only companion," she tried, softening. "I need him."

Laroby pouted.

"I am your companion now," he said. "The cat is, eh, how to say it? 'Far niente.' And that is that." He chuckled at his little joke.

She lunged at him.

"You bastard--" But he was too quick for her. He disappeared from the bench and manifested leaning against the porch rail, where he idly cleaned one index nail with the other.

"You mustn't be so physical, little one, I'm only supernatural." He looked at her absently. "There is a limit to my willpower, you know."

Valarie began to cry.

13

"This is for the cat," he sighed and looked up at the moon. "So now I must compete with a cat."

He stumbled against the rail.

She opened her eyes at him.

"What's wrong with you tonight," she peered at him. "You're...different."

"What of it?" he said.

She took a step toward him, looked into his face and nodded. "You're drunk!" she said, poking his chest with a finger.

He lay his hands against his heart, and swooned.

"Poisoned," he agreed. Then he vanished, reappearing seated in the rocking chair behind her. She turned to find him settled with his elbows on his knees and his head in his hands. He tapped his boots together idly.

"The man I drained tonight was in love." He sighed.

"You drained a man?" she blinked.

He laughed disdainfully.

"Always the innocent, eh? I have told you what I am. How many others before me have you invited in, then blamed for your own seduction? I am a vampire. I drained his veins."

He gave her a lofty look over the top of invisible spectacles. "It's what I do."

"And you didn't know he was in love, this man? Don't you--"

"We only read your minds, my dear, not your hearts. This man did not himself believe he loved her."

"You killed a man who was in love, and now you're drunk on it? On love?" She squinted at him. "What if he'd been drinking alcohol?"

"Chemicals are a mortal coil," he responded. "I am spirit. I respond to the spiritual."

"And if your victim is homicidal?"

"Then I will kill again, until I am filled with a fonder element. Dead souls leave the spirit wanting."

"Ah, of course," said Valarie, "of course. Like us all." She cocked her head at him. "So how long...does it last, this love spell?"

His pulled his lip, pondering the question.

"How long am I intoxicated? How long infected by the heat of this man's desire for a woman I have never met?" He rose and walked to the rail, leaned out, and blinked sadly at the moon.

"Sweet potent poison," he whispered to the unhearing night.

"How I love you tonight, Valarie," he said suddenly, turning back to her. "A monster's hunger is a raging love, that is all." He took a step toward her. "I am not so different than you."

His face seemed to unclose, like a well-read book opening to a favorite scene. This was a thing Valarie understood. If the scent of death was on him, still the illusion of his lovesickness gave him mortality. Now she could see her own reflection in his mother-of-pearl face. Now she could believe in him. She could trust and forgive.

She stepped toward him, gingerly reaching out to touch his hand.

This time he did not disappear, but looked down on the offering instead.

"What does a monster do with love?" he crooned. His glittering eyes were two emerald moons in the pale sky of his dead face.

"How consummated once achieved, this despair of the soul." He licked his lips. "Touch me, touch my hand."

She set her fingers against his wrist.

"You're on fire," she breathed. "That poor man. He must have been insane for her."

"Come closer," he invited. "Love me."

The ferocity was gone from the feral eyes. Valarie lifted her face to his and stood on tip toe.

"How long will it last?" she whispered.

"The same as for him," he answered. "Until I forget her."

"Her?" she swallowed, feeling suddenly empty, robbed.

"She is, for me," he whispered back, "you."

He closed his jeweled eyes and bent to her. Black lashes fanned his pallid cheeks. He brushed his mouth against hers, then pressed it there, so that for her the only supernatural element that remained of him were the two muffled incisors behind his now ravishingly warm and mortal lips.

Three

Laroby did not return the next night, or the next. On the third evening of his absence Valarie awoke from "the Dahmer dream" at 3:33 a.m., prompt. In this, another of her recurring nightmares, Jeffrey Dahmer lived in the attic of her little house. She could never convince anyone he was up there, but when nightfall came in the dream, he would invariably turn on the attic light and go to town. She could see slivers of light through the ceiling tiles and around the frame of the attic door and hear him humming to himself as he worked. Sometimes he would pass her little notes through the slit between the doorframe and the pull-down stairs. Sometimes she was up there with him, trying to find a way out while he boiled pieces of corpses in a soup pot on a gas range. One night he ate her grandmother's eyes like jellied eggs. One night he offered her a slice of her husband's heart like a piece of roast beef on a bloody plate. Tonight, it was her father's head he had pulled from the pot. Having mumble-screamed herself awake, she got out of bed and walked miserably out of the house and down the drive to the street. There she waited, under the hiss of the mercury lamps, for the vampire's great lurking silhouette to appear.

"Laroby," she whispered into the stillness. The moist night air was heavy with the scent of lilac blossoms and honeysuckle. The privet hedge that ran the length of her yard on Edna Pelano's side loomed above her head, long in need of a trim. But nothing moved among the shadows.

"Larobya," she said to no one, "where have you gone?"

Finally she padded back to the house, slipping in the dew on her bare feet and frightening a rabbit into the shrubbery.

"Hey wabbat," she said to the little beast. "hey, I'm not gonna hurt you. Come back and eat some clover, sweetie." But the rabbit only stared at her, wide-eyed with fright, under the cover of a rhododendron, and waited for her to pass.

She stepped on to her porch and looked in through the parlor window. Behind the lace curtain, a silhouette darkened the interior.

"Laroby!" She let herself in. "Where have you been?"

He was lounging on a love seat, his long calves slung over one arm, his back propped against the other. The couch should have come apart under his weight but it barely indented where his body pressed it. In his hands was her copy of "Le Cure' d'Ars" which she always kept on the coffee table next to the sofa.

"You have been reading this?" he glanced at her casually over the cover.

18

"Now and then," she answered, shutting the door behind her.

"And this?" He picked up a second volume, which she saw he'd been hiding in his lap. It was Sister Faustina's "Divine Mercy in My Soul." Valarie held out her hand for the book.

"I'd appreciate it if you'd leave those alone," she said.

The vampire let out a laugh. "Pah!" He said. "Leave them alone?" His lips curled in contempt. "That would be difficult, my dear! Impossible, I think!" and he bellowed out another laugh. Then his face became serious and terrible. He vanished from the love seat, reappearing behind her, so that his breath was at her ear.

"Where is your God in the middle of the night, when your dreams drive you out of your house and into the street looking for me? I am here, Valarie. Has the world taught you nothing? Evil is always with you. In the flesh. In the blood. Is there anything in you that still believes in a God of love? He is the great Abandoner. When has he ever heard your screams, Valarie? When has he ever answered?"

He reappeared before her, lifting his arms from his sides so that his greatcoat spread like a cloak. "Love me, Valarie. I am with you, and will never abandon you. I am substantial!"

She watched him, horrified by his words. Behind his broad back the parlor mirror reflected the braid hanging like a leather whip between his shoulders. Had she lost her mind? This was no dream. This was really happening. The books he had mocked lay at his feet between the toes of his silver-tipped boots.

"Why do you cling to these myths? Let me be your master, Valarie. Love me." He stepped over the books and reached for her. "Am I not magnificent?"

His green eyes glinted in the dark.

She flinched from his embrace but did not struggle when he caught her in his arms. A sigh escaped her throat when the needle cold incisors touched it.

"No, I don't..." she whispered.

The teeth withdrew, replaced by a gentle human kiss. She turned her head into the kiss and found his mouth.

The vampire growled, a damp, voluptuous sound that stopped her breath. His kisses trailed across her cheek, her jaw, to the pulse that called him. He found her throat, and groaned in selfish passion as he pressed his mouth to the artery. She closed her eyes and clenched her teeth, knowing what must now come, because of what he was.

The first pangs of grief hit her when the dagger-sharp canines found their mark. Then came the towering rapture, as he took her life in his mouth. She swooned, but he lifted her easily, flowers on the back of a mule, and continued his one-sided feast as she died.

Four

She had become the vampire.

The deadly vampire kiss was the resolution of the vampire's hunger for her, for upon his having her, upon his feeding on her, she was no longer desirable to him. She was like him.

Corruption spread though Valarie quickly, feasting gleefully on her innocence, devouring her wholly. It spread, leaving in its wake a hunger so insatiable that Valarie feared it. She learned quickly how to dampen it with regular kills. She overcompensated and made herself sick on the innocence of others. Still, her frame became leaner. Where she had once owned a woman's softness, a thin layer of subcutaneous fat, she was now hardened, vascular and athletic. Strength loomed in her as the vampire had loomed over her. Her strength astonished her. There seemed to be no limit to it. So monstrous was it that she feared its detection in the simplest gesture, a shrug, a turn, the lifting of an object. Her walk too, was new. The feminine sway gone, this new walk was a long, quiet, dangerous thing. She prowled.

"The sun will not burn you right away," Laroby told her before he left her. "You will bear it for some time before it scalds you as it does me." And he laughed. "It takes many feedings to corrupt so wholly that the sun itself is unendurable. It takes time," he said, "to kill a soul."

He had in fact lost interest in her almost immediately. "We do not love one another," he said, "except under... extraordinary conditions. All vampires find themselves repulsive. Which is why we cannot see our own reflections. We are, to one another, putrefied food. It is the living we lust after."

And she found it was so. She retched at the sight of him when from his fangs he released her. She lay shuddering with something like guilt until he left, but later found her own mirror an ugly thing. For she was fading.

She ate the things she hated after that. Red meat, mostly, a little wine. It did not satisfy. At night she hunted. She despised the killing. But there was nothing to be done about it. The hunger was too terrible, a bottomless grave of emptiness and isolation from humanity. As each night passed the hunger choked her, nearly driving her to seek the food of her new life in daylight. But Laroby had warned her against feeding on the living by day.

"The blood is poison, then, too rich, too whole. It will inebriate you. Then the world will discover you for what you are and destroy you."

He told her, too, that despite the hunger, it was not necessary to feed each night.

"Your hunger will convince you you are dying. But you cannot die of hunger as you could when you were mortal. You cannot die at all. You can only starve, the desire burning hotter as time passes. Take the innocent and leave those who, although still mortal, are corrupt, like you. They are the Chinese food of the dead, and will leave you hungrier than before. Do not over kill. Too much blood will make you sick. Then you will lose what you have in your belly."

"I tell you these things because I made you what I am, by stealing what you were. You will discover the rest in time. Your nature will instruct you."

Then he was gone.

The rest of her life did not change dramatically. She was too young a vampire to be threatened by the sunlight, so knowing nothing else, she continued to substitute teach and to live in the little cottage. Then, in the fall, she received a letter informing her that she had been hired by the Suffern County Probation Department.

It was a strange feeling. She had taken the County exam in the spring, before the vampire had made her.

The woman they believed they were hiring was dead.

But the letter was what she had been waiting for. A chance to disconnect from her acquaintances at the school and avoid their questions. She took the job.

It might be decades before she would need to avoid the daylight. In the meantime, she would live a human life. She would function normally, work, perhaps even marry, though it was soon quite evident she would not reproduce as a human woman. She would survive by deceit, moving though her new life like a pirate ship on an open sea. She would continue.

Five

Valarie Lorraine had grown up not a mile from John Barry Howell III's Old Inlet estate.

When he first noticed the little girl with the waterfall of raven hair bicycling through town with a schoolmate, he had already occupied his grandfather's rambling estate house for some thirteen years, having moved in not long after his appointment at the Suffern County Probation Department, a young field officer with old money, fresh out of Yale, his first child on the way. In fact, it had been his wife, Joan, who'd called his attention to her.

"My god, look at that child's hair!" she'd exclaimed, and Jack took his eyes off the road momentarily to see the most extraordinary tresses of blue-black silk cascading down the back of a girl of six or seven.

"Wow, I didn't know kids could grow hair that long. She Indian?" Jack had responded.

"I think she's the landscaper's daughter, what's his name, George something-French... you know... he takes care of the Tuthill place. I've seen her weeding their beds with him after school. I think he's greens keeper at the club, Jack. You should know him."

"They ought to make her cut that hair, before she gets it caught in something," said Jack, but in fact he wished no such thing. Old Inlet was a clannish little town, and although there was a small settlement of poor blacks across the railroad tracks up north, it was rare to see anything so exotic as this little girl on Main Street. Mostly, the village was a melting pot of second generation German, Irish, and English families and a few wealthy Jews. He knew the greens keeper, for he was a fanatic golfer. Yes, the child could be George Lorraine's daughter. Jack checked his rear-view mirror as he drove past her. He caught a glimpse of her little face and saw a diminutive replica of the greens keeper's handsome French-Italian features.

A few years later, when the children were small, Jack hired Lorraine to keep the property around his oversized old house. And in the summer the girl, now in her teens, came on Thursday afternoons to weed the beds. All summer long, when Jack came home from the office at 5:15 p.m. he'd see her first, squatting on haunches or kneeling in the flowers in a pair of cut-off jeans, her long tanned legs and feet exposed to brown in the sun. Before any of his own brood came out to meet him with their list of complaints and demands, the girl would turn her head for him, sending ripples of black music down the ebony keys of her hip-length hair, and wave.

"Hello, Mr. Howell."

And Jack would wave back, and somehow find a fatherly smile for her as he rolled the County's Ford down the drive toward the house.

Is that what girls look like at eleven, he'd wonder? He tried to picture Kelly with legs like a colt, and forced the idea from his mind. Perhaps the French matured early.

But the girl was a pleasant addition to his routine and when she stopped coming a few years later, he found he missed her.

There was a period of time it seemed she disappeared from Old Inlet, although he knew that was not altogether true. Now and again he'd see her at the dock, taking off with the Grayson's older boy on his motor boat, headed for Bird Island. One late-summer evening, passing his own driveway to find a few moments of peace at the end of Beach Neck Lane before going home, he saw two ten-speed bikes leaning on the guard rail. He made a quick perusal of the Lavin's property of his left and saw it was empty but for the catamarans pulled up on the beach. He looked over at the Wyandott's deserted beach hotel. There, in the tall grass, the girl sat cross-legged with a boy he didn't recognize. He could hear their laughter over the breaking bay waves and a dull, even pain caught in his throat. The boy was dressed in an olive-green flak jacket. His dark blond hair hung in ringlets over the exaggerated shoulders of the garment. The girl shoved him, and he obliged her by rocking over onto his back. She leapt up from her Indian squat

27

and sat on him, bending so that the black satin sheets of her hair covered them both as she kissed him.

Jack pulled away from the dock as quietly as he could and left them. Across the untended Wyandott acre, over the canal, the girl's father would be cutting fairways tonight in preparation for tomorrow's tournament. Perhaps he saw his daughter cavorting with the boy, across the waterway, and felt the same dull pain.

The years passed and, as his concern for his own children's lives intensified, Jack no longer noticed George Lorraine's daughter, or realized her absence when she left Old Inlet for college. Certainly Kevin's death in '82 drew his attention away from the world completely enough to explain his loss of interest in the pretty little girl who had tended his estate with her father when his own children were still toddlers.

Of his four surviving children, one daughter remained at home with Jack and Joan. Patrick was in medical school, Kelly was married with kids of her own, and Colleen was in Miami with the Dade County P.D. Joan began drinking after Kevin's accident and it seemed that as each child left the nest her drinking intensified. Only Lisa, the baby, was still a source of daily affection and joy for him.

For Jack, except for the brief relief of an occasional affair, life was to be endured with patient acceptance. But then the girl returned to him in the most unlikely and remarkable way. The Department hired her.

At first, it seemed she neither recognized nor noticed him despite the fact that she was assigned to his section. Had she forgotten him entirely, he wondered? He checked her personnel file and saw that she still lived in Old Inlet, a mile north of his home and across the highway, on North Beach Neck. It was not George Lorraine's house. The greens keeper had passed away a year after Kevin was killed, and his widow had sold the place and moved upstate. So she had found another place in Old Inlet, perhaps one of the summer-cottages-turned-year-round. Or she may have inherited it from Lorraine's mother, whom he recalled also lived in the village. Old Inlet was like that. Families passing homes down through the generations. Jack's house had once been a hotel, owned by John Barry Howell, his grandfather. But when the Hamptons became the "in" spot for New Yorkers to vacation in the late fifties, his family shut it down and gave it to Jack as a wedding present.

He let the girl alone a week, then two, waiting for her to acknowledge him. Every newcomer made an effort to gain the approval of the Assistant Director of Investigations with smiles and gestures of respect. But the Lorraine girl not only ignored him, she seemed to studiously avoid him. Finally Jack could no longer bear the insult. He decided to act.

Did he send for her that afternoon to force an acknowledgement from her? Yes, she had once knelt bare-legged in the beds under his den window, weeding for summer cash. Yes, she'd worked for him before, the gardener's daughter, his servant's servant, before his neighbors' boys discovered her and took her away. He didn't know, exactly. He only knew that the woman who leaned now against the door frame of his office, her arms crossed, her sable hair swept back into a knot and secured by a red chopstick, was too breathtaking to question.

He saw George Lorraine's Mediterranean features, made delicate, refined by femininity. Her face was a sculpture designed of soft planes, all cheekbones and brow and tipped chin. It was a feline face, the only makeup a bold black liner emphasizing the tilted almond eyes. The lashes, dark brushes against the palette of cheekbones, were untouched, feathery. The lips were sepia.

"I wonder if you remember me," he said to that face, wincing at the unexpected tremor in his voice.

Her dark eyes riveted. They seemed to look not at, but through his, as if piercing his head to tally the sum total of his worth.

"Of course, Mr. Howell."

Was that sarcasm he heard in her voice?

"My father used to bring me over to your estate on Thursdays to do the weeding." Now she smiled graciously. "Those beds! They went on forever!" She watched his face.

"Still do," he said. "Well-" What else was there to say? You've grown into a beautiful woman? Nice to see you again? It was all too trite and embarrassing.

30

She shocked him by stepping up to his desk and holding out her hand to him. "I'm sure it will be a pleasure to work for you again, Jack." she said smoothly.

He could do nothing but accept the slender offering, though a moment before, he could not have imagined touching her. Her handshake surprised him. It was cool, dry. Like stone. But strong! Its strength gave it substance, even authority. She held his grip a moment too long. Then she released him.

"Yes, I hope it will be," he said. He hardened his face and withdrew his hand. This woman! This creature! His stomach had clenched at her touch as if with fear. He wanted her to leave, but couldn't bear her leaving.

Instead, she looked over his shoulder at Lisa's school portrait on his window sill.

"I remember her in diapers," she said, her eyebrows lifted a little. Her face seemed to sadden. "She wouldn't remember me," she murmured, dropping her gaze to his face. Then her expression brightened.

"But you do," she gave him a warm smile. "I wondered if you would." And she stared into his eyes a bit too long before she turned and left him.

Within six months of her appointment, to Jack Howell's horror, Valarie married her immediate supervisor, Dean Valanchuk. She did so with no fanfare, in fact told no one of her plans until the deed was accomplished. Then she changed the lovely music of Rossetti to the Slavic cacophony of Valanchuk, forcing Jack to listen to the new title each time she was paged over the office intercom system.

With a bit of politics Jack managed to maintain Valarie in the Sharon Investigation Unit and had Dean transferred out to the Riverdale Office where he was assigned a Supervision section. Rumors flew. Dean Valanchuck was not a well-liked man. He was a stickler for detail, a social blunderer who frequently stepped on the wrong toes to champion his own dogmatic opinions, a tall, balding divorcee' of Ukrainian decent who could tweak the most self-assured nose with his air of self-imposed authority on every subject. Valarie was an enigma, better liked by the men than by the women, who found her an easy target for gossip and speculation. The steno pool hummed. What did she see in him? If she had married to service her biological clock it was not evidenced by a pregnancy. Perhaps Dean could no longer father children, though he had two by a previous marriage. Jack made it his business to avoid contributing to the scuttlebutt although this last secretly amused him to no end.

In the spring Jack took his traditional five week vacation. But instead of spending it on the Old Inlet golf course with Gil Stuart and Brix Tuthill, he conceded for once to Joan's yearly demand for a cruise to the Caribbean. When he returned to work at the end of May his appearance in the Steno Room was a debut. He was visibly slimmer, browned by the equatorial sun, and he sported a new wardrobe. Even more dramatically, his eyes, (his best feature, according to Joan) were no longer hidden behind his signature horn-rimmed glasses. Jack accepted the obligatory teasing with good humored sportsmanship. The attention he received, after all, was not unexpected for he had orchestrated this transformation. True, his face was showing his age, but it was still a good face, a square, Ivy League face, in late middle age, full of brooding authority. And he still had a thick head of black hair at an age when other men were donning "hair systems". All in all, he was not an unattractive man.

There was more than one embarrassing moment as a result of his new image, as female members of his staff responded to it with their own provocative preening. But Jack was no flirt. One cool and disinterested look was all that was necessary to curtail unwanted attention and remind the unintended victims of his charms that he was above such nonsense.

As for Valarie, her initial reaction was negligible. For the most part she remained respectfully distant. Still, it seemed to Jack that she did not avoid him as deliberately as she had in the past, and on occasion she came directly to him for direction rather than asking Cole, her immediate supervisor, for guidance. And sometimes, yes, he was sure he'd seen it, her eyes would leave his and drop to his mouth or his throat, and she would lick her lips with a quick flash of pink tongue, catch herself, and turn away.

By this slight flicker of physical interest, he began to believe that a reciprocal attraction had sprung up at last in this creature who had, for so long, eluded him.

Six

Jack had a plan.

It was early autumn. Valarie had been working in his section for over a year and there was no longer any question that she was the most efficient investigator he had ever supervised. She seemed to have the instincts of a hunter, and tracked down the details of a case like a raptor after a rodent. A good investigator needed to be a diligent hunter. Most of the subjects of these reports were themselves predators and it took a particular stamina to separate the true from the apocryphal. Valarie was especially tenacious with drunk drivers, and it had become Jack's habit to give her the worst of them. Even so, she never complained.

Now the court calendars were jammed with cases set back by the judges' summer vacations, and Jack had ample work to justify assigning heavy caseloads. He could also justify his own late hours. Often he stayed on till six-thirty or seven, proofreading reports that his supervisors had been unable to finish by five. This practice left him alone in the building, except for office reports on the opposite side of the lobby. But by inundating Valarie with enough cases to force her to work late as well, he knew it would only be a matter of time before he had some very attractive company.

It was not long before the desired effect occurred and Valarie began staying on after five. The investigators' offices were located across the hall, separated from administration by file rooms, a typing area, and the steno pool. But at least Jack knew she was in the building. He could all but feel her presence near him.

Eventually, she would realize he was staying late as well and come to talk to him, perhaps recall their shared past, ask after the children. And after that? Well, he only needed a little encouragement, a flicker of interest, a sign of reciprocal feeling. Just enough to convince him she had not ignored him all these years. He wasn't looking for an affair, just a sign of recognition, of respect. After all, he was a family man.

"Oh, crap, another Vehicular Homicide." Valarie threw the new case file across her desk with disgust. It arced across the room and sliced into the opposite wall like a Ninja's star.

There was that strength again, showing off when it was not needed. It was a hard thing to camouflage, especially when it was surrounded by the puniness of humanity. She had to be constantly vigilant of it, checking her temper, watching her speed and her movements. Among mortals in daylight, she had to pretend mortality.

Night time was different, of course.

Night time was for killing, and killing required strength.

Normally she killed with as little effort and as much compassion as her vampire nature allowed her. But not always.

One evening she realized she was being followed to her favorite hunting ground, the village dock. She knew this in the same way that a wolf knows when a coyote or fox has trespassed in its habitat. The soul of man was her food, but the blood of another predator was of little value to her. Nevertheless she would not tolerate his presence in her domain. He was a competitor for the innocence that she must now feed upon, therefore she would remove him from her world. It was of no consequence to her that he would not be missed.

He had followed her, in a blue van with smoked out windows, down the back roads of Old Inlet to the bay. Then he parked in an unlit corner of the dock and slipped out of the cab to come up behind her as she wandered along the bulkhead, pretending to be unaware of him. Before she turned to face him he grabbed her by the hair and slapped the palm of one dirty hand across her mouth. She lifted her lip and let him feel the cool length of her incisors before he pulled his hand away and clamped it to her throat. That was when he seemed to notice he was in trouble.

She let him bruise his fingers on her neck a moment as he realized he was dealing with a sheath of steel. Nor could he budge her an inch from where she stood. She was as solid, as implacable, as an iron girder.

"Fucking whore!" he blubbered as she turned like a lioness in his pathetic grasp and snarled. His throat was ripped clean through before he hit the ground.

Without mercy she watched him die, staring up at her with terror in his milky blue eyes as he worked to stop his own blood with the same strangle hold he had intended for her. "Worthless," she spat, kicking his corpse over the bulkhead into the black bay.

It was not the first time she had tallied the inherent worth of a soul with her vampire senses. At the office, that vision pierced human hearts like cold metal in warm fat, and there was little she did not know about her co-workers.

She knew she was surrounded by the half-corrupt, the self-righteous, the proud. But there was also innocence here, and in the most unlikely of places. For it was often the old who were most innocent, not the young. And when the old were innocent, how magnificent they were! For their innocence was earned by a lifetime of dignity, while the young often owed theirs simply to a lack of opportunity for sin.

Dean Valanchuk, for example, had been an easy thrall, innocence longing for corruption. But Jack Howell! For all his human intellect and privilege, he was as daintily pure in his soul as a newborn. She saw with supernatural clarity his devotion to his family, his grief over his son's death, his many years of marital chastity and his guilt over the two recent inconsequential affairs.

Because it was sinful she saw, too, his desire for her, and this made her veins itch and her teeth pound. For his desire was gentle, unformed, confused. A father's love, a lover's lust, a boy's crush. Her head spun in his presence. His lovesick blood sang to her. It was dizzying to speak to him, requiring all of her strength to subdue her strength. She felt her muscles flex rigid at the sound of his breathing.

Could a kill be more enticing? Less deserved?

To bite the throat that employed and provided cover would be foolish, she knew. It could lead to her discovery and destruction. And she did not intend to be stamped out now, in the prime of her death, because of her own lack of discipline.

To thrall was better, to usher in that slow transport to immortality. Thralling Jack would secure her human masque. But did she have the stamina to endure it? The terrible letting go, time and time again, when his throat was in her mouth, his blood in her lungs? No. She could not imagine letting go of that neck once her teeth were blissfully embedded in it.

And yet these were not reasons enough to spare an innocent man. The real reason was a flaw in her unfinished vampire nature. The real reason was the fondness she felt for him.

He had, in a manner of speaking, been part of her life once. Valarie cherished the short history of her human existence and

Howell had been an integral part of it. His Ivy League face, his upper class facade, brought back to her another face, the sun-browned, French-peasant face of her father, profiled under the brim of a yellow golf cap above a tan greens keeper's uniform. It was a link to memories of George Lorraine, sitting across from her on the red Naugahyde seat of his old Ford pickup, an eight-track of Anne Murray stuck in the console, and Butter, her half-collie mutt, sitting between them, panting dog breath into the cab. It brought back the smell of cut grass, (mounds of it, yellowing, fell from her father's pant cuffs when he turned them out at night) and gasoline, pungent on his work clothes. It brought back the sound of her own bare feet slapping on the hot blacktop of Howell's immense driveway as she ran to meet her father's truck, to hop back into the cab next to Butter after an afternoon of weeding at the estate.

Yes, it was fondness that kept Valarie's lips drawn over her teeth in Jack's presence. Nothing else, after all, not fear of detection, nor lack of stamina, could have.

Jack sat in his office in front of his computer terminal. The single oblong window at his shoulder gave him a perfect view of his staff's five o'clock exodus to the parking lot.

Dennis Cole had been on vacation since last week. It was Thursday and already his work was piled high on Jack's desk. Jack always read vacationing supervisors' cases in order to facilitate his section's productivity. Judges didn't care if supervisors were on vacation. Neither did Griffin, the Director. They expected work to get done.

There was a glaring flaw in one of Valarie Valanchuk's reports. She had neglected to contact a victim, or at least had not included that contact in her final draft. Jack could have brought it to her attention during the day when her office was occupied by three other officers but, of course, he had preferred to wait until she was alone.

He looked outside. It was nearly dark but he could still make out the line of county cars that always remained in the lot overnight, the custodian's van, his own Ford, and Valarie's Honda. He waited a few minutes longer. Then he picked up the offending case and carried it, through the labyrinth of the Sharon office, to her door.

He tapped twice and cleared his throat with his customary politeness. He expected a "Come in," or a "Yes?" but instead the door flew back on its hinges as Valarie slammed into him on her way out. She hit him square in the chest, then withdrew so swiftly that it seemed to him she disappeared for an instant.

She clapped one hand over her mouth what appeared a gesture of embarrassment. But her eyes cut into him. There was no abashment there.

"Oh,... I'm so sorry. Did I hurt you?" It was an odd thing for her to say. She was only a slip of a woman.

But in fact, she had hurt him. His chest stung where her shoulder had struck it, and for one crazy moment he wondered if something were broken. He fought the urge to check his ribs with his fingers.

"No, no," he managed a smile. "On your way out?" Humor was best.

She didn't seem to catch it. "I'm ... yes. Sorry," she lifted a hand as if to soothe the bruise she had given him, then her eyes flicked to his face and she clenched her teeth. He lost track of his thoughts as he watched the little muscles bunch along her jaw.

"I just had a question--" he said.

Her eyes shifted to the case file in his hand.

"I screwed up a case, huh?" She leaned toward him to take it. Her perfume was oddly old-fashioned, flowery and over-sweet, like a funeral bouquet. It reminded Jack of his grandmother's bedroom. Yet it suited her. On her, it was dizzying.

He lifted the case from his side and offered it to her as she stepped back into the office to let him in. Then she returned to her desk and hopped up to sit on one corner, her short black skirt hiking up as she crossed her legs.

"I was wondering if you ever tried to contact the victim on that one. There's no statement from her in the report but the police information indicates she was taken to the hospital after the accident."

Valarie flipped through the case folder as he spoke.

42

"Rudolph Katz?" She looked up and narrowed her eyes at him, pondering. "Did I do a Rudolph Katz?"

The fine brown hairs of one eyebrow feathered into an arch.

Jack's head swam. He was falling into those eyes, and his chest still hurt where she'd slammed into it. What was wrong with him? Was he having a heart attack? He forced himself to answer her.

"I'm afraid so," he said, grasping for good humor while his senses failed him.

She was still staring right into his eyes as she let the case file slip through her fingers onto the desk top beside her. She seemed to be rocking, ever so slightly, as she perched on the end of the desk. Like a cat watching a bird, her lips were slightly parted.

Jack swallowed.

"Jack."

Now she slipped off the edge of the desk and stepped toward him. She said nothing else, only his name. But he felt it sliding over her tongue and through her teeth as if it were a piece of him.

Something hot thrilled through his body, into his groin. Yet he stepped away from her involuntarily.

She measured him a moment longer with that ruthless feline stare.

Then she made a noise in her throat like a wet growl.

Dark, old! innocent eyes. A lifetime of innocence behind them. Unthreatened by her like until now, gentled into one solid Protestant work of spiritual purity. He and his kind were a dying breed. Near extinction.

She looked down the length of his body, past the clean, white shirt (always white! always crisp!), the middle aged belly, the silly, conventional slacks. This was someone's Dad! Oh, how delicious.

One drink? One sip? Can I take just one? I'm starving!

She rose from her perch in one sinewy movement and came toward him.

And he stepped back.

She thought of picking him up by the shirt front and throwing him against the door. Nailing her palms on either side of him, caging him in flesh and bone. Fastening her mouth to his throat and drinking, and drinking.

She felt the bloodlust rise in her and she knew her eyes must be hot and heavy-lidded, as if with human passion. She forced them closed, stopped in her tracks, put her palm to her forehead and groaned. It was only partly an act.

Immediately she felt his hand on her arm, and his human heat burned through her shirt.

"Are you alright? You look as if you might faint..." he said.

She drew back, unconsciously raking her fingers through her hair. A fine bead of sweat crowned her forehead. Her eyes were dull with hunger.

"Valarie?"

"I...have to go..." she whispered. "I can't...do this."

"Of course," he was quick to accept a solution. "I'll walk you out."

"NO!" She looked up at him in panic, then managed a weak smile. "No, no, I'm just tired. Hungry... I haven't eaten...in a while. I'll be fine."

"You're sure?"

"Yes." As she moved away from him she mumbled, "And I'm sorry about Katz. I'll get you a statement tomorrow."

Seven

It had been over a year since her death, and it was becoming more and more difficult for Valarie to get out of bed in the morning.

In the old days, before the vampire's kiss, she might have attributed her morning stiffness to a lack of sleep, or to too much wine. Certainly she slept less as a vampire, hunting at night and rarely retiring before three o'clock. But sleep itself, like breathing, was no longer a necessity. It was simply a habit. Laroby had warned that eventually the sun would become so unbearable she would be forced to avoid it entirely during daylight. Then she would not sleep so much as lie in state during the hours of its reign. But he had never mentioned the arthritic inflexibility that had begun to plague her mornings.

Nor was it the wine. True, she drank more than she had when she was alive. It took the edge off the hunger. But she drank far more blood than wine. And alcohol, as Laroby had once said, was a mortal coil.

No, these could not explain the immobility she'd been waking up with lately, a paralysis that had started in her eyelids, cheeks and lower jaw, pulling her face into a gruesome smile, but had in recent weeks begun to affect to the larger muscles. The hands and feet, the arms, neck, shoulders. The legs and buttocks.

There was no pain. Her body simply went rigid, board stiff, paralytic, while her mind remained active, sending frantic messages of locomotion to her limbs which her limbs could not respond to. Lately it was only with the most intense effort and determination that she rose at all.

My God, she thought. Is there no antidote for this? What about Laroby? Does it happen to him? Is it just a phase, or will it get worse and worse, until I cannot move at all?

Then she remembered. She'd read it in a mystery novel. In death, rigor mortis was exactly that. A phase the body went through as it decayed. It started with the small muscles of the face, then moved to the larger muscle groups. Once it spread through the whole body, involving all the muscles, it began to disappear in the same progression. Smaller muscles first, then larger. After about thirty-four hours, it was all over. The muscles relaxed as the body decomposed, and the corpse became soft again.

So it was all a part of dying.

And it wouldn't end until she experienced complete paralysis.

For Valarie, terror had found a new height.

Then one morning as she struggled out of bed, she was struck by a possibility. It often seemed that during these periods the more she moved the more movement she was capable of. Perhaps activity was an antidote for this new torment. Inspired, she limped into the parlor. As she lurched back and forth across the room, forcing the blood of her victims to circulate through her veins, she noticed movement through the parlor windows.

It was not yet 7:00 a.m., too early for most of her neighbors to be up and about. But there was a figure bobbing up the lane in slow motion toward her house. She stumbled to the window and peered through the white lace curtains. A tall, lean runner dressed in red shorts and a torn grey sweatshirt was jogging up the lane. Valarie squinted. The tousle of straw blond hair and the well-tanned face identified Old Inlet High's Phys Ed teacher, Daniel Kincaid running with the measured ease of a marathoner, his body trim as a boy's though Valarie knew he must be closing in on fifty. Mr. Kincaid had been new to Old Inlet High when she had started her freshman year there almost 15 years ago.

"What's your secret, Kincaid?" she mumbled through numbed lips. "How do you cheat the clock like that?"

But it was obvious. It was the cliché of the age she lived in, after all.

She had been watching Daniel Kincaid jog or cycle or race-walk through the streets of Old Inlet for nearly fifteen years now. Rain or shine, wind or sleet or snow. Kincaid was out there, doing what he believed in. If anything, he looked better now than he had at thirty.

Could it work for a vampire?

She hobbled back into the bedroom to find a pair of sneakers.

At twenty after seven Jack was normally in the shower or at the breakfast table having his first cup of coffee. But today was Saturday and he had promised to meet Gil Stuart at the Country Club at eight. So Jack was turning the key in his new import, a dashing black teardrop of automation, and pulling out of his immense driveway. The end of the drive was hedged in by two enormous hemlocks. They made it impossible to see up and down Beach Neck Lane without nosing out slowly, which he did automatically every morning. This morning was no different, except that this morning as he pulled past the hemlocks he nearly ran over Valarie.

It was the baseball cap that gave her away. The baggy grey sweatshirt and black bicycle shorts could have been anyone's, but the black, rhinestone-studded baseball cap was hers. She'd taken to stuffing her hair under it and wearing it to work lately. It was inappropriate but no one had said anything to her as far as Jack knew except to compliment her on it. In fact, she looked damned good in it, all eyes and cheekbones. A pretty little boy. Certainly Jack was not about to bring it up. He liked the playfulness of it.

Besides, she wasn't a field officer. As far as he was concerned she could wear what she liked.

Jack rolled out onto the lane and watched as Valarie continued jogging steadily down Beach Neck to the water. From his vantage point it appeared she could go on forever. Her stride was still long, her body centered, not leaning forward, although he knew it was a good mile from his house to hers, and another half mile to the beach.

He smiled to himself as he pulled down the street. He could use a little exercise himself. Maybe it was time for him to take up jogging.

For three weeks he did not run into her. That was fine, in his opinion, because it had taken him that long to work up the stamina for a three mile run. But he was getting frustrated. It wasn't much use exerting oneself for no reason. He was too preoccupied to notice that his fifty-two year old body was already responding to the new regime. He only knew that he was wasting his time unless it brought him into closer contact to Valarie.

Then one morning, following an evening of bridge at the Curtis' with Joan, he awoke an hour early.

That night Joan had been drinking martinis. Jack had lost count after her fifth. Now she lay fast asleep beside him in an alcoholic torpor, her brittle, platinum hair still holding its coif as she snored softly into her pillow. Jack gently covered her with the lace spread that had been kicked to the floor during the night. Then he padded on bare feet to the bureau and pulled out a pair of sweat pants and a shirt. As he dressed he took a quick look down to the street from his second story bedroom window. His heart lurched. There was Valarie, jogging down the opposite side of the lane in a black baseball cap!

He finished tying his sneaker laces quickly, brushed back his hair, and stepped into the bathroom to examine his face. The black shadow of a beard would have to remain. He had no time to shave. He washed his face and brushed his teeth. Then he padded across the hall, down the stairs, and across the kitchen to the back door, careful not to wake rest of the household.

And he was free.

Outside, the morning air was chill. A layer of grey mist blanketed the front lawn. Jack took a few deep, rapid breaths and started down the drive toward the beach. There was no outlet on Beach Neck beyond his house. The road terminated in a dead end at the water's edge. So when he didn't run into Valarie half way down to the bay he knew she hadn't doubled back. She was still down there, hidden somewhere in the fog. He smiled to himself.

"Got you," he chuckled as he approached the guardrail at the end of the lane.

She stood at the water's edge, staring out into the fog over the bay, toward Bird Island. There was a mild breeze and it played

51

with the tendrils of hair that had fallen loose from her cap. Only the screech of a gull, cloaked in the fog, broke the stillness.

Jack slowed to a walk. He knew he should continue jogging, right around the guard rail, offering a wave should she turn in the last minute and see him there. But he could not take his eyes from her. He was transfixed. When she turned, as if expecting him, and came toward him across the sand, he could not speak.

Under the brim of her black cap her eyes were enormous, luminous. They bore into his, disturbingly intimate, and he immediately felt an about-face. She was now the voyeur; he the object of unwanted inspection.

When she reached his side she looked up at him and smiled.

"Hey, boss, where you headed?"

"You choose," he answered, amazed at his own temerity. But she only grinned at him and nodded.

"Ok," she said, and took off at a trot down the road.

After the briefest hesitation, he followed.

They jogged together up Beach Neck Lane to the highway, then east into town, and at the corner of Robin's Hill Road, south, single file, to the village dock.

When they'd rounded the Yacht Club he called to her.

"That's it for me. I'd better start back."

"Sure," she nodded over her shoulder and began the climb back up Robin's Hill toward town.

After a moment Jack caught up.

"How about Tuthill Lane? It's shorter." He had tried to sound casual, but his voice betrayed his distress. It was nearly daylight, after all. He did not want to be seen jogging through town with the greens keeper's daughter. She gave him a sly sideways glance.

"Escape the prying eyes of the townsfolk, hmh?" But she obligingly cut in front of him toward Tuthill Lane.

"You don't seem winded. How long have you been jogging?" he panted after he managed to catch her again.

"Oh, I just started," she answered. "I've been getting a little stiff in the morning lately."

"You're too young for that."

"Not really," she answered humorlessly.

"I won't walk for a week," Jack laughed as they reached the corner of South Beach Neck.

"Nonsense," said Valarie, tipping the brim of her hat in 'good-bye' as she jogged across Tuthill toward home.

"You're stronger than you think," she called back, and then she disappeared into the fog.

Jack jogged on only a few more paces. Then he pulled up short and bent over, holding his knees and gasping for breath.

Valarie burned. With each new kill she felt her own damnation drawing nearer, and yet the hunger raged on, demanding more blood, more victims and more death. It was an addiction that forever called to itself, required itself, campaigned for itself, all at the expense of its host. By degrees, death was happening to Valarie, and it demanded her absolute complicity.

Her body, except for the morning rigor, did not seem to suffer from this condition. In fact, if locomotion was life, then she was more alive than ever. Her body had become as powerful, as quick and as deadly as any predator, and her body fat neared zero. It confused her that this added strength did not show as muscle mass or body weight. Each morning she checked her scale in the familiar human habit, and each morning she was greeted by a lower number. She now tipped it at 98 pounds, twenty pounds less than she had weighed when she was alive. Somehow, the uncanny strength she had discovered in Laroby's gift could not be measured in the material world, and unless in motion, did not seem to effect the world around it.

She still ate meat, a bit of bread, and an abundance of wine during daylight, which had no effect at all except to temporarily quench the bloodthirst. At night she hunted, taking the evil from the world by making herself a target and then turning on her attacker and relieving him of his blood. Her thirst for innocence heightened with every draught of wickedness.

At work, she watched Jack display the plumes of his innocence like an unsuspecting peacock preening in the range of a leopard. Her thirst to consume that innocence was like a fever in her blood. She was inflamed.

It was becoming harder and harder for Jack to endure Valarie's presence each day at the office. If he saw her, the agony was in the longing to close the physical distance between them, to catch the scent of her perfume, to hear her voice, her footsteps, so impossibly light! to touch her, even for an instant, so that he might never again wonder at the texture of her skin. Yet if she were not in, if she were interviewing at another office, the torment became even more intense. Then his office was a tomb, devoid of light, of life. His concentration suffered. He often went home early on these days. It was wrong, it was obsessive, but he could do nothing to control it.

And then one day, when the worst of it was on him, a memo came over his desk that threatened his very reason. Valarie had requested a transfer to the Riverdale office, twenty miles away.

Of course, he had the power to deny such a request based on any number of considerations. He needed her in Sharon, for example, nearer the County Courts, since he so frequently assigned her the most notorious cases. There was also the fact that Griffin, the Director, frowned upon husbands and wives working together in the same office, and Dean was currently stationed in Riverdale. Nevertheless, the memo was a blow. How could she request such a move? Didn't she enjoy his proximity at all? This request would take her completely out of his daily environment. They might not see each other for weeks on end.

Jack took the next day off. It was a crisp autumn Tuesday, a perfect morning to play golf. He met Gil Stuart promptly at eight, played nine holes at the club, then begged off lunch with a lame excuse about paperwork and spent the remainder of the afternoon at home nursing a bottle of scotch and staring without interest at the Sports Channel. He was still sitting in a self-induced trance on his favorite sofa, holding an unlikely glass of ice and peering out the den window to the street, when Joan came home from the University at four and interrupted his reverie. He might have pretended not to notice her if she hadn't stepped deliberately in front of the TV and turned down the sound when she entered the room.

"Have a nice day off, hon?" she smiled at him. In her grey wool suit and scarlet blouse, her hair recently cropped to a chin-length bob, his wife was still an attractive woman. But when Jack turned to answer her he was surprised to find that he was more cognizant of the age in her face, the delicate crow's feet that bracketed her blue eyes, the puffiness in her jowls, than of the remaining sweetness of that once coquettish smile. She was still slim. She ate like a bird to keep her weight down, but age and gravity were having their way with her body. Under a half bottle of scotch Jack's mind swam to the image of that body underneath his in bed. It flopped onto the deck of his thoughts like a flounder. It had seemed acceptable, the soft, boney, flaccidity of her, until now. Now it repulsed him.

Jack forced himself to get up from his chair, approach his wife and brush her mouth with a dry kiss. She reacted instantly.

"Is something wrong?" she said, a little warning in her voice.

"Not at all," he responded woodenly. "Everything's just fine."

He was past her, half way down the hall, when she called after him.

"Are you going out somewhere?"

"Just a jog before dinner," he replied.

"Don't go too far, Jack," she volleyed back. "I'm having the Dahls over for bridge at eight." Then she went to the bar to fix herself a highball.

Eight

"Jack?"

It was a breath, a whisper for him alone.

His name, in her mouth.

"Can I see you a minute?"

Jack was standing in the steno pool, chatting with Patty Kinsemmi, Stan Gould's secretary. Patty was a big girl, tall and mannishly built, with colossal green eyes and huge hair. Despite her size and stature Patty had a lovely, ebullient laugh and a natural flair for flirtation. In her presence all the men in the department felt desirable, and Jack was no exception. Right now he was enjoying her uncontrolled giggle, which he had triggered with one of his best anecdotes, one which undoubtedly had gone straight over her enormous perm. But what did that matter? Patty always availed a man of that giggle of hers, which was sexual both in its yielding and in its abundance.

In fact, he might have stood there for the rest of the afternoon, ringing that happy little bell, if Valarie Valanchuk hadn't spoken his name, like an incantation, at his ear.

He turned to her with the what he hoped was cool detachment, only to see the foolishness of his flirtation reflected back at him in the intrusive mirror of her gaze.

"Something wrong?" he said, drawing back into the safe shell of professional posturing.

"Well. Yeah, actually. I've got two different sentencing dates for this indictment. Which one do I honor?" She might have added, for her eyes said it, that the incompetent fool who had assigned her the case had missed this obvious error. She did not. She handed him the documents, her bottomless eyes fixed on a point somewhere between his chin and his collar.

He moved closer to her, ignoring her offering, so that he could peruse the referral over her shoulder. That vantage point became quickly alarming, as it revealed the architecture of her upper body from such an angle that heat rose to his throat as if an oven door had been opened in his face.

"Oh, that's ridiculous. Let me make a call and see what's going on." He took the file and fled to the sanctuary of his own office, hoping she would let him get back to her on this one.

The little vampire hesitated an instant, wondering if he had meant for her to follow him.

It wasn't always so easy to read minds, especially when they were occupied, as his was, with visions of her own violation.

Sometimes it was best not to try. Sometimes it only made things worse.

Clearing her throat and her thoughts, she stepped out of the steno pool to follow the Assistant Director of Investigations to his office. She knocked politely on the closed door, then let herself in without waiting for his consent.

She found him talking into the telephone at his desk, his white-shirted back turned to her, and she settled into a chair across from him and waited.

Behind him, on the window sill, stood the picture of a teenage girl with a mop of red-blond hair that seemed to explode in all directions from her scalp. The girl had Jack Howell's square jaw and broad brow, but these gave her a mulish appearance. Valarie puzzled how features, quite pleasant in one sex, could wreak such havoc in the other.

"That's Lisa?"

But Jack was still speaking into the phone.

Her eyes came to rest on his throat again. Today it was neatly dressed in a floral tie, like a gift waiting to be opened. She ran her tongue over her incisors. They were still human enough, though razor sharp. Even a dentist might not notice that they were a bit too long.

His conversation ended, Jack placed the receiver back in its saddle and turned to her.

"I think His Honor wants the defendant sentenced on separate days on each indictment in order to give him more jail time," he said.

"So I'm supposed to have a report ready for the first date on the earlier indictment."

"Right," he said.

She stood. "And a completely separate report on the second."

"Right."

She turned to the door. "Even though it's the same goddamn criminal in front of the same goddamn judge, with the same goddamn criminal record and social history."

He cleared his throat.

"I didn't know you were such a linguist," he made a wall of his face.

She lifted a brow, smiled a lop-sided grin of amusement and stepped toward his desk, then deliberately unnerved him entirely by leaning over it. Under a little black bolero she wore a poet's ruffled silk shirt, the collar of which now fell obediently open to her breast.

"Jack," she said, "Did you read my memo?"

"Pardon me?"

"Look," she picked up a plastic paper clip from his blotter and turned it in her fingers. "I'm finding it ...distracting in this office. Working together..."

His face had turned to rubber.

"I think I need... a change."

"A change," he repeated.

She clenched her jaw. A change? No. Not a change. I need blood. Sweet, innocent, nicely aged... Blood red, all American, Ivy League educated blood. Just there, beneath skin grown delicate with age, wrapped, like a present in a collar and tie,...lovely, living, everlasting BLOOD.

The dizzying thirst was on her again. For a moment her muscles tensed, bunched to spring, and the fight to deny them their locomotion was a marathon. He was talking, offering her a new room assignment, something quieter, maybe closer to his office. She heard herself agree with the solution while she imagined with a rush opening his throat and lapping the lovely elixir of his lifeblood into her mouth. Her canines pounded. She had to have it, that magnificent drink.

Yet she could not harm him. He was her childhood.

Miserable, she backed away from his desk and disappeared down the hall.

When his phone rang a moment later Jack was glad it was Joan, until he realized he couldn't hear a word she said.

His blood was singing in his ears.

Nine

Dean was covering her with kisses.

"You're amazing. You're all muscle. There isn't an ounce of fat on you," he murmured into her hair.

"It doesn't bother you that I'm dead," said Valarie, turning her chin from him to avoid kisses on her mouth. Undaunted, Dean kissed her neck.

"You're not dead. You're more alive than anyone I've ever known," he answered.

"I'm dead. Or dying," she said.

"We're all dying," he countered, and turned her chin back to him. "I love you," he said.

"They won't give me the transfer," she said. "They're assigning me a new room instead."

"They who?"

"Jack."

"That ass." Dean kissed her right eyelid, then the little dark fan of lashes beneath. Valarie made a sound in protest and pushed him gently away.

"Stop that." She sat up on the bed.

"So is that OK with you, a new room assignment?" asked Dean, leaning back on one elbow.

"I guess," she said, standing.

"I need to get out of Old Inlet, Dean. I need a fresh hunting ground. I've been looking out east, out by the wineries. There's a house in Pequot Bog. A friend of mine built it a few years back. It's gorgeous."

She picked up a hair brush, turned to her dresser mirror, flinched, and turned back to him with a determined look. "I'm going to have it."

"You're serious?"

"Mmm-hmm." Valarie dropped the brush on the bed and disappeared into the closet. She came out with her black leather jacket half-shrugged over her shoulders.

"Does this look appropriate? I can't tell if its cold out anymore."

"It's fine," Dean nodded. "It's a little raw out tonight."

"I won't be too late," she said, grabbing a small handbag from her bureau and checking its contents: a pair of latex gloves, a pack of razor blades, a roll of duct tape.

"Be careful, honey," said her husband.

Outside it was crisp and clear. A half-moon bathed the lawn in bluish light. Valarie moved silently on stiletto heels to her little red Civic.

Although tonight's kill would be different, she wore her usual hunting gear, a lace bodysuit under the leather jacket, a short black-leather skirt, and calfskin boots with four-inch heels. They slouched over her ankles like stockings loosed from their garters. This particular outfit didn't always lure the wicked, and she had once been offered a considerable sum of cold cash for a certain service she could not have rendered had she wanted to. That kill had been especially sweet, for there had been no malice in the heart of her prey, only longing and loneliness.

Valarie pulled the little car out of the drive and gunned the engine as she headed toward the highway. At the corner of Beach Neck she looked south, as if she expected to see Jack's Miata purring at the opposite corner. Her night vision was extraordinary now and she could see as well as in daylight, but Beach Neck curved to the west and out of sight long before it reached Jack's house. No cars interrupted the first quarter mile of the lane. Valarie turned left and headed east.

It took half an hour to reach Pequot Bog. At quarter to eleven she pulled into the First Presbyterian Church parking lot, killed the engine, and slipped out of her car. A light rain had begun to fall and she quickly found her rhinestone-studded baseball cap in the back seat and tucked her hair beneath it. She was at least a mile from her destination, a mile through deserted fields and vineyards. It would not take her long. She had, in her transformation, developed an uncannily light tread and she rarely left a footprint, even in mud. She laughed to herself. Her boots would be pristine when she reached the house, the only sign that she had travelled some distance by foot, her water-stained jacket.

The house she was headed for was an immense square structure with two opposing wings set apart by a patio of flagstone. It was located on a cul-de-sac flanked by a hay field. Valarie knew the house. It had been built in '85, during the real-estate boom, by a retired railroad engineer. He'd built it for his daughter and her new husband, adding a separate wing for himself and his wife.

It was an odd house, oversized and extravagant. It was composed of two apartments, each with its own staircase leading to a master suite with marble-tiled bath. Beneath these were the living areas, joined by a common great room and central foyer. A chef's kitchen, tucked under the west wing, was shared by both households.

Valarie had seen the house first when it was still under construction. Cecile Dumont Gagnon had invited her to stay for a few days not long after Claude's death. But living with newlyweds had proved too painful for Valarie, being so newly widowed herself, and she had remained only one night.

Now Cecile and Guy were divorcing, and with only the old man's pension to live on, the family could barely afford the place.

66

So the house had been put on the market, but because of its peculiar design it was difficult to sell. As yet there had been no serious offers.

Valarie moved across the wet fields swiftly, leaving no trace of her passage. Locomotion was different as a vampire. Too fast, too thoughtless a movement and she would vanish. But moving over rain swept fields of grapevine in the middle of the night did not require that she remain visible, so she moved at a comfortable pace and disappeared.

Presently she stood in the field behind the house. She scanned the second floor windows and saw that the Dumont's apartment was unlit. But across the patio, Cecile's bedroom glowed with light.

Valarie moved over the flagstone patio to the row of French doors that opened into the great room. She tapped her nails lightly on the glass. CECILE, she thought.

Soon a slight figure appeared on the landing of the central staircase.

CECILE, thought Valarie. LET ME IN.

A small woman with a tired face and dark circles under her eyes crossed the great room floor. She peered through the door at Valarie. Her hair, a mess of dark curls around her head, appeared to have been slept on. She wore a white nightshirt with a great wedge of yellow Swiss cheese silkscreened on the front. The cheese was inhabited by three mice, each poking a tapered snout from a different hole in the wedge. Curved above the graphic was the jingle, "What's a housie without a mousie!"

The woman's eyes were bright with alarm. OPEN IT.

A look of nausea reached the woman's little oval face but she pushed on the latch and the door opened inward.

"Valarie?"

NO, CECILE. DEATH. DEATH HAS FOUND YOU, CECILE.

The woman stepped back as the vampire entered.

THAT'S RIGHT, CECILE. Valarie looked around in the dark. NOW GO BACK TO BED.

"Back to bed..." repeated Cecile, her voice dreamy.

AND REMEMBER NOTHING.

"Nothing," said Cecile.

The woman in the rodent-riddled nightshirt obediently turned and marched back up the staircase, turning only once, at the top, to say "Good night, Valarie" before retiring into her own apartment.

Valarie moved across the rose-beige carpeting to the second staircase, which ascended to the north wing from the back of the kitchen. She moved up the stairs soundlessly, her heels barely denting the thick carpeting. When she reached the landing she turned only briefly to Mrs. Dumont's door at the head of the upstairs hall. SLEEP. Then she crossed the corridor.

The old man slept here, at the far end of the corridor. The Dumonts no longer slept together, hadn't since Philip started smoking Tiparillos a few years back. But Mr. Dumont was a good man, kind-hearted, hard-working. The kind of second generation European who lived for his family. Valarie had a momentary pang of human guilt, but it faded quickly as she opened his door and the bloodlust attacked her.

Old. Sweet. Innocent as a rose on the vine.

Valarie let herself in to the old man's room.

By midnight she was on her way back across the fields to the churchyard.

She moved quickly, for it was best now to distance herself from her crime. She had drained the old man in his bed, then carried him into the bath and laid him in the whirlpool, where she had opened his wrists. She'd left some evidence of foul play and a suggestion of suicide. After all, one could never be too careful. She would let the police muck about with the two possibilities, it would keep them busy longer.

Now she was filled with innocent blood and for the moment, she was satisfied. Philip Dumont's death would not be in vain. His widow and his daughter, horrified by the circumstances of his death, would sell the house at any price now to be rid of it. And Valarie would benefit a second time by their bad fortune.

The churchyard was nearly in sight. Valarie scanned the quiet graveyard for bloodscent before she slowed her pace. She did not wish to reappear before mortal eyes. But there was no life here. She began to cross the burial ground toward the parking lot and her car.

Suddenly a shadow moved across a headstone. Valarie stopped in her tracks and stiffened, listening. The cemetery was silent. But her vision was too keen to be wrong.

She took another step. Another. She skirted the headstone where the shadow had moved. Just as she began to believe she had been mistaken, Laroby materialized.

It seemed as though he sprang directly from the ground beneath him. There had been no sound, no motion, yet suddenly he loomed before her, larger than life, his face pale alabaster, his eyes gleaming jade, an outrageous highwayman's cloak fluttering from his massive shoulders like a flag from hell. Beneath it, the great expanse of his chest strained at the buttons of a leather vest. His narrow waist was cinched by a blood-red cummerbund.

He seemed to hesitate a moment, his eyes skimming her. Then he crossed his arms over his chest and his face twisted in a cynical grin.

"Well, well, well," he said.

Damn you, thought Valarie. You murderer. You thief. Yet within her, reason cautioned. He WAS a murderer, and a thief.

What did he want?

70

The answer came with the nausea that his presence demanded. A belly full of blood! Veins flowing with fresh life!

"Stay away from me you clown-from-hell," she growled through clenched teeth, and the blood she had taken flushed though her body, hardening it. Pumped with the old man's adrenaline, she felt herself grow resolute, implacable. This thief would not rob her twice.

The older vampire watched her, amusement dancing in his emerald eyes.

"Death becomes you," he said. "You no longer cower from me like a whipped dog."

Her teeth clenched at the insult.

"Get away from me, you bastard! I know what you want from me, and you can't have it!" she snarled, advancing.

"It is you who are drawn to me," he observed.

She stopped.

"Why else have you come, if not to steal, you thief!" she demanded.

Now he smiled.

"You called me here, my dear," he said.

"That's a lie! I want no part of you!" she screamed.

The brute raised his brows.

"Valarie, your voice will carry to the ears of the living. You have just committed murder. Do you really wish to call attention to yourself at this most crucial moment of your get-away?"

Valarie's eyes widened with alarm. She looked about, as if expecting a posse to appear out of thin air.

"Nice touch," said Laroby, gestured to her cap. "The hat. Not very traditional, but... cute."

He moved to her side and draped his arm over her shoulder.

"We must talk, you and I," he murmured softly in her ear. "You misunderstand me. I do not come to steal what you have stolen. I am full of blood myself and have no need of it."

He was steering her to her car.

"There is a more important matter between us. A matter of a certain gentleman. Very sweet, very innocent. Getting on in years, you might say. It seems you've been awfully careful with him. Seems you don't want to tarnish his goodness, infect him with your evil and all that. I find this amusing. Amusing, yes. And a little... disconcerting, too. After all, you are like me now. You can do as you please. No need to spare the innocent. If you don't corrupt them, well," he shrugged, "someone else will!"

He released her in front of the Civic's driver door and went around to the opposite side. Then he leaned his elbows on the roof and waited for her to speak.

She looked up at him over the top of the car.

"What do you want, Laroby?"

"What do I want?" repeated the demon, nodding for her to get in.

"This is about what you want, Valarie, not what I want." He opened his door and climbed inside. "This is quite snug," he murmured to himself as he made an effort to arrange his considerable bulk in the tiny compartment.

"Claustrophobic, even for me," he winked across at her. "Hah!" he laughed at his little joke.

Valarie grit her teeth.

"Tally-ho!" said the fiend, gesturing for her to start the car.

"Where?" she asked quietly.

But his answer was a question, whispered in the dark. "Why, where else but Jack's house, Valarie?"

Valarie shook her head, staring unbelieving at him.

"Oh, no. No I won't take you there," she said, but her eyes were glittering.

"DRIVE!"

He bellowed the command and his magnificent baritone rumbled through the cabin of the little car like a thunderclap. Valarie turned the ignition and pulled out of the parking lot before the windows stopped rattling.

"I don't want you to hurt him," Valarie whispered after a time.

"Well, we're quite the little Florence Nightingale tonight," chuckled the fiend beside her. Then his features flattened. He peered through the windshield into the rain, his viridian eyes glimmering under doll-length lashes.

73

"Bloodlust is not love, Valarie," he muttered, staring into the dark. "You confuse the two. But love is no longer in you. What you possess now is passion."

"I always had passion," she answered.

He chuckled again.

"Are you so sure?" he said, turning to her.

She fell silent. When they came to the turn off at Beach Neck Lane he nodded. GO ON.

Valarie took a dry breath and swallowed.

"Does he die tonight?" she whispered.

The demon smiled.

"That is your dilemma."

Valarie pulled the Honda on to the grassy shoulder across the street from the Howell's mansion and killed the engine.

"Will you let me go on from here alone then?" she asked quietly.

"Very well," he unfolded himself from the tiny car and regarded her over the hood.

His emerald eyes twinkled in the dingy street light. With a conspiratorial wink he snapped his cloak over his head and vanished.

Valarie exhaled, her breath misting in the cool air. They had driven ahead of the rain. In Old Point, the air was heavy with expectation.

She turned to face the great old house she had come to rob. It was flooded with artificial light. From the road it looked warm and safe. A fortress.

Sadness enveloped her. She did not want to hurt this man, or his family. Tears stung her eyes, and when she wiped the first of them away she was not surprised that they were bloody. She slid to her haunches, crumpled in a sleek black heap against her car, and wept silently.

Ten

In the dream, he heard her voice against his ear. She was weeping his name and hot, blood tears trickled from the corners of her almond eyes to stain his white shirt. She was holding her body against his, begging comfort as the scarlet tears spilled generously down the front of his shirt until his shirt was soaked with them.

He felt her cheek turn against his shoulder. Now her lips brushed the hollow under his chin, searching, nuzzling, like a calf at its mother's belly. Then they withdrew, and he felt her teeth tug at his collar, heard the soft moan in her throat as her mouth found what it sought, and her tongue lay against his pulse.

He was awake.

Joan had turned over against him in her sleep. Her arm was folded over his chest, and her fingers, splayed against his neck, twitched spastically in a dream.

He jerked away from her reflexively and sat up in the dark to peer at the clock. It was midnight.

The sensation that someone watched him, impossibly, from the second story bedroom window, invaded him. He rose quickly and pulled on a pair of sweatpants. Avoiding the window, he moved to the doorway. He was perspiring although the room was chill.

Where was he going?

He sat back down on the edge of the bed and dropped his head in his hands, recalling the dream. The feeling lingered that he had been holding Valarie, allowing her moist lips to nuzzle against his throat, until Joan's fingers wrestled her from him.

And a chill went through him, leaving the hairs erect at the back of his neck. He turned and looked at his wife in the dull light. A lock of damaged, platinum hair fell across her cheek, creating the illusion of a gash. He could not force himself to return to her side.

Slowly he rose and moved around the room gathering what he needed: sweatshirt, socks, sneakers. Then he checked once more to see that Joan was sleeping before he left her and padded down the hall to the stairs.

The click of the Howells' screen door latch was enough to bring Valarie to her feet. Her vampire hearing told her that somehow, at midnight, someone was leaving the Howell house.

"Oh God," she choked. Her hands were bloody with vampire tears and she knew her face must be also. She scrambled into the

Civic, turned the ignition, and shot down the road to the bay. There was no time to make a U-turn in front of Jack's house and return to the highway.

She cut the engine at the end of Beach Neck Lane and opened the moon roof, sighing with relief. But her confidence was misguided. The distinct, crisp sound of sneakers against pavement was steadily approaching. Someone was jogging down to the water at this ungodly hour!

"Damn you," she muttered, closing her eyes and leaning her head against the wheel. "Hell of a time to go jogging, Jack."

She stripped off her jacket, cleaned her hands and cheeks on the lining, and snapped on the overhead light to check her face in the mirror. There was still a smudge of scarlet under her eyes. Instinctively she dabbed a corner of the jacket lining to her tongue to blend it away. But a blot of crimson appeared on the dampened material.

"Oh, Jesus, saliva too?" She checked the mirror again, wiping away the last smudges with a dry portion of the lining. "This never happened before," she moaned, running her tongue over her teeth, then checking them in the mirror. The rhythmic footfalls were fast approaching. She rolled the jacket into a ball and threw it in the back seat, then looked over her shoulder out the back window. She could see a figure bobbing down the lane toward her through the mist.

"Damn." She raked her fingers through her hair, checked the mirror once more, and stepped out of the car.

She had stepped from her car and turned toward him in the mist as though it were the most natural thing imaginable that they should meet there, at the end of his street, in the dead of night. Moonlight bathed her. She wore only a silk blouse and a short skirt but she did not appear to feel the damp wind at her back. Her hair was tousled by it, gathering like dark smoke about her shoulders. She did not smile. She did not speak. Like a specter she stood motionless, watching him, her blouse billowing in the rough air, her dark eyes glowing like black diamonds.

"Valarie."

He stopped an arm's length from her.

"You're out here alone?"

She didn't answer at first. After a moment she turned abruptly away from him and sighed.

"Til now," she glanced up at him, then leaned against the car beside him.

"What brings you out, Jack?" She gave him a measured look. "Bad dreams?"

A jolt of adrenaline shot through his veins at her casual accuracy.

"As a matter of fact," he answered, "I dreamed of you."

"Oh?" Her eyes narrowed.

"Yes," he said. It was nearly a whisper. "You were crying," he gave her a gentle look. "And your tears were made of blood."

Her eyes widened at him. She took a step away and combed her fingers over her scalp.

"What is it?" he asked her softly, moving closer. "What's happening between us?" he lifted one hand as if to reach for her.

"Please," she took another step back. "That's not a good idea."

He let his hand drop to his side.

"I know," he said. "But I get them anyway." He searched her face. Then he reached for her again, this time drawing her without resistance into a spontaneous embrace.

She moaned, a feral sound.

"Valarie," he muttered against her hair.

He kissed her mouth. She had become corporeal at last. He pulled her to himself, amazed at the compact density of this creature who had for so long seemed ethereal to him. Then a lovely surprise as her elegant hands came up to lie against his face and she returned his kiss, drawing herself up against him and arching in an embrace so tight that it took his breath.

It required all of his strength to push her away.

She made a little cry of disappointment as he did it, and a cloud of anger passed over her features. Then she drew back.

"Jack," she breathed. "I can't do this. I don't want to do this to you."

He looked at her quietly. He shook his head, frowning.

"You don't want to do this to me? You've done nothing. I'm to blame. I should know better." He thought a moment. "I do know better." And he turned to leave.

But she caught his arm.

"You don't understand. You don't know what you're up against here. You aren't in control this time, Jack Howell. You're over your head. Listen. Stay away from me. I'm deadly. I'll destroy you."

"Like you destroyed Valanchuk? That bastard's never been happier." He smirked.

She let go of his arm, her lids dropping over her jeweled eyes.

"Suit yourself then," she said, shoving him out of her way as she turned to open the door of the Honda.

She had swooned in the cage of his mortal embrace. She had fought the urge to coil around him, to crush his bones in the viperous vampire grip, though her body burned with the dizzying heat of the bloodlust. Vampire mouth against mortal, her thirst had become a panic of greed. She had felt her lips pull back over her teeth, her canines pounding for the soft relief of his throat. But his sweet mortal mouth had been oblivious to the danger. He had kissed her tenderly, worshipfully.

She would kill this man if he touched her again. There was no longer any doubt. There would be no further reprieves for the Howell family.

81

Valarie gunned the engine of the little Honda and sped, into the impervious night, from her worst nightmare.

PART TWO

One

The little priest sat with his back to the sun, comically diminutive behind the expanse of the great mahogany desk that separated him from his penitent. He was nearly bald, and what was left of his silver hair was trimmed close to his round little head. His black cassock was serious, censuring, but his brown eyes sparkled with mirth behind his glasses and a broad smile never left his features, even as he spoke in prayer.

He was praying now, leading Valarie in the Apostle's Creed, his sing-song accent betraying his Polynesian origins. As he spoke the words of the devotion, she repeated them in tandem with him, her eyelids shut so tightly that she could see the feathery pinkness of her own blood vessels pulsing within them. When he had finished the prayer, Father Tito folded his hands together on his lap.

"Now, my child," he said. "What brings you to Immaculate Mary's today? What is it that you wish to confess to the priest?"

Valarie looked up sadly at the little man behind the ornate desk. She sighed and bowed her head to recite the correct penitential response.

"Bless me father, for I have sinned. It has been seven years since my last confession."

"Oh, yes, yes. You come for absolution," he nodded, waving his hand abruptly. "But you asked to see a priest immediately, Valarie. Something is troubling you deeply, something you have told no one else, and can no longer hide in your heart. Something only the priest can hear. What is it you need to tell Jesus?"

"Father, I--I've taken what isn't mine, I'm a thief. I've stolen what was never meant for me, sucked the blood out of people, destroyed families, thought only of myself. I'm a bloodsucking parasite, and I'm never satisfied. I'm always hungry for more."

She blinked at him, shocked by her own admission. Then she dropped her face into her hands and moaned.

But the priest was not perturbed.

"My child, the Lord knows your sins before you speak them, and yet His arms are ever open to you. His blood has washed away all of our sins, yours and mine. We are all hungry. But the only bread that satisfies is the Bread of Life, the only blood that heals, His Blood. And the only drink that quenches us, the Living Water."

She looked at him through her fingers. "What did you say about blood, Father?"

The priest had come around his desk to stand beside her chair. He laid a diminutive hand on her shoulder, reciting the passage as if to a truculent child.

"Whosoever eats My flesh and drinks My blood has eternal life. For My flesh is food indeed and My blood is drink."

"Jesus Christ said that?" Valarie blinked at him.

"Oh yes, these are His words!" he laughed. "Oh, Valarie, you have been away a long time! But you are welcomed home like the prodigal son whose father waits for him on the road with open arms!"

She shook her head. "You don't understand, Father-" "But the Lord understands you, Valarie, and knows the depth of your sin, and he instructs his priest to offer you forgiveness in his name. And so, if you will give me an act of contrition--" and he began his absolution.

"And now, for your penance, Valarie, I would like you to read for us a poem, written by the English poet Francis Thompson in the late 19th century, and one of the most famous tributes to God's unfathomable mercy and divine faithfulness .."

The little priest prattled on as he flipped through a volume that had been sitting on the corner of the great desk, sandwiched between several other volumes of poetry. Valarie watched, uncomprehending, as he found what he was looking for and handed her the opened book.

She took it from him, hesitating briefly before looking down at the text.

"'The Hound of Heaven?'"

"Read please," gestured the priest. He settled himself into his chair, tilting his head back and closing his eyes as if readying himself for a sunbath.

And read she did, thought the meaning of the voluptuous verses were lost on her. Now and then she stole a glance at the priest as he sat quietly in his chair, his face a picture of contemplative ecstasy, his lips curled in the peacefully vacant smile of a corpse.

When she was finished Father Tito opened his eyes and clapped his hands together, chuckling merrily.

"Oh, isn't it beautiful, Valarie, and do you see how the Lord has waited also for you to return to him at the end of your searching and like the Hound of Heaven has kept from you what you desire 'Not for thy harms, but just that thee might'st seek it' in His arms..."

She stared at him. She closed her eyes, squeezed them shut, opened them. Father Tito was still talking, it seemed, in one continuous run-on sentence.

"Father," she interrupted finally, "what if I do it again?"

"Valarie, we all will sin again and again on this earth but 'not by works are we justified but by faith.' You see, just as gold is tested and made pure by fire, we are tested and made pure by trials and tribulations but the Blood of the Lamb sanctifies all who believe in Him."

The vampire covered her face with her hands. He was making no sense. All this talk of sanctity. Faith. Blood. Blood.

Not just innocent but...she lifted her head, her eyes glittering... Divine.

"Communion," she whispered.

Father Tito, for once, was reticent.

"I want Communion, Father," demanded the vampire.

"Then you will come celebrate mass with us on Sunday?" asked Father Tito.

"Sunday," agreed Valarie. "Yes, I'll come to church on Sunday, Father." And she rose and, thanking him, she left the rectory.

Two

It was a simple Vehicular Homicide, a typical DWI fatality. The victim, a young marine, driving home on leave in a yellow Karmann Ghia, was instantly decapitated by a collision with a nursery truck on Southern State Highway. The operator of the truck, a thirty-two year old alcoholic, had stopped for a few shots on his way home from work. He had been weaving on a wet road for a quarter of an hour when the Karmann Ghia pulled onto the parkway from an entrance ramp. The truck was in the center lane, but veered into the right lane just as the little sports car was accelerating into traffic. The collision sent the Volkswagen rocketing off the roadway toward a lone hitchhiker, who would later testify that she saw the marine cut his wheel in the last minute in a desperate attempt to avoid her. That final act of mercy threw the Karmann Ghia into a roll, down the steep embankment and into the trees at the bottom of the hill. The marine's head remained attached to his body by a shred of erector spinae. He had been belted in, which saved the emergency team from searching for body parts, but did nothing for the marine. It was the hood of the little car that had done the job. Smashed open by a frontal impact with the trees it flipped open and back, slicing through the windshield and knifing through the driver's cabin to remove the driver's head with diabolical accuracy.

The case was in Valarie's rolling file at 9:00 a.m. It was her habit to stop in the steno pool and check her mail for new cases as soon as she came in each morning. This morning there was only one, the Homicide case, and as she read the D.A.'s material, standing over her unit's rolling file, her face clouded with rage. She looked up from the referral, her eyes flicking about the room in search of the miscreant who had assigned her the case.

"Where's the boss?" She had directed the question to Karen James, Jack's private secretary. But the steno room quieted instantly.

"He should be in any minute," Karen offered. "Want me to tell him you need to see him?" She pushed her glasses in place with an ink-stained finger. "No," answered the vampire, quietly letting the referral file slip from her fingers. It fell apart as it hit the floor, documents scattering on little puffs of air in all directions.

"Just tell him I'm not doing it," she said. She felt an unexpected satisfaction as the hen heads turned, one to another, around the room.

"And don't put it back in my rolling file," she said quietly to her own steno, Donna Deluca.

"Whe--whe--well--" began Donna, who had a bad stutter under the best conditions. "Jack ref-ff--ferred it t-t-t-"

"Don't," said the vampire, her eyes glittering under half-closed lids. "Don't even pick it up. Don't touch it." She looked deliberately about the room at the other women. "Let him step on it when he comes in."

She waited for an argument, but none came. Only Joanne Harris rolled her eyes dramatically as she swiveled around to return to the work on her desk.

At 9:08 a.m. Jack stood in the steno pool doorway looking down at the scattered pages of the Puentez file. Valarie's initials, printed in bold red marker across the referral page, lay at his feet. He blinked in dim confusion at Karen, his initial impulse to quip about the poor housekeeping in the steno area quelled by seven pair of eyes riveted to his reaction.

"Valarie doesn't...um...I don't think...she wants that case." Karen offered.

"What?"

"She just...sort of...dropped it there...for you."

"WHAT?"

"She seemed pretty upset," Karen tried.

His black eyes fell to the papers at his feet.

"Why did you leave them there?" he asked quietly.

"She to-told us not to tou-touch it," Donna jumped in, before realizing this was a rhetorical question. She hopped off her chair to gather the documents.

"Whe-where do you wa-want it?" she stuttered.

"I referred it to Valarie Valanchuk," Jack responded with chilling calm.

"You...sure you want to give it back to her?" Karen asked gently.

"Yes," replied Jack, "I'm sure." He paused for effect before disappearing down the hall toward his office.

Jack tossed his Newsday on his blotter and stepped behind his desk, shoving his fists into his trouser pockets. What in hell had gotten into her?

Normally a blatant act of insubordination like this would be met by an official memo, perhaps even a formal disciplinary hearing. But this was Valarie, and Jack had no intention of marring Valarie's perfect record as an investigator with a hearing.

It might get her transferred into the field.

Which would be unbearable.

No. This would have to be handled a bit differently. A memo would brand this little misunderstanding "official." It would involve others. Like Griffin.

All in all a private, face to face confrontation seemed a more agreeable alternative.

"Jack wants to see you in his office." Karen poked her blond bob through Valarie's closed door timidly, an expression of surprise crossing her face when she saw that Valarie had never taken off her leather jacket and was leaning back in her chair, her boots crossed on the edge of her desk, her arms folded in front of her, staring blandly out of her narrow office window toward the parking lot.

As if roused from sleep she pulled her feet off the desk and turned listless, red-rimmed eyes toward the boss's secretary.

"Ok," she said.

"Are you alright?" Karen's voice was conciliatory.

"Ah," sighed the vampire, "no. I am not alright." She cut a row of parts through her hair with her fingers. "None of this..." she waved a hand, "is alright." She stood, then looked down at herself and gave a weak laugh. She looked at Karen helplessly.

"Is it cold in here?" she asked.

"Well, I'm not, but... maybe you have a fever or something, your eyes don't look right."

"Mmm, a fever," Valarie shrugged off the jacket, tossed it across her chair and followed Karen out.

Outside Jack's office Karen gave Valarie a concerned frown.

"Good luck," she said, knocking on his door before leaving the vampire there to let herself in.

Valarie pushed the door open with the tip of one finger and closed it behind her with a spiked heel. It shut with a crack.

When Jack looked up from his desk his expression was studiously nonchalant.

She licked her lips.

"I thought it was common knowledge how my husband died," she said, taking a step toward his desk. Her eyes were hot and heavy-lidded.

A flicker of sudden realization crossed Jack's cool expression.

"I've... given you DWI fatalities before," he said.

She dropped her lids to half-mast and lowered her body into the chair in front of his desk.

"Yes," she agreed, "you have. But this is different, Jack." She spoke softly, setting her chin on her palm and drumming a set of long white nails along her cheekbone. "This is heartless."

She watched him.

Jack looked down at his desk. He opened the Puentez file and thumbed through to the coroner's report. After a moment his face lost all expression and his gazed returned to her.

"I don't generally read the police reports, Valarie. If there's a similarity...I didn't know," he said softly.

"Didn't know? Didn't know what? That my husband was beheaded by a drunk in a Karmann Ghia? That he was a military man? Or that this poor bastard met with the same fate?"

"I honestly didn't know either," he shook his head. "Of course I'll reassign the case." He closed the file as if the problem had been neatly solved by their discussion. But the vampire only stretched her legs out and folded her hands together under her chin.

"Is there something else?" Jack asked uncomfortably.

"Yes. I think so." Her eyes settled on his tie.

He made a mask of his face, meeting her hostility with his own blank glare.

She didn't flinch.

"What I don't understand," said Valarie, watching him with jewel-bright eyes, "is how an innocent man can be so cruel. You like me. You think you need to possess me. Yet you blindly inflict pain, without intention, and then dismiss it, without apology." Her brows lifted.

"Where is your innocence now? Can I have misjudged you? It seemed to me your heart was decent, but maybe what I've mistake for decency is only a lack of deliberate malice." She sighed. "Without generosity, without compassion, what good is that?"

"Would you like to convince yourself that I have no feelings for you, Valarie? Pretend what you like. I feel-- a great deal," he clenched his hands on either side of the Puentez file.

She rose and leaned over the desk, aligning her hands with his.

"Be careful, Jack," she said, tapping his knuckles with a finger. "I'm very hungry."

"What makes you think you've cornered the market on hunger?" he whispered, turning his palm up to catch her finger.

Her ears pulled back across her skull like a mad cat, elongating her face. She snatched her hand away. When she had regained her composure she turned abruptly to the door.

"I'm sorry for you then," she said, and stepped into the hall, shutting it behind her.

Three

"It's too late for me," she moaned in the dream to the crimson bird at her bedroom window. But the creature only opened its wings to her, beckoning.

"Stay away from me! Don't you see? I'm wicked, I'm dead!" she cried, but the bird continued to unfold its wings to her, like the petals of a rose opening in the rain, or like a fountain, rising, spreading crimson until it was no longer a bird but a man, robed in red, and scarlet with wounds from head to foot, his arms lifted to her as he offered his embrace.

"Did I do that to you?" she sobbed, seeing that the terrible gaping wounds at his neck and wrists and feet were bleeding freely. But the apparition only gazed down upon her with the tenderest compassion in his tormented face. His cheeks were washed in bloody tears that mingled with the rivulets of blood coursing from his hairline.

He did not answer.

"It must have been me," she said, and ran her tongue over her teeth, anticipating the unnatural sharpness of the canines but finding none. "But where are my fangs?" she whispered to the

96

beautiful victim. He no longer stood at her window but sat beside her on her bed.

"Valarie," he said. And his voice! The one word was a symphony of sounds and chords, unimaginable to the human ear.

"Drink," he said. His eyes were sapphires. "I am innocent."

"NO!" cried the vampire, as the vision lifted his bloody hands to his breast and tore open the robe to reveal a terrible fresh wound at his side. From it flowed a river of blood, impossibly abundant. His blood was everywhere. It soaked the white sheets she lay upon. Valarie froze, unwilling to accept the terrible feast, yet unable to refuse it.

The blood angel smiled and bent to touch her mouth with an immaculate kiss before he disappeared.

Valarie was awake, but immobile. Her body lay, as if in state, across her bed. Her skin burned in the bright summer sunlight that poured through her bedroom window. Her preternatural vision found the clock on the nightstand peripherally and made out the time: 7:51 a.m. Dean had already left for the Riverdale office. She was alone in the little cottage. And she was completely paralyzed.

Her first inclination was to scream out in terror. That desire died in her throat. Her vocal chords were unresponsive to her will.

An eternity passed. She lay in the brilliant daylight, burning with heat. Bloody perspiration trickled down her sides, soaking the white sheets about her. She fought with every fiber of strength she had to make her body obey her. But it would not. She felt her tears mingle with the bloodsweat and run down her temples, over her scalp and onto the bed sheets.

8:16 a.m. A sound. Finally, a sound broke through the horrifying stillness. A beat. A tiny drum. The precious music of her own heart had reached her vampire hearing. Now she managed a swallow, to flex her fingers, and finally, to move her arms and legs with large, grotesque gestures. She heaved her body off the bed. The bloody print of her perspiration on the sheets repulsed her and she lurched away from them, stumbling, mummy-like, into the bathroom and the shower. She turned on the cold water and began to wash the bloodsweat from her body, but the icy water did nothing to cool her burning flesh. The shower floor was pink with blood and water. When her body was finally clean, she shuffled out of the bath and dove into the black safety of her closet. For a moment she merely stood there, pressing her bare back against the closed door. The coolness of the darkened room was a caress.

But it had happened. Death had found her.

Her vampire vision had no difficulty discerning colors in the dark. She dressed in a black turtleneck tunic and leggings, taking the extra precaution of boots as an afterthought. Only her face and hands were exposed now.

She shuffled gingerly out of the closet, testing the light. Her eyes adjusted immediately. Her face felt warm and she imagined it was flushed, but it did not burn. Her hands were cool.

"Extremities. They're not affected yet." She considered the idea briefly before kicking off a boot and baring her right foot. She felt the unnatural warmth immediately, but it did not burn.

And then the dream returned to her in a thunderbolt of clarity. The crimson bird at the window, the man, dressed in blood, offering himself. And the kiss. The kiss that woke her to paralysis and agony.

Who was he? What was he? She thought of her promise to the little priest, her promise to return to church for Communion on Sunday. That had been two weeks ago.

She had put the idea aside, forgotten it almost entirely until now. Now it seemed time was running out for her. And she had to do something before it was too late.

Perhaps the crimson bird and the priest were telling her the same thing? Perhaps an antidote for death did exist? Could it be Communion?

As she considered this insane solution, the two sides of her nature collided in the battleground of her flesh. Her stomach turned, bile rising in her throat, yet her skin tingled with a quenching chill like a curtain of cool air under the wings of a bird.

A crimson bird.

And she knew what she must do.

Four

"I've been to see a priest, Dean," said Valarie to her thrall that evening. "I've been to confession. I received absolution and I haven't killed since. Tomorrow I'm going to receive Communion."

"What?" Dean was incredulous.

"It's true. I saw a priest two weeks ago. I confessed and I told him I'd come back for Communion. I'm going to do it, too."

"But do you feel...any different?" he asked. "I mean, since you spoke to him?"

She pursed her lips and looked down. "No."

"Not at all?"

"No," said the vampire. "Except I haven't been so hungry. And I haven't fed in a long time, Dean." She picked up her black leather jacket as she moved toward the door.

"So then where are you going at 8:00 p.m., honey?" asked Dean, looking from the jacket to his wife.

"Just a walk."

"Just a walk?"

"Yeah." She shrugged the jacket over her shoulders and pecked him on the cheek.

"Be careful," he said.

"Don't worry," said the vampire.

"Dad, could you drive me over to Nichole's? We're going to the game tonight and then I'm sleeping over." The girl with the corkscrew red hair was talking from behind the refrigerator door where, Jack assumed, she searched for something dietetic.

"And anyway, you said you would yesterday." She popped her head out from behind the door, a hard-boiled egg making a white 'O' of her open mouth.

"What kind of diet is that?" Jack asked abstractly. He was sitting at the kitchen table with a cup of coffee and the Saturday Suffern News. Now that construction on the Bird Island sanctuary was no longer blocked, the paper was filled with ecstatic reports from developers and real estate brokers that the Suffern recession would soon be over. For Jack, the loss of the sanctuary was an environmental tragedy. He had no appetite this morning.

"High protein," said his daughter, popping another egg into her mouth.

"Mm," he responded, her original question escaping him.

"DA-A-A-D!?" the girl screeched.

"Lisa, you don't have to raise your voice, I can hear," said Jack, looking up from his paper.

"Will you take me?" repeated Lisa.

"What time?" he looked at his watch, sipping coffee thoughtfully.

"Eight o'clock," she replied, and bumped into her mother coming around the dining room doorway.

"My God, Lisa, watch where you're going," said Joan. "No game today, honey?" she asked him as she pulled a mug from a cabinet and poured herself a cup of black coffee.

Jack looked up. His wife was wrapped in her favorite silk robe. She appeared shapeless in it, a blur of vague beiges and creams. On cue, an image of Valarie in black pounced through his thoughts like a panther. His wife invariably lost in physical comparison to Valarie, and when he reminded himself of this fact, which he frequently did, his social and financial stature plummeted in his own estimation. The enormous house, the prestigious position, the bridge and the golf games, they all seemed pathetic and empty to him, an old man's pastimes. The true prize in life was a woman whose value diminished the value of all else.

He fought back the urge to lash out at his chosen companion with a cynical comment. It was a mindless urge, vicious and completely foreign to him. He shrank from it, forcing himself to go to her instead and plant a sexless peck on her forehead before closing her feeble upper body in a cold embrace.

"I'm all yours," he lied. "What do you have in mind?"

"I thought we might spend the day together, take a ride out east in your new toy, maybe stop for dinner at Pandora's."

Jack's heart sank. He had no desire to leave town. Old Inlet, at least for the moment, was still where Valarie was. Here he might run into her at any moment, unless...

"You know," he offered nonchalantly, "that might be fun. One of my officers is looking at a house in Pequot Bog. We could take a ride out there and see it. It's supposed to be pretty unusual. Would you mind?"

"Well, no, of course not." Joan's bottle-blue eyes scanned her husband's face with special interest. "Which officer?"

"One of the supervisors. He and his wife want to move back out east where he grew up. He works in the Riverdale office," he added perfunctorily.

Joan gave him a wary glance before turning to the back stairs. "I didn't know you took such an interest in your staff, Jack. I'd like to meet this couple sometime."

"Sure." Jack watched her ascent. When she was out of sight he crossed to the dining room and lifted back a curtain to check the street. No joggers interrupted his view of the neighbor's white Victorian. He pushed his clenched hands into his trouser pockets and shuffled through the parlor to the front stairs. It was risky driving past a house he knew Valarie intended to buy and might even be visiting today for that purpose. Still, he could think of no other reason to acquiesce to his wife's wishes, and if Valarie (or Dean) did see him, he could simply stop and say he'd been curious about the place from Dean's enthusiastic description of it. It was

Dean, after all, who'd mentioned his possible new address to Jack at a supervisor's meeting earlier that week.

The day passed uneventfully, but Jack's mood was black from the moment he laid eyes on the house he had gone to take stock of. It was an enormous rectangular contemporary, faced with horizontal cedar planking. The low roofline and frontal breadth of the facade gave it a brooding look, and it was tucked away behind a stand of tall spruce at the end of a lonely cul-de-sac. Like a fortress, it was unattainable but from one direction.

The thought of Valarie moving here, so far from Old Inlet and from him, was a dagger resting squarely in his heart.

Joan was no help. She speculated on the spacious modern rooms inside, commented on the rather warren-like style of their own three story dinosaur, and suggested that the new owners would be quite content here, except for the rural location perhaps.

Jack barely touched the stuffed flounder he'd ordered for dinner, said little on the drive home, and spent the rest of the afternoon in the den drinking gin and tonic and staring at a ball game. At 8:00 p.m. he drove his daughter to her friend's house. Then he took the Miata down to the village dock and parked.

It was a clear night, warm and still. There were two other cars parked at the end of the dock, a cream-colored Pontiac and a grey coupe. Both were occupied. Jack relaxed against his headrest and drummed his fingers absently on the steering column. He was, he realized, exhausted from driving all day and from the emotional backlash that came with the visit to the house in Pequot Bog. Valarie was leaving. Moving away from him. He was losing her, and somehow it seemed he was losing a piece of himself.

He crossed his arms over his chest and closed his eyes.

He was just beginning to doze when the click of the passenger door latch caused him to start. His face darkened with anger but just as quickly lightened with delight when a lean, black-clad form settled beside him in the passenger seat.

Valarie clicked the passenger door shut, ignoring him, and ran a hand over the surface of the dashboard in front of her.

"Nice," she said, turning to him with a devilish smile.

"Yes," he had to clear his throat before the word would come. "It is," he added, returning her smile.

She looked into his face for a long moment, then, perversely, frowned down at the seat beneath her and made a little growl in her throat.

"Something warm-blooded has been sitting here for a very long time," she said, lifting her eyebrow at him.

For a moment he had the urge to prevaricate, to tell her that he'd been driving with his daughter all day. The desire confounded him. He had a right, after all, to take his wife for a ride in his new car.

"Well, I don't know about the warm-blooded part but I have been driving all day with my wife," he answered.

She ignored the humor, even seemed to grit her teeth for an instant as she looked out at the bay through the windshield.

"I thought I'd lose the desire if I confessed it." She was talking to herself. "But," she looked back at him, "it has a life of its own."

"I haven't heard you confess any desires, Valarie," Jack whispered. "In fact, you've been doing a pretty good job of rejecting me for some time now."

"Hmph," she made that feline sound again. "I have, haven't I?" Then her brows screwed up in a little frown. "But am I forgiven?"

Jack swallowed. "Yes, of course," he said.

"Then I'll keep my end of the bargain," she affirmed.

"What's that?"

For the first time Valarie blinked at him as though she had expected a different response.

"Never mind. I just mean I don't intend to hurt you, no matter what. I'm not going through that hell again." Then she lifted a hand and stroked his head once. It was an odd gesture, utterly unexpected and too familiar. He waited for her to repeat it, to cross that line again, but she only withdrew her hand and placed it harmlessly in her lap.

"What am I going to do with you," he said.

"Nothing," she answered.

"I want to be with you," he heard himself confess.

"I'm not capable," she responded.

106

"Then why are you here?" he whispered.

She looked at him evenly.

"I guess I was testing myself. To see if I could really do it, could be with you without," she looked up again but her gaze leveled at his throat, "tearing you apart."

"Oh God," Jack turned back to his steering wheel and grabbed it with both hands. "You'd better go now," he said, noticing the cream-colored Pontiac backing up and moving slowly around the Yacht Club House toward Robin's Hill Road. "Someone could see us together."

"Hah?!" she lifted her brows in surprise, threw back her head and laughed merrily. "Is that what you're worried about?" She ran her index fingers under her eyes and checked for tears, still giggling. "Hey!" she said, looking down at her hands, amazed. "Real tears! I'm human!"

"I don't see the humor," Jack murmured.

But Valarie had already slipped out of the car. She clicked the passenger door closed as she leaned over it to give him her answer.

"Your idea of sin, Jack," she said.

Then she straightened and he heard her take a deep breath and sighing contentedly before she sauntered off.

Five

"Blessed are You, Lord God of all Creation, for through Your grace we have this wine to offer. Fruit of the vine and work of human hands, it will become for us our spiritual drink."

"BLESSED BE GOD FOREVER."

The priest who raised the chalice of Precious Blood above the altar towered over his congregation. He was an enormous man and the hooded Franciscan robe he wore under his white vestments only amplified his abundance.

Father Thomas was the pastor at Saint Luke's in East Patton, the next parish over from Immaculate Mary's, where a vampire had received absolution from a little Polynesian priest two weeks earlier. Father Thomas knew his flock by name, and greeted them individually each Sunday morning in front of his church before Mass.

Valarie learned this when she appeared the next morning on the church steps.

"And what have we here? A new face! Well, very nice to have you!"

Father Thomas, towering over her from a height that rivaled Laroby's, embalmed her in his ample embrace. But not until he had released her did she look up into his face and flinch with recognition, for there a pair of marine blue eyes regarded her with angelic affection. But no. This was no angel. This was only a priest. A priest with a halo of curly blond hair framing his apple-cheeked face.

"I've come from Immaculate Mary's," she offered, drawing back from the intimate embrace. She smoothed her hair.

But Father Thomas's smile only brightened.

"Oh-hoh! Another defector!" he laughed in his incongruous alto, shushing her toward the foyer doors. "We've got another defector from Mary's!" he shouted to his arriving congregation.

But now Father Thomas was at his altar, lifting his arms at his sides so that his vestments spread to their full dimensions, and for an instant Valarie was struck by an opposing vision, a vision of a demon in a black cape opening his arms to her before a grave in a misty churchyard.

"So then pray my brethren that our sacrifice may be acceptable to God," said Father Thomas, and his parish responded with the appropriate devotion.

"MAY THE LORD ACCEPT THE SACRIFICE AT YOUR HANDS, FOR THE PRAISE AND GLORY OF HIS NAME, FOR OUR GOOD AND THE GOOD OF ALL HIS CHURCH."

Valarie looked up from her prayer. She was standing in a rear pew, behind which was an aisle and then a final row of seats against the back wall. The church was filled to bursting. The chairs behind her were occupied and people were standing along the side walls, under the Stations of the Cross and the statues of St. Frances and St. Claire. Most peculiar to her in this strange church was the crucifix, which was not the usual Christ in Agony, but a Risen Christ with shining countenance and outstretched arms. He was handsome enough, and his eyes seemed to watch her from any angle, but she missed the Crucified Jesus she knew, the familiar suffering servant hanging in torment in his terrible final hours on earth.

"This is the Lamb of God who takes away the sins of the world," said Father Thomas, "happy are those who are called to His Supper."

"Oh Lord I am not worthy to receive you," said the vampire, "but only say the word and I am healed."

It was a different priest, a short, chubby friar with silver-rimmed glasses and a complacent aspect who gave the vampire Communion in the form of the consecrated Host. And a parishioner, one of six who approached the altar to help serve after the consecration, offered her the cup of Precious Blood. She took the bread and wine like any human, carrying the Host gingerly and

110

reverently on her tongue as she returned to her pew and kneeled obediently when she arrived there. Then she let her dark head drop into her hands as the quiet tears of gratitude came. Clear tears. Uncomplicated, human tears.

"I won't betray You again," she said to her new Master, and in her soul she believed that she would not.

The fangs were gone, the morning rigor mortis, too. Valarie was mortal again, or so it seemed.

Two things remained of her vampire life, the predatory strength in her body, and the complexity of her feelings for Jack. But both of these were altered. For although her body remained lean and muscular, her strength was no longer a bizarre, supernatural manifestation. She was robust for her sex, but no stronger than any athlete of equal size. She wondered if perhaps she'd earned this one advantage during the trial of her spiritual death, when she ate only a little meat and wine and prowled most of the night, making nothing of a physical battle with a male twice her size.

As for the feelings she retained for Jack, these too had altered in her mortality. She no longer starved for his innocence, but merely for his company. She did not understand this emotion, imagining that it was a desire for forgiveness from one whose life she had coveted, or perhaps a desire to earn his affection as a mortal, and to know that his affection was for her mortality, and not for the vampire, who was extinct in her. He had, after all, loved only the vampire, and the vampire was no more.

"Bridge at the Curtis' tonight, Jack," called Joan from the shower. She'd heard her husband come in and snap on his electric razor, and she knew she'd have only a few moments with him this morning to solidify the obligation.

Ever since their drive out to Pequot Bog on Saturday, her husband had been behaving oddly, in fact he was fast becoming downright unpredictable. He spoke to her in single-word sentences or not at all, never initiating conversation, and his once charming, if cynical, sense of humor had been displaced by an abstract veneer which only barely hid an unheard of temper. The man she had married for his gentle disposition and intelligent good humor (not to mention his family's money) had overnight become as rejecting and as frightening as her father.

She heard him clear his throat over the razor's hum. "Can't make it," he said.

His response was disorienting. She shut off the water in the shower and composed herself for battle. Jack had never cancelled a bridge game in the eight years they had been playing with the Curtis'.

"What did you say?" she tried to sound even-tempered as she opened the shower stall door and reached around it for a towel.

He had been standing at the sink, his razor to his neck. Now he snapped the instrument off and cast a black look at her mirror image. It was a dead look, devoid of feeling. She shivered in her plush peach towel and pulled it closer around her torso. That look was not unfamiliar. It told her she would not win this battle with tears. It also suggested that there might be more at stake here than an embarrassing last minute cancellation.

She looked up at her own reflection, standing behind her husband's, and drew away from the mirror. She didn't like her reflection any more, especially after a shower. Her face was puffy and freckled, her over-processed hair a mat of pale gold straw. Where had youth gone? She felt faded in the shadow of her husband's dark indifference.

The dead black eyes continued to watch her from the mirror, the razor poised against his throat. He was waiting for her to challenge him. He wants me to, she thought. She forced herself to maintain her composure.

Turning from him as she toweled her hair she said, "Any particular reason?", an edge surfacing in her voice. But she couldn't help take a peek in the mirror to gauge his response. The hostility remained in his eyes although he had casually resumed shaving.

"Well, for a start, I'm sick of the Curtis', bored with cards, and tired of being tied to your itinerary in my free time." He stared at her back in the mirror as he said this, his eyes never losing their disconcerting hardness.

Now her temper flared. "This is rather sudden, isn't it?," she responded acidly.

"I suppose so," he answered. "But I'm growing to like spontaneity." He watched her through the mirror.

The words fell on her ears like gunshots. She took a painful breath. If she pushed him further would he would tell her what she was coming to suspect but was not yet ready to admit?

She came to his side and put a hand gently on his shoulder.

"Oh, let's not argue," she said and made a little, ineffectual rubbing motion. "I suppose it does get tiresome, week after week. I'll call and tell Miriam you're just not up to it."

The peck on the forehead she anticipated for her deference didn't come. He snapped off his razor and reached instead for his aftershave. The black bottle was an ill-disguised phallus.

She did not recognize it.

"Any other items of this morning's agenda?" he said to her reflection before turning and leaving her in the bathroom.

Her nerves nearly snapped then, but she waited, using that unerring patience she had learned over the years, that patience that had always worn him down in the end. She waited, listening to his soft masculine footfalls pad down the staircase, and then she picked up a wet washcloth from the sink and threw it at her own pink reflection in the wicker mirror.

Six

Valarie had expected Dean to leave, to abandon her when all that was left of her was mortal and human. But he did not.

Dean's affections for her remained constant. Regarding this new turn of events as an unavoidable act of God, he explained to her that they would weather it together. What she was, he desired, whether she be vampire, mortal, or angel.

"But don't you see? I have no power over you now. You, too, can choose. Why do you stay with the one who made you a slave?" she asked him.

"Love makes us all slaves," he responded. "I was always your willing victim. That hasn't changed."

And it was true. He was still devoted to her. Yet it soon became clear to her that a change had occurred in him, too. He did not seem aware of it, and would have probably denied it had she confronted him, but he was becoming domineering and protective of her. He was becoming more a husband, less a thrall.

It evidenced itself in little things at first, a new concern for her safety now she was mortal, a lack of faith in her judgments. He no longer trusted her physical strength to protect her from the world, and frequently he questioned her comings and goings as he never had before.

He questioned her decisions now, as well, arguing that her ideas were often foolish, ill-conceived whims.

"Maybe we shouldn't sell this place and move to the house in Pequot Bog, honey. It could get pretty expensive, taking on that big dog."

"It's what I want, Dean," was Valarie's reply. "Besides, it's my money."

"Well," he retorted, "I'd hate to see you jumping into something that might not make you happy."

There were other clues that he doubted her ability to handle mortal life. He criticized her diet, which was still mainly meat. He insisted she supplement it with vitamins. He expounded on the dangers of too little sleep and too much wine. He even began correcting her diction, which frequently fell short of perfection, for she emulated her father's second-generation French when she wasn't vigilant.

"Maybe you should just leave," she said one day. "We can get an annulment. You don't seem to like me much anymore."

"I don't want to leave you Val," he replied, "I love you. I'm just trying to improve your life, to be helpful."

Initially she fought a running verbal battle with him in an attempt to regain the supremacy and independence she had lost, but he denied repeatedly that he had changed or that the observations he made were of a critical nature, and so the battle degenerated into an illustration of the very incompetency she sought to disprove.

Her spirit was injured by this tiresome combat, the very act of defending herself giving weight to her opponent's position. She kept this injury to herself, and Dean was not aware that she secretly wished she had never enthralled him at all, creating the obligation of their marriage from a need for the social acceptance she no longer required.

It was autumn.

Valarie had been mortal for a season.

Every Saturday she received absolution from Father Tito at Immaculate Mary's, and every Sunday she took Communion from the Franciscans at St. Luke's.

Now it was Halloween, the season of death, and Valarie was forced to watch it being celebrated all around her. She witnessed its jollification in the jack-o-lanterns that grinned on the porches of her neighbors. She saw it glorified in the store displays on Main Street. It was even commemorated at the office, where cardboard witches and ghouls with gleeful cartoon faces decorated the doorways of the steno pool.

Even her roommate, Richie Childs, whom she had come to know was more interested in pornography than classic cinema, had pasted a black-and-white of Bela Lagosi on their office door.

Valarie tolerated the festivities with hard-earned patience. They know not what they do, she reminded herself, and ran her tongue over her incisors self-consciously.

"S-so you going tri-tri-trick-or-tr-treating tonight, Val?" Donna Deluca stuttered as Valarie scribbled in her time and whereabouts on the clipboard hooked above Donna's head. She'd been scheduling her interviews in Riverdale just to avoid the celebrations in Sharon this year, and had just returned from that office.

"Not hardly," she mumbled under her breath.

But Joanne Harris had overheard. "Shit, she wears black all year anyway. What's she need to go trick-or-treating for. She thinks she invented Halloween."

The little growl that vibrated in her throat startled Valarie. "I'll be interviewing out at the county jail this afternoon," she murmured to Donna, backing out of the steno pool uneasily.

"You look like you saw a ghost," Stevie smiled from her desk under the window as Valarie came through the door.

"If one more person mentions this bloody pagan jubilee to me..." Valarie sighed.

"I don't think she likes my poster either," Richie laughed.

"I don't think she likes you, period." Stevie shot the back of his head a disgusted look and gave Valarie one of sympathetic camaraderie.

"What's the matter, somebody comment on your wardrobe, Val?"

"What are you psychic now, Stevie? Jesus..." Valarie threw her black satchel under her desk and dropped into her chair.

"It's not exactly subtle." Stevie's face was calm.

"I just don't like all this devil worship, that's all. People don't know what they're celebrating. Death isn't fun. It's nothing to celebrate."

"Christ, what a crab. It's just a holiday. You got your period or something?" Childs quipped.

Valarie narrowed her eyes at him. "That'll never be any of your business, Richie."

"She wants me," he snickered over his shoulder to Stevie before ducking the file Valarie threw at his head.

It was 5:30 p.m. when Valarie returned from the Suffern County jail. The parking lot was nearly empty, but for a few county cars and Jack's Miata. Valarie smiled to herself as she pulled up and parked in the space to the left of it. Jack had been taking his sports car to work in favor of the county's Ford recently, and the little black teardrop suited him somehow.

She was just stepping out of her car when she noticed him approaching from the building.

"Long day, Valarie?" he smiled warmly at her as he stepped between the two cars and fumbled for his keys.

"Too long," Valarie sighed. Then she looked back at him with unusual interest.

"Hey, Jack, you..ah..going out to celebrate death tonight?"

Jack gave her a peculiar look. Then he opened his car door and reached under the driver's seat.

"That's an odd question," he said, turning back to her with a package in his hand.

"Well isn't that what Halloween is all about?" she mumbled, looking at the parcel. "What's that?"

"Something for you, Valarie," he said, and he handed her the package over the roof of her Honda.

"I've been saving it for you. I didn't want to give it to you in the office," he said.

It was a rectangular object wrapped in plain brown paper and tied with twine. She leaned over the roof of the car to accept it.

"Thank you," she said, puzzled.

"I know," he said. "It's inappropriate. But I came across it unexpectedly and it jumped out at me. I thought you'd know why."

She slipped the package into her jacket.

"Well-" she could think of nothing to add.

"Happy Halloween, Valarie," said Jack. He opened the door of his little sports car, slipped inside, and pulled away.

She stood there a moment, waiting for him to maneuver out of the parking lot. Then she slipped the package out of her jacket and tore it open.

It was a book, antique, by the look of it, leather bound and overplayed in gold. On the cover was one word, the raised lettering done in elegant calligraphy, and once gold, were now faded or rubbed pale by a history of hands.

Blood drained from her face as she sank back against the door of her Civic and read the title out loud.

"Vampires."

He had come across the volume at his favorite used book shop in Watertown. He'd driven up with Joan a week earlier to visit Kelly and her brood, and on the way, as was his habit, he had insisted on stopping at The Watershed to browse. His literary tastes were generally inclined to historical novels and political commentary, but something drew him that day downstairs to the occult section. When he saw the title in tiny gold print on the leather binding he reached for it immediately, charmed by the style and delicacy of the thing.

It was a history of the vampire legend, from ancient times into the 20th Century, and it intrigued him. It conjured up in his mind images of lethal yet beautiful human predators, tormented beings whose unquenchable hungers drove them to commit acts they did not wish to commit, and to betray those they did not wish to betray. Lonely, lovelorn creatures doomed to an eternity of isolation, yet superior to mortals in all else, in strength, in beauty, in intellect.

How could he not think of Valarie? Valarie in black at the water's edge at midnight, eyes like black diamonds and skin, by moonlight, like mother-of-pearl. Valarie in his dream crying tears of blood, and kissing his throat as though his throat were a feast.

He was not a superstitious man. Categorically pragmatic, he did not subscribe to religion, nor to mythology. But in a poetic sense, in a purely romantic interpretation, he could imagine Valarie a lovely little vampire.

He tucked the book inside his coat, peered through the book stacks in search of Joan, and saw she was browsing in the self-help section. Quickly, he approached the counter, paid for the volume in cash, and slipped outside to the car to deposit it under the front seat. Once this was accomplished he returned inside to collect his wife.

"Do you think we could get going? It is getting late," he said to her coldly.

"Oh," she looked up from an annoying looking volume called "What Men Want".

"Sure," she said. Why don't you go start the car, I'll be right out." He obliged.

Valarie's first reaction was to run, to pack a small suitcase, take her savings out of her account, and disappear.

North, she thought. Canada, Ontario. Quebec. I'll use my maiden name, or Rossetti. Before it's too late. Before...

Before what? Before he drove a wooden stake through her heart? No. It was pointless to run. Even if Jack had guessed her true nature, he could never convince anyone of it. Besides, she had been restored to life by the Church.

Valarie pulled open her car door and sank behind the wheel, tossing the unopened book onto the passenger's seat.

There was no point in panicking. She would have to trust Jack with this secret

Seven

Nikolai Larobya was hungry.

From his lair he heard the siren's song of a new victim calling. It was the music of loneliness, despair, and anger turned inward. And it was coming from the Howell house.

The woman had been grieving for years. But that early grief was a drink brewed of love, a chaste emotion untouched by jealousy, hatred or even fear. Her son's death had been sudden and had, for a time, driven her into herself and into the oblivion of alcohol. But it had not ruptured her confidence in God, and it had not removed her from the world. She still had her home, her remaining children, and of course, her husband.

Until now.

But now even that was threatened.

They had never had a close relationship. Jack was an introspective and unemotional man, and seemed to her at times an enigma she would never completely fathom. The children had come early and were a welcomed focus. They were, by necessity, her primary interest for many years, and they enhanced the superficiality of her marriage, upon which she relied heavily. Children gave her life another dimension beyond that of wife and lover, the latter of these being a role she had never been adept at. Her initial fraud on this score had cost her, in the end, the intimacy and sweetness of a romantic alliance.

She did not feel she owed her husband her honesty in this respect although in her heart she had, from the very beginning, understood that another woman could have provided him with that feature of their relationship breathlessly, and from the center of her soul. She hated women like this, women who could play the wife and mother in the parlor or at the club, then bed their mates with the base and primal passion of beasts in heat. She had never known this kind of love for a man, though if she could have conjured it, she felt she would have given it to Jack, whose very presence gave her life stature and meaning.

Now that meaning seemed to be coming to an end. The children were all but grown. Jack was in charge of the finances as he had always been, having brought most of their assets into the marriage. Her contribution, in comparison, was negligible. And with one rehab under her belt and one breakdown, she knew her chances of winning the house in a legal battle, especially in light of his connections, were almost nil.

He had not asked for a divorce, and perhaps he never would. But his behavior toward her of late had become so hostile, so rejecting, so cruel, that it was beginning to look to her as if he were deliberately setting out to drive her from him.

She had been drinking heavily, sneaking vodka in the morning from a bottle she kept hidden under the vanity in their bathroom, and getting up at night when he was sleeping to fix herself a drink from the bar downstairs. It wasn't difficult to hide it from him. He spent most of his evenings in the den watching TV, often sleeping through until morning on the sofa.

On those nights Joan would sit up waiting for him, curled in a chair by her bedroom window and staring vacantly down at the street below. Then she would allow herself to think of the day Kevin took his first steps out on the back porch, or rode his bicycle without training wheels, or pitched his first winning game.

And the hollow terror in her heart would come, and the panic. Could Jack leave her now, after all they'd been through together? Could he do it? And what would become of her then, without Jack? How could she go on? Who would she be?

The vampire sensed all of this where he lay in wait under the earth. Human despair always awakened him and charged his appetite.

He knew the woman longed for the fulfillment of death, the absolution, the peace, and he longed to give these things to her.

That it was all a lie was of no consequence to him, that there was no fulfillment in the death he offered, only hunger, no absolution, only an eternity of regret. This soul was ready for him, ripe with hopeless self-loathing. And he would not disappoint her.

When Jack opened the kitchen door that evening his house was vibrating with feminine rage.

"Mom's drunk," Lisa announced, as he closed the door behind himself and shrugged his topcoat over the back of a chair. "I tried to get her up to bed before you got home, but-"

A torrent of foul four-letter words from the den interrupted her. Lisa stormed up the stairs to her bedroom in tears, returning her mother's verbal assault with her own arsenal of epithets. Jack waited for a moment's respite in the battle. When it came, he picked up his coat and walked calmly through the dining room to the den, where he found his wife lying on the sofa he'd been using as a bed.

His first emotion was an odd mix of territorial rage and revulsion.

Joan was in her street clothes, a parsley green blouse, a tan, box-pleated skirt. Her favorite peach and cream afghan was draped over her legs. He watched her with vacant patience as she lifted her platinum head from a pillow he recognized as the one he kept for himself in the coat closet. She blinked at him from her resting place, her head wobbling a little. A stubby highball glass sat on the corner of one mahogany side table near her head, an inch

127

of vodka still cooling in a piece of melting ice. The room smelled of metabolized alcohol.

Joan met his composed countenance with drink-dulled eyes. Even drunk, she could not fail to recognize his feigned detachment and know it for the mask of rage it was. Contrition kicked in too late. She made a lurch off the couch, stupidly trying to remove the sight she had so deliberately planned for him. Instead, she bumped into the coffee table and stumbled, breaking her fall on the arm of the sofa.

He would have struck her, back-fisted, to the floor, had she reached him. He knew that even as he watched her grope for purchase on the arm of the couch. He had never hit her, not in 27 years of matrimony, but he would have hit her then, had she not been stopped by another force.

Her blue eyes filled with tears as she steadied herself on the sofa arm. She began to babble his name, spittle leaking from the corners of her mouth as she did so. He squinted, a facial flinch, watching the detestable scene. But he refused to move, neither forward, nor back out the door.

"I can't, Jack," the woman whimpered, rocking herself as she clutched the pillow like a child with a teddy bear in its arms. "I can't live without you, too. Don't leave me, Jackie, please, don't," she choked, sucking air noisily between sobs.

He stood quietly in the center of the den, watching her histrionics without sympathy. The heartstrings she sought to play had long broken. No, he thought, I will not leave my home. Not for you. You are the intruder here. I did not marry this. You are strange to me. Your lover lives in a bottle. You are the adulterer here, not me.

But to her he said nothing, only watched as she reacted to his silence with even greater heights of hysteria. Finally, she fell back down onto the couch, whimpering.

He walked to the doorway, lowered his head, and said "Get out of my room," before he left her.

It was dark out, although it was barely half past five. Jack walked heavily up the stairs to his bedroom, stripped, and pulled on a pair of jeans and a polo shirt. Then he found the suede coat that Patrick and Lisa had chipped in together to buy him for Christmas, and put it on.

He padded past Lisa's room in stocking feet, stopping briefly to listen at her door. He could hear her telephone conversation within, youthfully uncomplicated. So she had recovered from the scene. Lisa was like that. Like him in that way. Never let them see you sweat, he thought to himself, smiling. He continued down the hall to the head of the stairs.

He heard the door open behind him and he paused.

"Dad?"

"What is it, honey?"

"Is Mom still crying?"

He looked at his daughter evenly. "Mom's drunk, Lisa. Drunks cry. I wouldn't pay too much attention to anything she says when she's been drinking. She won't remember it in the morning."

Lisa gave her father a confederate smile.

"O.K." she said.

"She'll sleep it off," Jack added as he descended the stairs. "She always does."

He imagined his daughter's shrug of resignation as she closed her door behind her and returned to her phone call.

He was about to leave the house through the back door when he heard an odd, scratching sound rake across the storm door screen. Like the chilling screech of chalk on a blackboard the sound irritated, thrilling up his spine and setting his teeth on edge. Some animal, perhaps a stray, had found his house and looked for comfort here from the bitter winter night. Well, there was no comfort to be found in this house. Jack's anger found its vent. He swung the door open, hostility burning in his eyes, and was confronted instead by the largest and most striking human being he had ever seen.

The man was an easy six foot six, and yet it was not so much his height that created his enormity but his breadth. Even under the bizarre black highwayman's cloak it was clear that his shoulders were herculean, his arms and chest massive. His face was not young by any means, yet showed no line, no furrow. His chestnut hair was caught in a tail behind the muscular column of his neck. His skin was pearly white. But most astonishing of all were the riveting, viridian eyes. They smiled in the white marble face with the fixed gaze of a man who has searched the world and lo! ... has found his love at last.

Jack's anger subsided. It was replaced by awe and not a little apprehension as he stared at the magnificent creature at his door. The man's dress, his attitude, suggested refinement. He was no local man, surely, but a foreigner, an adventurer, a man with miles and countries under him. This was no burglar, no common thug. And yet he was a fearful thing to behold. He was not a man whose presence could be taken lightly, nor a person one ought to usher into one's home without serious thought.

And yet how mysteriously the green eyes sparkled! What could one learn from such a stranger? This man was all that Jack was not, and Jack did not wish to send him away.

"May I help you?" asked Jack in his most urbane voice.

The creature's lips tightened into a smile to match the one that twinkled in his eyes.

"I do believe it!" he said, his voice a surprisingly resonant baritone. There was a slight accent there. What was it, Russian? Jack only hesitated for a moment. Then he stepped back from the doorway and gestured for the stranger to come in.

"Do you need a phone?" said Jack as the visitor stepped over the threshold. "I'm Jack Howell," he added, extending his hand.

"And I am Nikolai Larobya Vasilyevich," said his guest. He took another step forward and Jack, a common five foot ten, became suddenly aware that he barely reached the man's chin. "But some call me Laroby," the intruder smiled slyly.

"That's a bit of a stretch," quipped Jack.

The stranger's eyes turned to green ice.

"Not really, Jackie," he said, and he picked up his host's hand and kissed the back of it before it could be wrested free.

When Jack looked up into the intruders eyes again he saw that amusement brewed in them. He lifted his chin and hardened his aspect, determined not to flinch. But his odd guest had created an ugly stalemate. Though the two men were still close enough to embrace, neither moved.

It was the visitor who broke the silence. He leaned suddenly over his host and breathed, "Do you not know me, little man?" into Jack's face.

Jack blinked up at him, startled by the question. "Know you?" he puzzled.

The intruder gave him no time to respond. He lifted Jack up by the lapels of his coat and slammed his back against a counter. Then he snarled, exposing two magnificent, inch-long fangs.

132

"Do you not know me?" he asked again, folding Jack in his arms like a lover and whispering, "I am your master," as he yawned his vampire yawn against Jack's throat.

Repulsion cracked Jack's dispassionate facade. He shoved at the creature's massive chest with all of his might but it was unyielding. Sickened as much by his own weakness as by the strength of the thing that held him, he turned his teeth toward it. The beast's neck was roped with muscle so thick that to bite it seemed hopeless. Desperate, Jack bared his teeth, but he could not cross that line that separated man from animal.

"Let me go, you freak!" He heard his own voice from a distance. The beast was squeezing the breath from his body, murmuring like a lover against his throat.

"Quiet. Do not struggle so," it said as it kissed the neck it meant to tear. "It will hurt you less if you surrender. You may even like it," and he drew Jack up into his arms, binding him against his chest with bone-crushing strength.

Dizzy with lack of oxygen, Jack succumbed to instinct at last. He brought his teeth down onto that sinewy neck just as the vampire fangs closed upon his own. He bit down hard, his teeth his only unbound weapon. He felt them slice through flesh, felt the vampire blood fill his mouth, tasting sour at first, then sweet, sweet as ambrosia, or any nectar a god might drink.

"Ah-ah-h!" keened the vampire, lifting his teeth away from their mark. He pressed his eyes shut and threw back his leonine head in ecstasy.

"Oh-hoh!" he sighed, "Sweet surprise! You are like me!" Then he lowered his head again, pressing the gleaming fangs into Jack's unprotected neck.

Jack opened his mouth to scream but could not. His throat was paralyzed. The sharp teeth were knives in his flesh yet the warm lips that pressed him were tender, even passionate. The vampire was drinking deeply, pulling his nourishment from its vessel with violent hunger. Jack felt a numbness move through his veins like a drug. His heartbeat rang in his ears.

Now the vampire grunted, like a weight lifter hefting an impossible stack, and the teeth withdrew. He shoved Jack from him, his face clouded, perturbed.

"Damn you, mortal, you are in love," he said. "Poisonous fool." For a moment the brilliant green eyes dulled. They seemed to hunt for some interior message. Then a wry smile touched the pulpy lips as recognition lighted the monster's face.

"Haha!" he laughed, looking heavenward with an exaggerated expression of surprise, "the woman, Valarie!" His eyebrows descended. He lifted Jack's face, embedding his long fingers into his cheeks. Jack blinked at him through blood drunk eyes.

"She that betrayed me," the vampire licked his lip. "She that betrayed me to Him," he cocked his head at heaven. "But you, my

134

little accomplice, you love her, yes?" He threw back his head and laughed suddenly. "Very well then! I give you an eternity to hunt her!"

He pulled Jack to himself suddenly, bared his own wounded neck, and forced Jack's mouth back to the scene of its crime.

"Drink, little devil. You are so thirsty. Drink," he crooned, and the new vampire drank, finding the wound open and sweet.

After a moment Laroby gave him a shove, and Jack fell back, blood spilling from his mouth.

"Greedy, greedy Jack," said the fiend. "You will make me proud."

Jack winced up at him, his head wobbling a little, his eyes glazed and staring. After a moment, he brought his hands to his mouth, touched it, and looked down at his fingers. They were smudged with blood.

"You have tasted eternity," said Laroby. "You have been born again." He turned toward the dining room, lifting his chin, and sniffing the air like a dingo.

"This house is a banquet," he announced, and turned toward the interior, shrugging his cloak back from his shoulders to reveal his powerful frame, his tapered waist.

"Come," he said to Jack, lifting a hand to him. "Let me show you what you are."

Eight

Jack hesitated momentarily, then staggered across the kitchen, following his new master into the interior of his house. He saw the great black-clad back of the beast disappear into the den and he followed after, the dream-like quality of his new vision causing him to step gingerly as he tested his balance. It seemed as if he were seeing the world in slow-motion, while his own movements remained in common time.

As he reached the doorway to the den he saw that the beast now knelt beside his wife, who lay on the sofa in a drunken sleep. The fiend lifted her wrist, testing her pulse, then gently lay her arm over her chest. He mouthed a word against her ear, and Jack's fantastic new vision zoomed in on the vampire's mouth. But the word was foreign to him. He could not discern it. The beast lifted his head and looked over his shoulder at Jack, his strange eyes bright with internal heat. COME.

The word exploded in Jack's brain like a mortar shell, yet the vampire's lips had never moved. Compelled more by his own desire to do so than by the command, Jack began to move awkwardly across the floor to his master's side.

KNEEL, came the telepathic blast.

And Jack settled on his knees beside the demon.

Laroby lifted Joan's wrist once more, yawned to expose his savage white fangs, and slashed it open in one arcing motion. Blood spattered his alabaster face, and the woman moaned, eyelids fluttering. He fastened his deadly lips to her pulse and drank, a guttural moan shuddering in his throat. Jack watched as the vampire squeezed his eyes shut in rapture, his black lashes forming dark fans under his tightened brows, his pearl white flesh growing radiant as he fed. He felt his own need well up in him, watching the vampire's lean cheeks cave as he sucked life from Joan's vein.

"Give me." He heard his own croaking voice under his body, under the earth. "Give me."

The vampire grunted, released the wrist, and held it up for Jack to take.

"Drink deeply," he said.

The shock of this first draught of human blood was bewildering. The vampire's blood was as nothing compared to it. Jack moaned. All of his senses flocked to his mouth and worshipped there. He heard his wife's whimpering as she succumbed to the poisonous bite but he could not stop, did not want to stop. The blood lust flooded his body, charged his veins, gave strength and locomotion to his muscles. In a rush, orgasmic in its intensity, he felt vitality and virility flooding him, replacing

137

his natural torpor. His mouth had become an organ of pleasure and passion. His tongue pulsed thickly in the current of life-giving mortal blood that coursed past it. He drank, drank, until the vein would yield no more. Still he knelt at the altar of his wife's death and sucked the white limb.

Finally, his pulse quieted, his breathing softened. He released the wrist and the dead white hand fell listlessly to the carpet. A tiny trickle of blood drained from the wound across the open palm, settling in the crease at the juncture of the fingers. The polished fingertips twitched and were still. The ring finger curled accusingly toward the palm, pointing to the antique silver wedding band nested there.

A wave of intense nausea volleyed through Jack's belly as he stared at the ring, the symbol of their matrimony.

"Oh-h-h," he moaned, as the fingers of nausea kneaded him. "Oh, God, no," he grit his teeth against the pain, clutching his abdomen.

For a moment it seemed to pass. A glimmer of ridiculous hope stirred in him.

"Joan?" from his crouched position he looked up at her paste-white face. It held no response. The nausea returned and he whimpered, collapsing on the oriental rug. Pain, more severe than any he had ever known sliced through his bowels as he vomited his wife's blood onto the carpet beside her lifeless wrist. It went on and on, crashing through his intestines in waves, a mad storm, renting and bruising as it made its path through him.

Finally the sickness passed. Jack raised his head to see Laroby perched like a demented marionette on the far end of the sofa. He was so immense it seemed his weight must topple the thing, throwing Joan's corpse into the air. Yet he sat quite steadily on the narrow arm, his own arms folded over his chest, his head cocked to one side as he watched his apprentice display his humanity on the floor.

"You have murdered your wife, you imbecile," he said.

"Wh-hat? No, you--" Jack cried.

"You finished her off, you fool. Now she's dead, and I cannot restore her to life. You will be convicted of murder, hunted down and destroyed."

Laroby repositioned himself, leaning one elbow over the back of the sofa, his fingers in his hair, as he gazed down at Joan's body.

"Unless we make a zombie," he considered.

"Oh my God," wept Jack, "my God..."

"Who? Hypocrite. You don't believe in God, you believe in golf," spat the demon. "Birdies and eagles. Pars and bogeys. That sort of thing. That's where your loyalties lie, Jackie, my boy. Now," he stroked his chin. "Let me see. She certainly has all the makings of a zombie, don't you think? All this should require is a little imagination."

Laroby lifted Joan's chin with an index finger.

139

"Awake, you sack of misery! Your master has use for you yet! Move about in this corpse as you always have, a vapid, sightless animation. The Other's brood will recognize you for what you are, but what of that? They are a scarce minority in my world. Your condition shall go quite unnoticed."

"What are you saying? She's dead. A corpse... in my house? The mother of my...? My God, Lisa!" Jack wept.

Laroby shot him a disgusted look.

"Your children will never know the difference," he said. "This woman has been half dead for years. Keep her out of churches, temples, away from charity events," he made a little flip with his hand, "that sort of thing, and no one will be the wiser. Oh she'll seem a bit stiff, perhaps a little too obedient. But..." he turned his attention back to Joan's body, musing, "she never was much trouble, was she?"

"Give me your hand." He reached for Jack, opening his palm to him as if he had asked him for a scalpel. Jack cringed and the vampire grunted with disgust and snatched Jack's forearm before he could flinch again. Without a moment's hesitation he brought the palm of Jack's hand to his lips and sliced it open on a fang. A lozenge of burgundy oozed from the diamond shaped gash in the center of Jack's palm. Jack gasped and yanked away but the vampire was too strong for him. Holding Jack fast in his steely grip, he set the bleeding palm over the corpses face like an oxygen mask and waited.

Suddenly Jack felt a slick, wormy flicker against his palm. Joan's body convulsed, her eyes flew open, and her arms shot out to grab at him as her ghoulish mouth sucked his wounded hand. Laroby released Jack's arm and Jack lurched back in horror, crab-walking backwards across the carpet into a corner.

"Oh God," he whimpered.

"Get hold of yourself, man, you are as dead as she," said Laroby. "Sit up," he said to the corpse.

The zombie jack-knifed into a sit and turned its doll-dead eyes to Laroby.

"Will she eat the living?" Jack's voice shook.

Laroby sighed intolerantly. "She's an animated corpse. She has no desire to eat." Then he sniggered. "Cheer up! She won't be doing much DIETING anymore."

Laroby wiped his eyes at his little joke.

"She looks awful," said Jack.

Laroby rolled his eyes. "Oh, do spare me. Now give her an order. Tell her to clean this mess up," he said, gesturing to the bloody rug.

"Why should she listen to me? You made her," Jack argued.

"Oh, really?" said Laroby, his brows raised. Then he leaned over the couch and whispered in Joan's ear. This time Jack could not see his lips moving.

The doll eyes of the zombie settled on Jack.

"She will obey you," said the vampire. "Do as I said."

Jack swallowed. He tried to think of his daughter, who might at any moment interrupt this nightmare by coming down the stairs.

"Joan," he said, "would you clean up, please?"

The doll eyes crinkled a bit at the corners as the corpse responded with a deadpan smile.

"Yes, dear. I'll get out the steamer. It'll take it right up," it said. Then it popped off the couch and shuffled across the carpet toward the kitchen.

Jack dropped his head into his hands.

"Lisa will know," he said.

"Know what? That her mother is a zombie? Please. She's far too sophisticated to believe it." Laroby chuckled. "However, if you are inclined to have her committed to an asylum, it should not be difficult to find a good doctor who will be happy to diagnose catatonia." He unfolded his long body and stood up.

"I leave you now to haunt and rape the world," he said, his wickedly luminous eyes somehow finding light in which to glitter in the dim room. "Make me proud, little accomplice."

Then he lifted his arms from his sides, snapped his cloak, and was gone.

Jack stood and stared dumbly at the spot where the vampire had been. He could hear his wife's corpse clattering about in the kitchen, assembling the Bissell. The awfulness of the situation had a numbing effect, not unlike shock. But he was no longer mortal, and there was no place for shock in his new world. He knew what

142

he had done, knew what he was. That information was available to him spiritually if not intellectually. He had become a spiritual being and his new senses told him the truth. There was no hiding from it now that he was dead.

"Oh God," he moaned. He made to exit the room but the strange vampire vision caused him to stumble. He would have to get used to this slow motion vision. He tried again, moving cautiously. His vision seemed to catch up with him when he did so. Like a marionette, he puppeteered his body out of the den and into the front hall one movement at a time. He grit his teeth, swallowed, and moved in front of the antique mirror that faced the foyer.

Nine

He was not unhappy with what he saw.

There were two dark drops of dried blood on either corner of his mouth. Except for these, the man in the mirror was quite handsome, even striking.

There were still the telltale signs of his mortal age about his eyes, tiny crow's-feet, little creases of flesh under the lower lashes, but these were not unattractive. The eyes themselves drew away from them. His eyes had always been... well, Joan had once used the word 'lurking'. Now they riveted. They were the same dark brown, nearer black, as they'd always been. But now they drew, invited, sparkled with their own light, and they were bottomless.

He imagined fixing Valarie with them. A new weapon against her indifference.

He peered closer, noticing his complexion. It was paler, but had a youthful radiance, a flush, almost sexual. And his mouth, the blood tipped lips, were fleshier and darker.

144

Could blood do this?

He lifted a hand to rub the blood crust from the corners of his lips. The mirror reflected no motion. First the hand was at his side, then at his mouth. He tried it a second time, lowering his hand at normal speed. The results were the same.

He stepped back from the mirror. Stepped forward. Stepped back. The mirror reflected only the two locations, no motion between.

"I'm too fast," he murmured to his reflection. "Too fast for the mirror. How can that be?"

He tried moving slower. Now motion was reflected in the looking glass, but faster, much faster than he believed himself to be moving.

So that was how Laroby had vanished. He had simply moved at a comfortable pace...which for the vampire was the speed of thought.

He realized he would have to train himself to move at mortal speed in order to conceal what he was, deliberately thinking out each piece of the motion. Or he would appear and disappear like a ghost.

He heard, with subsonic hearing, the zombie clicking off the Bissell, wrapping the cord around the canister top and rolling it out of the den and across the dining room floor to the laundry room behind the kitchen. Under these noises he heard it breathing, a shallow, mechanical whoosh and suck, shoosh and suck. It needed

145

no breath, and yet it took the air in, polluting it with its dead lungs. Jack shuttered, then realized with a flinch that he was breathing also. What on earth for? He stopped and found he had no difficulty holding his breath indefinitely. So it was simply a habit. And why not? He'd been doing it for over half a century.

He began practicing his walk, thinking out each piece of the motion as he moved down the hall and back, in front of the mirror.

PART THREE

One

It was mid-winter and a bitter wind blew from the east across the barren fields behind the Dumont house.

Valarie stood in the courtyard between the two wings, wrapped in a red woolen cloak. She still thought of the place as the Dumont house, or Cecile's house, although the remaining Dumonts had packed weeks ago and were now staying in a mobile home in Jitney Bay. Most of Cecile's furnishings had been sold, although the front parlor sofa and chairs were part of Valarie's spoils. These were sturdy pieces done in a Herculon of green and rust plaid, not especially charming, nor in keeping with the oriental decor of the house, but of sentimental value to Valarie, who had been curled in one of the armchairs a year earlier when Cecile first suggested that, having lost her husband's income, and with her father's impending retirement, she might soon have to sell the house at a loss.

A cold February sun was falling slowly earthward on its journey across the grey winter sky behind the house. A small "V" of geese cut across the tree line below it, their wild honks filling the bitter cold air. Except for them, there was silence.

It was a silence, a peace Valarie had long yearned for. Now, at last, she was far from the little cottage where she and Claude had begun their life together, far from the daily reminders, the dull and constant pain of living in a place where her sweetest memories were made, and later lost forever. And yet, she was not content.

Valarie hugged herself inside her woolen cloak. What she felt was not cold, but a numbness she carried with her in all climates. She had come here to escape it, but it had followed her. And with it, a new demon had taken up residence within her soul as well. For the guilt of Philip Dumont's death lay heavily on her conscience.

Inside the house she knew that Dean was spackling the closets, which Dumont had covered with scrap cedar in an attempt to emulate the aromatic cedar closets of the rich. Valarie hated the scent of cedar, nor was she fond of the slap-dash effect created by the old man's mosaic of hammered-in scrap wood. She had insisted Dean remove the uneven pieces and spackle and paint the closets. Dean, delighted as always to be helpful, had made the task his first priority.

Valarie had also insisted on separate bedrooms. She now occupied the wing that had been the Dumont's, while Dean had Cecile's apartments. Of course he had balked at this arrangement at first.

"It's either this, or separate lives," she had replied, and the bland indifference in her eyes told him this was true.

Valarie turned as the sound of a neighbor's car moving into the cul-de-sac disturbed her thoughts. She had made no attempt to meet her neighbors. She had no desire to know them, only wondered about their feelings on the topic of Philip Dumont. Did they know the old man? Had they liked him? Would they sense on some invisible level that she'd been responsible for his death? Would they look at her and imagine, behind their smiles, "this is his murderess?"

She pulled her collar over her ears and walked to the back entrance of the house, pulling open the French doors and stepping over the threshold into the enormous, cathedraled great room. Two black kittens charged her and began making eights around her feet. She had found the kittens mewling under a bush at Immaculate Mary's when last she'd visited Father Tito for confession. Apparently someone had left them there for God to look after. And maybe he had. Valarie brought the kittens home with her to Pequot Bog and her charity did not go unrewarded, for she soon found that their presence added life to her great, empty home.

She stopped to fluff Andy's belly as he tumbled over the toes of her boots. "Silly cat," she murmured, lifting him into her arms and nuzzling his fur.

The sharp tang of paint hit her as she closed the French doors and pulled off her coat. Apparently Dean had finished the spackling and begun to paint.

She crossed to the foyer and snapped on the transom light. The sun was setting and it was growing dim indoors, but she could still see out to the street quite well. The sound of another vehicle entering the cul-de-sac drew her attention to a sidelight. She peered out onto her front lawn, not knowing what it was she hoped to see there.

A cement Buddha, which in the summer spouted water from its upturned hands, stood in the center of the front lawn. He was surrounded by a circle of bonsai trees which seemed, in the glow of the transom light, to dance about him like misshapen elves.

Out on the street a white Lexus pulled slowly around the circular cul-de-sac and disappeared down the lane.

It was not a little black Miata, and Valarie's disappointment startled her.

Someone had told her, after her father's death, that of all things it was hardest to lose unconditional love. She had not understood the magnitude of that observation then. But she was beginning to understand it now. Jack had changed, especially toward her, since her move. He came to work later, chatted less with the staff and laughed less with the stenos, and he spoke to her almost not at all. Even more disturbing, his eyes had changed. The light of innocence had gone out of them. His soft, deep brown eyes had become the hot black eyes of a shark. Unblinking and hungry.

Valarie turned from the window, setting Andy gently down on the foyer tiles. She had murdered her friend's father for this house. She had taken away one of Cecile's last resources of unconditional love. She had believed then that she had to do it, that it was the only way she could keep herself from hurting Jack Howell.

But something had happened to Jack in spite of her desire to protect him from herself. It may have even happened because of it. Her move to the house in Pequot Bog seemed to have precipitated it. Valarie shuddered.

"Maybe I'm imagining things," she said to Andy, who pawed at her toes as she pulled off her boots and set them on the boot rack by the front door.

"Maybe he's just got a lot on his mind," she sighed, tossing one last look out at the street before wandering up the kitchen stairs to find her husband.

Two

When Jack hunted, he hunted women.

Did all male vampires hunt women, he wondered? Did all females hunt men? It had nothing to do with sex. His sexual desires were dead. It had little to do with blood. If it had had to do with blood, he would have hunted men, who generally had more of it. And despite stereotyping to the contrary, his soul had quickly discovered, in its newly omniscient state, that women were every bit as evil-minded as men. Innocence had no sex, and except for the very young, no age.

No, he hunted women because while they initially desired him and frequently played the predator at the onset, they inevitably feared him more in the end and were more tormented by their culpability for their own deaths. This, he found, excited his hunger.

Men generally believed that they could overpower him, fight him off. They were as angry as they were afraid, and trusted in victory through sheer pugnacity. By the time they understood the truth, they were already dying.

Women, on the other hand, could not believe he truly meant to do them harm. He was too urbane, too civilized to be a monster. Once they realized that they had finally encountered the grim reaper of their worst nightmares, they expected to be kidnapped, sexually assaulted and tortured. Women were frequently relieved, so terrified were they of the options, when they realized they were simply going to die in his arms.

Jack found this most satisfying. First to gain their trust, (which took almost nothing), allowing them their flirtations, their coquetry, never really responding nor giving them the mildest provocation for such boldness but rather remaining unreadable, unreachable. Then he would utter a word, a phrase, to shock them. Something cruel or unreasonable but always true. And they would try to rebuff, or overlook it. Finally, he would growl. That throat growl he'd first heard when Laroby purred it against his own throat. That vampire moan of passion. The blood-growl, an almost wet, tiger-purr emanating from the bottom of the throat. Oh, happy sound.

And that sound and the dead black shark stare in his once beautiful Black-Irish eyes, would send most women over the edge, over the very edge of their sanity.

At the height of which feeding was most sweet to him.

Of course, it didn't always happen that way. Not at all. There had been the Haas woman, for instance.

She was a local. The wife of an architect who spent most of his time in New York. She was an active community member, a real organizer. She'd been hosting an annual charity auction for the homeless for the past few years and she was becoming quite famous for it. If he hadn't intervened when he did, she just might have been single-handedly responsible for putting Old Inlet on the map.

Her own home rivaled Jack's in size, but was only a dozen years old. It flanked the beach on one side, the canal on the other, one street over from Beach Neck Lane. Her husband, the architect Jerry Haas, had designed it. Actually it was a hideous contemporary, shouldering in among the stately old homes that had been brooding over Old Inlet Bay since the early part of the century. But they were that kind of people, the Haas', intruders with money for ripping up the dunes and filling in the wetlands to build their ostentatious eyesores.

He'd met her at the Curtis' twice before. She'd behaved quite haughtily to him in front of her husband, a fat man with an abundance of curly grey hair and small, greedy blue eyes. But she'd flirted boldly when Jerry's back was turned. She'd made a point of sitting across from Jack on a low love seat when the party had retired to the parlor for drinks. Then she crossed her naked legs, the gesture hiking up her little white linen skirt naughtily, and she gave Jack a quick, appreciative wink when she caught his eyes on her. For his benefit she held her drink with both hands,

154

caressing the stem with her fingers as she pretended to listen to her husband drone on about business and politics. Droplets of sweat from the glass, slipping off her fingers, fell silently onto her knee, and her eyes flicked to Jack's face again as she smoothed the drops into her skin like lotion. She had an impeccable figure. A tall redhead who'd modeled for a top agency at one time, she knew she was devastating and used her looks to her advantage. Jack was convinced she'd slept with at least one village trustee to get that damned colossus built on what had always been protected property. But she'd had no use for Jack, except to tease, until she saw him again at Lisa's birthday party.

Actually it had been a sleep-over and her daughter, Nichole, had been invited. When Leslie showed up to drop her daughter off, Jack met her at her car and invited her in for a drink. Then he shot her a hot, feral look with the bottomless black eyes of a cobra, and her curiosity eclipsed her judgment.

"Where's Joanie?" she smiled casually as he escorted her to his bar in the den. The girls could already be heard giggling and squealing upstairs.

"Tied up at the campus," he lied. "She won't be home until very late tonight, I'm afraid. Ice?"

"No, thank you." She took her scotch and sat down on a the sofa, tucking her long, elegant calves under her like a cat tucks its tail around its paws.

"You look as if you've been up to something," she touched the rim of her glass with her tongue, licking away a droplet of scotch. "Been working out at a gym somewhere?" Her eyes caressed him.

Jack finished pouring himself a glass of gin and came to stand beside the sofa.

"What is it exactly that gave me away?" he lifted his brows.

She took the bait like a retriever. Her eyes dropped to his pelvis, then she cocked her head a little, pretending to peek behind him.

"Oh, this and that," she purred. "A woman notices when a man takes the time to stay in shape, you know."

At that moment a crowd of teenage girls tumbled down the center stairs to the front hall.

"See you later, Dad!" called Lisa. "We'll be back about twelve."

"Be careful, honey," said Jack. "Who's driving?"

"Tonia." Lisa peeked into her father's den. "Hi Mrs. Haas," she said, a little surprised.

"Have a good time, Lise," smiled Leslie.

The herd of girls disappeared out the front door.

Jack turned his back to his guest to watch them through the den window, squeezing into Tonia Messina's Scrambler like insects swarming into a nest.

"Your daughter dating?" he said over his shoulder.

"What?" she was caught off guard. "As a matter of fact she's seeing the Dahl's boy." She got up and stood beside him. A remarkably statuesque woman, she was eye level in a pair of espadrilles. He looked at her dispassionately.

"Don't you worry about her? She's only sixteen."

"Honey," said the redhead as she opportunely slipped her arm around his waist, "you can worry all you want, but you can't fight nature."

His brows dropped at her words.

"Mmmm," he said.

"Hey," she rubbed his back. "Come on, you were young once, remember? They'll survive it."

They watched the little Jeep disappear down the drive. Then Jack turned suddenly in the woman's arm and faced her.

"Are you flirting with me, Leslie?" he said quietly.

"Yes, Jack," she answered after a moment, moving her body closer to his. "I guess I am."

Ah, thought Jack. He lifted a hand to capture a wave of her auburn hair in his fingers and lost himself in its brilliance for a moment. Then he looked into her lovely turquoise eyes and smiled.

He made his own eyes vacant.

Leslie Haas leaned forward, toward the unfathomable mystery that lay behind them.

"You should go, Leslie, you have a man at home."

157

He took her glass out of her fingers and walked to the bar. "I'm sure he's waiting for you," he added.

She crossed her arms over her breast, a look of amusement on her face.

"You are a perplexing man, Jack Howell!" she said.

He turned and gave her an even look. His jaw tightened.

"Am I?"

She walked to the bar and retrieved her drink.

"Very," she purred, touching his chin with a finger.

"And you are a very obvious woman," said Jack, stepping toward her.

In a heartbeat he took her by one wrist and brought her to her knees. He had not hurt her, had only moved her where he wanted her with the least resistance. Still, when he drew her head back, twisting his fingers in the beautiful red brush of her hair, she cried out.

"It is intimacy you want, Leslie?"

He was looking down at her with the concentrated stare of a big cat.

"Because I can be very intimate if you like."

He pulled her back, by her hair, until she lay on the carpet.

Now he was on top of her, crushing her deliberately to camouflage his lack of substance. She sighed, wrapped her arms around him, and began to move beneath him in an ancient female dance of invitation. He nuzzled her mouth, not kissing it but

158

searching her lips, her tongue. A wet, tigery growl shuddered in his throat.

"God," she panted, "you're wicked. Let me-" She managed to move her hands between his body and hers and began to tug at his belt.

He pushed her hands away. "Don't."

"What?" She whispered against his ear. "Oh no, you're mine, I found you and you're mine." She was pulling the tails of her silk blouse out of her skirt.

He lifted himself off her for an instant and she moaned.

"No," she drew his head down and kissed his mouth. "Don't stop."

His eyes slid down the length of her body.

"All right, Leslie," he said. He pushed her skirt up and her panties down in a single motion, and keeping her hair tangled in the fingers of one hand, he moved his mouth down the ridge of her sternum, his tongue stopping to worship the heartbeat between her breasts, before following its nature to the pulse in her belly, and beneath, where her blood had rushed in wait for him, to the femoral artery, at the base of the pelvis, just above the adductor muscles. And there he buried his teeth in her and drank, and drank, until she was still.

Three

Jack was pleased.

He was sitting at the kitchen table with the morning paper and a mug of black coffee, scanning the Sunday cover story on Page Two. It seemed that a prominent Old Inlet architect, Jerry Haas, whose wife had committed suicide about a month earlier, would be putting his fantastic contemporary up for sale at a give-away price and moving back to Manhattan with his daughter. Apparently, Haas didn't agree with the D.A.'s decision not to investigate the case as a homicide. He was convinced that enemies in high places had murdered his wife, and were out to get him as well. He was finished with Old Inlet and corrupt County politics and he was taking his business elsewhere.

That made one less astigmatic architect in Old Inlet to spoil the austere, old-moneyed beauty of South Beach Neck Lane with his post-modern exhibitionism. One less uncultured lout from the city come to pave over the dunes and fill in the wetlands, and turn Old Inlet into another Hampton, another affected length of Dune Road.

As for Leslie's death, the police felt that the circumstances left no room for a homicide case. They concluded that the woman had returned home after dropping her daughter off at a neighbor's at about 7:00 p.m., had walked deliberately up to the third story landing, and had hurled herself through an immense plate glass window which peaked into a huge half-round, showcasing the canal side of the house. Since the landing ran dangerously parallel to the window on the third floor, all Mrs. Haas had to do was to take it into her head to make a running start from the stairs and smash through it. Her body had been found on the front lawn in the freezing rain, her back broken in two places, and her right arm nearly severed at the elbow by a sheet of falling glass. There were no prints but hers on the car, which was neatly parked in the garage. Her prints were on the entry door from the garage to the back hall as well. Her shoes were at the bottom of the stairs on the first floor. Apparently she had changed into slippers (her husband said this had been her habit) before walking up the oatmeal colored carpeting to the third floor landing. One slipper had been found against the front of the house behind some shrubbery, the other was found further out on the lawn, about four yards from her body. By her blood loss, which was considerable, it was suspected she'd died of her injuries on the ground, over a period of half an hour or so. Time of death was estimated at about seven thirty, which corroborated the neighbor's story that she'd left his house after a drink at about seven o'clock.

Jack Howell, at any rate, had an immediate alibi in Gil Stuart, a local school Superintendent, who had called him at 7:10 about a golf tournament. That hardly left Howell time to slip out unnoticed by his wife and sprint over to the Haas mansion to sneak in after Leslie, rush up the stairs behind her, push her through the window, then turn around and sprint back to his house without leaving footprints or tread marks outside either house. There were a few oddities in the case. The woman had lost a great deal of blood and the blood found on and about the body couldn't account for all of it. No traces were found anywhere else in the house. So she hadn't been bleeding before she took the fall. And the woman clearly went through the window before she died. It was speculated that the freezing rain that began at quarter to eight that evening must have washed it away, across the gently sloping side lawn to the canal, though not everyone was convinced of this. The other peculiarity was the way in which the woman had gone through the window, like a projectile, head first, the impact being quite high up, as if she'd taken a running leap into it, or been flung through it by more than one person working in tandem.

But what mortal could have surmised the truth, a truth that Jack himself could still barely believe? That evil delights in itself, reproduces itself, and protects its progeny. That the laws of nature, that the very laws of the universe were his accomplices that night. So that John Barry Howell III of Old Inlet, New York, who not a month before was a decaying mortal in the twilight of his years, had, with newborn vampire speed and strength, simply driven the unconscious Leslie back to her house in her own car, let himself in with her keys, and hurled her through that abominable cyclopean three story window to the lawn. That the slippers had been something of an artistic touch, and that, seeing the mules at the foot of the stairs, he had simply made the swift observation that Leslie would have left them there for a reason and that people were creatures of habit. So he had exchanged them for her espadrilles, carried her up the stairs, and thrown her in a magnificent arc, like a football, through the plate glass window, head first. Then he had feasted his supernaturally enhanced vision on the slow motion shatter of the glass, a stalactite of which broke free with diabolical accuracy in time to challenge her rate of descent and slice through her upper arm, creating a useful explanation for her excessive blood loss on the ground. He was at the ledge before she hit it, to watch her bounce off the herringbone brick patio below onto the lawn, and to hear her back and leg snap before she came to rest. Finally, he had let himself out as he had come, careful not to leave prints. Then he had returned, with the weightless tread of a vampire, to his house.

Jack had not hunted again for a fortnight, so satisfying was his brief affair with Leslie Haas, the beautiful redheaded architect's-wife. But then he saw the blond in the black leather jacket, and the bloodlust returned with a vengeance.

Four

He had seen the girl crossing Main Street in Old Inlet Village on his way to work. He could not have helped but notice her. She had the confident stride of a New Yorker, and he had never seen her before.

She had bright blond, shoulder-length hair, cut in an attractive wedge except for the bangs, which were dyed pink and crested like a rooster's comb. A huge black and silver jacket hid her hands but revealed her petite derriere, which was clad in devilishly tight, acid-washed jeans. She wore silver-tipped boots and carried a capacious black leather pouch over one shoulder. A row of silver earrings rimmed the edge of one ear, and a tiny silver hoop flashed at the peak of the opposite eyebrow.

He saw her notice the Miata instantly as he passed her, attracted, no doubt, to its shiny, organic shape. Her hair fanned over her shoulders as she turned to catch a glimpse. Then she hopped up onto the curb and disappeared inside the corner deli. A bald man in a bomber jacket turned to watch her go in.

Jack did not stop then, but made a mental note to look for her later. He often stalked a victim during daylight hours for his evening kill, but he was later than usual for work today and did not relish the idea of arousing further suspicion.

At nightfall he took the Miata out for a drive. There had been a heavy snowfall two days earlier and now the frozen drifts sparkled in his headlights like mounds of sugar. The village was white, pristine, encased in snow, and deathly still. It was a fine night for a murder.

He purred around town aimlessly, down to the dock and back, parking on Main Street to kill some time. Finally he pulled away and took the ride he had been longing to take past Valarie's little cottage. He noticed a white Toyota in the driveway and boxes stacked on the front porch in the lamp light. The red Civic was conspicuously absent.

Loneliness bit into him like a rodent and chewed at his heart. He winced and continued down North Beach Neck to the highway, turning east at the corner, back into town.

He passed the Carmody mansion, shrouded in stillness and snow, and Beacon Savings and Loan. He slowed to an idle at the four corners, where he'd seen the blonde cross the street around lunchtime.

Two teenage girls sat on the brick planters outside the deli. A boy called to them from across Main Street.

He turned to survey the row of storefronts on the north side of the street. A group of well-dressed adults were walking into Foo Long's Chinese take-out. Behind them, a yard or so behind, the blonde in the black and silver jacket was gesturing emphatically to the tall young man at her side. The boy's head was shaved on one side, a brilliant orange on the other. The unshaved side was cut in a spiky crew-cut. He wore an oversized grey topcoat, and black combat boots under his faded jeans.

Jack waited for the light to turn, watching the girl in his rear view mirror as she and the boy disappeared into Foo Long's behind the others. Then he continued through the intersection, scanning the cars parked on Main Street. There were only two parked on the north side, a red van and a black late model Lincoln. He guessed that the van, license plate IPLAYSAX, was the girl's escort. He drove on a few hundred feet past it, parked on the south side of the street, and slipped out of his car.

He sprinted across Main Street to the van, his vampire tread leaving no mark in the crust of snow on the street. In the shadows of a tiny alley between the A&P and Hartnett Liquors he waited patiently for the girl to return.

He did not have to wait long. When the couple returned they were carrying two brown paper sacks of take-out food reeking of garlic and ginger.

"Let's go down to the dock," he heard the girl suggest. As she climbed into the van, her jacket hiked up, revealing a tight little derriere beneath it.

Jack trotted back to his car unseen, waited two minutes, and made a U-Turn on Main Street at the firehouse. Then he turned

166

down Robin's Hill Road and drove to the dock to park beside the red van.

He could not feel the bitter cold, but he left the engine running. He parked on the driver's side of the van so that he was hidden from view under the roof of his own car. After a few moments, he slipped noiselessly out of the Miata. Crouched, and moving too quickly to be detected by human eyes, he pressed one sharp nail to the valve of the van's rear passenger tire and let the air leak out. When he was finished he returned to his car, slipped behind the wheel, and waited.

By quarter to ten the boy with the half-shaved, half-scarlet hair was half way up Robin's Hill Road in pursuit of a phone. By then there were no other cars at the dock but Jack's Miata and the lame van, and the boy had had no choice but to approach him for help. The driver's window of the Miata was down in anticipation by the time he came around to knock on it.

The boy never opened his mouth. GO FOR HELP, Jack though, looking into his eyes, and the boy straightened up, peered up Robin's Hill toward the village, and said, "I'll go for help."

YOU NEVER SAW ME, Jack added as an afterthought. The boy rubbed his chin absently. Then he started up the hill, without the vaguest recollection that he had ever seen a man in a Miata.

Jennifer Tate rolled down the window of her boyfriend's dilapidated van and watched as he marched up the hill toward town. She had sent him to ask the man in the sports car if he had a jack, or if he might be nice enough to offer them a ride. But now Eric was striding up the hill, oblivious to the fact that he hadn't left her the key so that she could at least turn on the ignition and keep warm. So here she was sitting in the van alone, freezing to death.

"Stupid jerk," she mumbled under her breath and then stuck her head out into the wind and screamed, "No jack?" but the wind off the bay whipped her voice from her throat and carried it away over the inlet. And Eric, the clod, continued trudging up-hill like a damned zombie.

It was then that she recalled seeing the little import in town earlier that day, seeing it and admiring its odd, organic lines, and the wealthy looking suit who was driving it.

She thought about leaving the van and trotting up the hill after Eric. But the prospect of walking in the cold to the nearest public phone was not a happy one. She was cold in the van, but it was windy out, and raw.

She leaned over the driver's seat and peered out at the little black car. It was purring warmly, puffs of pale grey exhaust rising from its tail pipe.

"Fuck it," she mumbled under her breath and jumped out of the van. Then she came around the Miata and tapped on the stranger's window with one short pink nail.

He rolled it down, smiled graciously, and said, "Looks like he forgot to leave you the keys. You'd better get in before you freeze to death."

"Yeah," she laughed, relieved that he was going to be chivalrous. "Thanks. I mean I'd definitely freeze in that old van by myself. Eric took the keys, do you believe it?"

"Hop in," said the stranger, and he reached over the passenger's seat to unlatch the opposite door. Then he snapped the heater on high while she settled herself beside him.

"I saw you in town today," he said. "But you're not local."

"I'm out from the City. Staying with Eric's friends."

"Live there all your life?" he asked.

"Connecticut, mostly," she answered, and she looked around the interior of the car, admiring.

A moment passed.

"Still cold?" the man asked, his voice kind.

"A little," she gave him a smile. "Do you let people smoke in this thing?" She reached for the Newports in her pocket.

"No," he said quietly. And he took her hand, the one that had gone for the cigarettes, and put it back on her lap.

Her hand tingled from his touch. Surprised at his boldness, she looked into his face and discovered there the blackest eyes she'd ever seen. Their intensity was narcotic. Before she could think what to say, he touched her again, lifting her chin with his fingertips.

169

"You're a pretty little thing, aren't you," he said, fixing her with those depthless black eyes. "Let's let Eric take care of the van," he added softly, "and I'll take care of you."

"Well..." she tried keep her mind on what he was saying but she couldn't. His eyes were so hypnotic. He was more striking than she had first thought. Hadn't she seen him on T.V.? A politician perhaps. So smooth, polished. And such an aura of control about him. He was leaning closer. His cologne reminded her of her father's. She had the sudden urge to cuddle against his chest in the cold.

The stranger lifted her chin again with a light touch, and suddenly his dark head bent to kiss her throat. She gasped. His breath was cold. So cold! But his mouth was fire.

"I'm going to take you home," he said, drawing back from her. He looked at her with that unnerving gaze. It was not a suggestion. It was a decision made without her. She tried to force a self-assured smile but could not. She thought of declining his offer and climbing back into the frigid van but his lips on her throat had thrilled her. He was a far cry from Eric, or from any boy. He was too old for her. But his kiss! It was wicked. And it excited her.

"Ok," she said, "I'll just leave a note for Eric in the van--"

"Listen to me, girl," the man lowered his lids and the timber of his voice at the same time. "Eric," he touched her hair, "is a baby. An innocent little baby. Like you. All dress-up, hmm? Black leather jackets and ripped jeans and angry hair." He bent and,

170

taking her head in his hands, he kissed her full on the mouth. His mouth was ravishingly hot, and she felt her own heat, the answering accomplice, rise in her to greet him.

"Now," he said, and he tangled her hair in his hand and drew her head back by it. Then he set his lips against her neck and she gasped again. "Do you want to come with me, or not?"

She felt herself swoon, her cheeks and throat flush with blood. She felt drunk, more than drunk, wasted.

"Woah," she swallowed. "You're a trip." She felt foolish the moment she's said it. The hard black eyes were watching her with predatory evenness. She changed her tone.

"Yes," she nodded, "yes, please."

He pulled the Miata around the Yacht Club and drove north, back into the village. The light on Main was green. He passed through it, continuing north until he reached the limits of Old Inlet. Then he turned left into the cemetery. "Hey," she said, becoming alarmed. "What are you doing?"

"Just a quiet place to get acquainted," said the stranger. His voice had returned to its pleasant tenor.

"I guess SO," she looked over at her companion. "So you don't like cigarettes, huh?" She was nervous and longed for one. But she also longed to feel his kiss again. It was bewildering and wicked, and undeniably dangerous.

He was pulling over near a mausoleum. He didn't respond to her question, just turned and fixed her with those depthless eyes.

"Come to me," he said.

She hesitated briefly. The command made nerves tingle she didn't know she had. She swallowed her fear and moved closer. He leaned toward her again and slowly, so slowly! he bent to nuzzle the base of her throat. She made a little sighing whispered and swallowed.

"Do you like that?" his voice was deep again.

"Mmm," she sighed and caught her breath as she felt his tongue lay against her throat deliciously.

"You are a little fool," he whispered.

He pulled her head back suddenly by the hair at her nape.

"Ow, you're hurting me," she protested, gritting her teeth at him. "Don't be so rough."

He let her go and narrowed his eyes at her.

"Why can't you be nice, like before. You're so sexy."

He laughed.

"Child. Would you know it? What do you know about sex. Or life. Or death. You're an infant. A sweet little infant," his eyes were glowing like coals. "And I," he kissed her again on the mouth, "am deader than anything in this cemetery."

"Hey, come on. Stop saying weird stuff like that."

"I tell you the truth," he murmured against her mouth. "Even now, you could escape me if you chose to."

He's one weird dude, thought the girl. But the maddening hot kisses, the little growl he made when he pressed his mouth to her throat, she could not resist.

He moved away again, leaning back and looking out at the graves. It seemed he had suddenly lost interest in her.

"Hey," she whispered, "Where'd you go?"

He turned and regarded her, a little frown of puzzlement passing over his inhumanly cool expression.

"Come on," she touched his hand with one pink-polished fingertip. "Be nice," and she said. "And keep me warm."

She pecked his cheek quickly, like a little girl saying goodnight to her father.

The wet growl vibrated in his throat at the contact.

He moved so quickly she had no time to scream. In an instant he was on her and her throat was open. She felt his inhuman purr resonating against her breast as her hands flew up, pressing vainly against his impassive strength, and she knew.

Her fingers splayed and clenched, splayed and clenched against his chest. Then she shuddered, and gave herself to the vampire.

Five

"Dad?"

"What is it, Lisa?"

"Can Nichole Haas come out for the weekend? Mom said I should ask you."

Jack cleared his throat. So soon? he wanted to ask. For God's sake, her mother isn't dead a month, what's wrong with that bastard, anyway, to let his daughter come out here so soon after...

"Lisa, do you think that's a good idea?"

"What do you mean? She's lonely in Manhattan. All of her friends are out here."

Nichole. Leslie's daughter. Oh God, here? Under his roof? At NIGHT? He couldn't have it. He just couldn't allow it.

Not that he couldn't make it look like a second suicide. He had all the time in the world to think under pressure. And things had a way of turning out in his favor, he was beginning to notice. It was as if he had fallen through some kind of vortex of nature and found himself in a land of mirrors. Even when he made mistakes, which was rare, something always assisted his nature. Something always protected him, focused attention away from him, nurtured his confidence and his cruelty.

No. Not Lisa's friend. Enough is enough. How close do I have to come to genocide before my own flesh and blood starts to look good to me? I am not a maniac. I still have self-control.

But on what grounds could he protest?

"Maybe after a little more time has passed, honey," he looked up from his paper to see his daughter's face twisting up in a fist of pain.

"Oh, Lisa--" Too late. She was crying now, full blown sobs. Heart-wrenching, innocent, undeserved.

"I feel so bad for her," she choked. "I thought...I thought it would help-" she'd lost her breath.

Her dead father got up from his chair and moved to put his arms around his daughter in the old reflex, like a corpse coughing.

"Daddy--"

"Ok, ok. Let her come for a weekend. Maybe it will help."

Lisa turned her face toward his and gave him an unexpected kiss.

He felt his brows lift instinctively like a jackal. Then he cleared his throat again, pushing his human offspring gently out of his embrace.

"This weekend?" she asked, her own brows lifted in an interrogative.

He felt his blood drain from his face.

"Dad?"

"Sure," he nodded, turning away.

"Honey," said the zombie behind him. "Nichole Haas is here. She wants to say hello."

"Hi, Mr. Howell."

He had been standing at the parlor window watching her approach the house with Lisa. A moment later he heard the front door slam as the girls entered the hall together and Nichole greeted his wife. Now she was standing in the parlor doorway, as tall as her mother, but waif-slim. Her bright auburn hair cascaded over her shoulders to her waist. She had been in his house a hundred times. She'd been to parties there, slept over, even spent a week one Christmas when her parents went to Spain. But today she was a stranger to him. Today she stirred his blood.

Her sweetness numbed the room and set his vampire heart on fire. He had thought he would control it. But it defeated him, this rage. He was a mouth, twin razor fangs, and a tongue that pulsed with heat and hunger. He was hunger itself, shaped like a man. Shaped like a father.

He knew his face was clenched like a fist. But the girl only responded by coming to him across the carpet, believing his pain to be compassion for her. Now she was in his arms, a child, clinging to him, begging kindness. She needed to be held, needed to believe that her friend's dad loved her, and could make up just a little for the love she had lost.

"Nichole," he heard himself say softly into her hair. "I'm so sorry, sweetheart."

And he wanted to hold her with mortal tenderness, but the vampire arms could only crush, the vampire mouth could only tear and draw into itself. He felt the sting of tears in his eyes and he made a fierce little noise in his throat. It masqueraded as grief. His teeth were chattering and he grit them against themselves.

He was going to kill her, there was no doubt.

Mercifully she drew away from him, demurely wiping her eyes. Mercifully too, she had not seen his tears, which were surely scarlet, had not felt him shudder with need at her nearness. He wiped his eyes quickly with a handkerchief and it came away blood smeared. He stuffed the evidence of his fraud into his trouser pocket.

"Nicki," he said, "any time you want to stay with us, you know you're always welcome. You're family."

The girl looked back at him and smiled, her eyes the same remarkable turquoise as her mother's.

"Thanks Mr. Howell, I really appreciate that. I miss everybody out here a lot." And she disappeared down the hall with his daughter.

He watched her leave, her little tennis skirt swishing like a horsetail behind her. A growl thickened in his throat. He felt eyes boring into his back and he turned, black fury clouding his vision. The zombie was staring at him with a deadpan expression. It was innocuous, but not innocent.

He narrowed his eyes at it.

"Go make dinner for them," he ordered.

But it continued to stare with its cold, dead blue eyes a moment too long, willfully. Then it turned and shuffled out the parlor door toward the kitchen.

Six

"Valarie."

"Jack?"

"I have to see you."

Valarie was alone in her great empty house in Pequot Bog. Even so she walked the cordless into the half-bath off the kitchen and closed the door before she answered.

"What is it? Are you alright, Jack?"

"No. No, I'm not. I...need to see you."

Andy had shoved a paw under the bathroom door and was clawing the air in search of his mistress. Valarie watched absently as his little foot slipped back and forth along the linoleum floor. She touched his center pad with a bare toe and his claws retracted instantly. He patted her toenail playfully. "Silly," she giggled.

"What?"

"Oh, nothing, just my..." she had turned to regard her image in the shell shaped mirror over the double vanity. "reflection..." she finished.

"Valarie?" Jack's voice was shallow. "Will you come?"

"Of course, Jack. Where? When?" she answered.

"At midnight. At the dock," he replied.

"Okay." She breathed, and pressed the hang up button.

"Okay," she said to her reflection, translucent even in the hard light of the florescent lamps that hung above the mirror.

Valarie's red Honda pulled up alongside Jack's black Miata at the Old Inlet dock at a quarter after twelve.

Jack licked his lips as Valarie, wearing her obligatory leather jacket and short black skirt, a porter's cap cocked over her brow, hopped out of her little car and into his.

"Hey, now. What's up?" she said casually, settling herself into the tiny seat. But her eyes were concerned. Jack sighed.

Here she was beside him again, a little black-clad package of femininity, her tip-tilted almond eyes piercing him like the stiletto heels of her dove grey boots. Something human stirred in him, stirred so fiercely that he thought his vampire heart would break open and bleed for happiness to see her. What was this feeling? It was not hunger. His heart was aching with joy and it was a stranger to him, a thing sated by her proximity alone.

He had meant to satisfy himself at her expense, to save his daughter's friend. And yet he found himself desiring her understanding more than her blood.

He grit his teeth.

180

"I can't stand what I've become," he whispered. "I don't want to be...this way...anymore."

"You have changed," she agreed. "And not for the better."

"You see it?" he wondered.

"Sure," she said. "Come on, Jack. Tell me what it is. I'm here."

Her compassion infuriated him. He felt his face contract in a spasm of anger as she stared at him with affection in her eyes.

"I wonder," he said, his voice vibrating through the cabin of the little car. "Will you give me what I need?"

She watched him quietly.

"What is it you need, Jack?" she asked.

He dropped his lids to half-mast and leaned toward her.

"Because of you," he said, "I'm burning."

She started to shake her head, confused. "I didn't seduce-"

"Because of you, this thing has come upon me," he continued. "I don't know how. I don't know what the connection is. But it all started with you. You. And nothing satisfies me anymore. It just goes on and on, and it's never over, it's never enough. No matter to what depth I stoop, it's never low enough to quench me."

She gave him a pained look, then turned from him and peered out through the windshield at the black bay. When she turned back at him, a pleat of guilty concern had settled between her brows.

"What can I do?" she said at last.

Again he felt his face betray him. She was offering herself, was she not? He regarded her with the narrow stare of a hunter. He would do this thing and be done with her. His answer came quickly, without regard.

"Feed me," he said.

He was at her throat so swiftly she could only gasp. He drew back his lips, finding her pulse with his tongue, and yawned. But something was wrong. He stiffened, breathing against her neck like a jackal panting over a deer.

He grunted and drew away.

"Look. If you want...me...that way," she said.

"No."

"Better me than someone who might betray you later, hurt you, or your family-"

"No."

"I'd cause you no trouble. I'd be safer. If it's what you need-"

"Damn it, Valarie, what are you?" he roared, shaking the little car with the volume of his voice. "You'd give yourself to me to save me?" He shook his head, bewildered. "But you don't arouse me to it. There's no innocence in you."

She smiled sadly at him in the dark. "No, I'm afraid not."

"You care for me," he said. "Is that it? Is that what protects you from me? Compassion?" He spat the word.

"You cared for me once, too, Jack. Maybe that's it."

"No, it wouldn't matter." He rubbed his upper lip with a finger, pondering. "It's something about you. There's something very wrong with you Valarie," he said, "if the Devil doesn't want your soul."

Her eyes widened at him in the dark. "Oh God!" her hand covered her mouth.

"Ah, God again," Jack sneered. "What about him?"

Valarie stared. A tear trickled from the corner of her eye, hanging on a lash a moment and then dropping to shatter on the console. In the half-light, it appeared colorless. "My God," she repeated, "you, too." And then she fled.

Seven

When Jack finally returned to his rambling mansion on Beach Neck Lane early the next morning, he slept in.

Nichole Haas was safe, at least for the time being. Jack slept, sated on the killing spree that had followed Valarie's departure. And in his sleep, he dreamed.

He dreamed of bodies, piled high all about him. Bodies stacked in pyramids along the sidewalk on Robins Hill Road. Bodies strewn across the parking lot at the Yacht club, bodies bobbing in the water at the dock. There were bodies in boxes on the porch of Valarie's little cottage. Bodies in his living room, in his den, in his car, even in his golf cart. Everywhere he went, whatever he tried to do, bodies piled up around him, surrounding him, threatening to bury him.

He began to run, trying to put some distance between himself and the dead. He jogged down Beach Neck Lane, jumping over bodies as he went, in sweats and sneakers. His neighbor's lawns were stacked with bodies, cars were stuffed with them. There was no one left alive.

184

And then he saw her, jogging down the opposite side of the street, the rhinestone studded denim baseball cap cocked over her eyes. She was there, as she'd always been. And she was so alive.

He called to her, but she did not hear. He tried to cross the street, but the street was littered with corpses, piled with corpses, and he could not maneuver around them.

"Valarie!" he shouted, but she continued to jog, casually trotting past the bodies as though they were perfectly normal, hurtling them like an Olympic sprinter.

"Valarie," he heard himself scream, his lungs filled to bursting. "Please don't leave me, don't leave me here alone!"

He saw the hat turn toward him, saw the soft brown, doe eyes light with recognition under the sky blue brim. She smiled, mouthed a word to him, waving in slow motion, beckoning.

He started to gain some ground, nearly reaching her side.

COME ON, she mouthed. FOLLOW ME.

Then his foot snagged on something. He couldn't break free of it. He looked down and saw that a hand was gripping his ankle, a hand with pink-polished nails. Then another joined it and another, until a nest of hands covered his feet and he couldn't take another step.

Valarie awoke with a start. In the dream she had been back at the cottage, looking for the cat. Not Amos or Andy, but Timmons, Claude's Siamese, the cat that the vampire Laroby had killed. She knew he was dead, knew she was dreaming. Still she called, "kitty, kitty, kuss, kuss!" as she walked around the back yard searching for him.

Then she heard the mewling behind the hedge, on the other side of the stockade fence, in Edna's yard. It was a fragile sound, not a cat's mew but a kitten's plaintiff cry.

"Here kitty, here Tim," she said, looking up through the hedges that covered the fence on her side.

The hedge towered over her, overshadowing the fence as it had never done. She peered through it looking for the familiar vertical pickets of the stockade behind the greenery, but found only a wall made of smooth, organically shaped stones, and of mortar. A child was crying, weeping on the other side of the stone wall, forlorn and forsaken. She pressed her palms against the flesh colored stones and called, "I'm here," to the child.

And her fingers sank into the rounded stones. For they were not stones but shoulders. Arms, hips, knees. Bodies. Corpses. The wall was made of corpses. She drew away, repulsed.

"Valarie!" cried the voice on the other side. It was a voice in agony. Tormented.

Whose voice? Not a child. A man. A hopeless, despairing, lost man.

She began to trot alongside the wall of bodies, looking for the end of it, for some way of reaching the forlorn voice on the other side.

186

"Valarie," it said. "Don't leave me here alone!"

Whose voice? She continued to jog along the wall of bodies.

"Find a way through," she told the voice. "It can't go on forever."

Then she realized she was running south, down toward the bay, and she knew that at the water's edge the wall of death must end.

"Follow me," she told the voice. "Follow me to the water!" Then I can swim across and find you, she though. And bring you to safety.

Above the mound of bodies she began to see the tips of trees, the roofs of houses. The mound was diminishing as she approached the bay.

She looked ahead. Fantastic blue-green water danced on the shoreline in the brilliant sunlight. Her heart soared at the sight of it. And she nearly forgot the voice behind the wall of bodies, until it called again.

"VALARIE!"

She turned back to the wall and over the top, above the uppermost corpse, she saw the second story of Jack's house. And in a window, Jack stood, staring down at her with Laroby's emerald green eyes.

"NO!" she cried, "No, no-o-o!" But the thing in the window nodded, YES. And then it lifted a bundle up, over its head, and heaved it at her. It bounced like a rag doll as it hit the ground, its gold blond hair flying up around its head in a crescent. It joined the other bodies littered all about the lawn, resting near a boy with half-shaved, half-scarlet hair.

"I'm Hungry!" screamed the thing in the window that looked like Jack, clenching its fists and raising them to heaven.

"I'm HUNGRY!" it cried, as Valarie's feet hit the water's edge and she plunged in.

PART FOUR

One

In the closet behind the kitchen, in the hallway leading to his gym, Dean was laying on the final coat of white paint over the newly spackled sheetrock.

He was a tall man and he found his workspace cramped, giving him an oddly claustrophobic feeling which unnerved him against the backdrop of the otherwise oversized house. The paint he used was latex-based, and in an open area it was not unbearable. But he was hypersensitive to fumes and the acrid odor impinged upon his sensibilities, making it hard for him to concentrate on his work without worrying about its latent effect on his lungs.

He was painting the last closet in the Dumont house in need of renovation, and he was glad the job was nearly over. Despite his large frame, as a child he had been fragile, allergic to a host of

189

substances before he reached his late teens. As a result, he was obsessively careful with poisons, edible and airborne, and he took great pains not to remain in toxic situations without protection.

He stepped back from the paint, adjusting his breathing mask. The grey appendage had two short snouts at the chin line, each capped with a filter. It resembled an antique military gas mask. Valarie had refused to wear one, despite the rather eloquent discourse he'd given on the dangers of airborne toxins just before he started the spackling two weeks ago.

"Never mind," she had said, shaking her head at him, "I'd rather choke."

"You won't. You'll just get cancer ten years from now," he reminded her.

"Cancer?" she gave an angry laugh. "What would cancer do with me?"

And he had not brought the topic up again.

Now he backed away from his work, breathing shallowly through the heavy rubber mask. In another half hour he would be done, his tools cleaned and put away. Then he would wash up, have a few 'carbs' and go back to the gym to work out. Maybe Valarie would even join him, as she had on more than one occasion since he had installed his weight equipment in the second largest room in the house.

The gym had been Mrs. Dumont's private sitting room before the Valanchuks had moved in, but with only Dean and Valarie living in the double sized dwelling now, there was already an abundance of sitting room space. There was the great room, separating the two wings, the front parlor, where the green plaid Herculon furniture remained, and the spare bedroom on the east wing, which had been converted into a small library. Dean saw immediately that Mrs. Dumont's sitting room was the perfect place for his gym. Situated behind the kitchen, under the back stairs, at the end of a hallway, it was big enough for his entire arsenal of equipment, including the leg press and the calf raise machine he had built the previous summer in the basement of the cottage on North Beach Neck Lane. Valarie had agreed to forfeit the room for a gym with reluctance at first, but became more enthusiastic about it as time went on. It seemed she believed she was losing some of the physical strength that had accompanied her bedevilment, and it frightened her. One morning she followed him into the newly arranged room and asked him to explain the purpose of each of the exercises he performed, and then demonstrate to her their proper execution. She benched sixty pounds that day, not bad for a woman. But she had not impressed herself.

"What can you press?" she had asked, looking up at him sadly.

"On a good day? Two twenty, two twenty-five tops," he'd replied, not a little smugly. "Well," she'd sighed, "I guess I'll try for half of that." And she gripped the bar again with the pair of pink

191

lifting gloves she'd bought at Sport World, and threw herself back down on the bench. "One-oh-five."

"One ten," he corrected.

That had been three weeks ago. Valarie had been working out every other day since then, pushing her top press up to seventy five pounds. It was a substantial gain, but she was not satisfied. Dean wondered if he might suggest at this point that the strength she feared she'd lost had been an illusion all along. Maybe it had ALL been an illusion.

"Finished?"

Valarie stood behind him in a grey leotard, a yellow towel draped around her shoulders. She had tied her hair back with a yellow headband that bisected her forehead and made her eyes enormous.

"You look nice." Dean's eyes travelled down the slender column of his wife's sweat-less body.

"So good-bye, Philip Dumont Memorial Cedar Closets, hmm?" She studied his work over his shoulder, ignoring his flirtation.

"Good-bye, Phil," agreed Dean, and follow her back to the gym.

"So, coach, wanna hand me the bar?" Valarie asked as she slipped a cassette into the boom box she kept by the squat rack. Van Halen roared through the hollow room.

"How can you exercise to that crap? It drains your energy level," Dean shouted over the music.

Valarie sat down on a straight bench, flexing a little to bring the blood up into her arms and chest. She began mouthing the words to the song, ignoring his ire.

"I doannoh wadabeen lookinfoa but iss, not enough to fill meup...hand me the bar," she laid back on the bench and grabbed the Olympic bar, "Ah want the best, uh, of, uh, both worlds, uh honey..."

"Wait a minute! Holy shit!" Dean rushed over to grab the bar from her, too late. Valarie was executing presses with slow, deep, perfect pumps. At the count of five she threw the weight back on the rack, cursing, and sat up.

"What the hell is your problem, Dean, I'm trying to do a full set here for Chrissake!" Dead black anger brewed in her root beer brown eyes.

"Valarie," Dean panted, "look what you just lifted, honey."

She twisted her torso and looked behind her at the bar. "Hundred, fifty, two, fif-"

She looked up at him, eyebrows peaked. "Two fifty?" Her face became grave. She pursed her lips. "Well," she said at last, tossing off her gloves, "I guess that about wraps it up for me."

"I guess," Dean swallowed.

Two

It was Friday and the Sharon Probation Office was ghostly quiet. No probationers waited in the lobby, for office reports were never scheduled on Fridays. Half the clericals had gone home, "flexing" or "pinking out" a few hour to make a longer weekend, and most of the field officers were in the field. Valarie had her office to herself. Stevie was home with a sick baby, and Richie Childs was dictating a case in the empty office next door. Valarie could hear his nasal James Cagney buzzing through the wall.

Her stomach growled and she looked up at the little clock on the base of Richie's automatic coffee maker. 4:15 p.m. She tried to think when her last meal had been but couldn't remember. Not today. Today she had worked through lunch on the Rodriquez case. It was another fatality, the victim, an 18 year old honor student with a football career ahead of him. His parents, who were divorced, had insisted on separate interviews. In the end, the Rodriquez case had taken her the better part of two days to write.

Valarie pushed herself away from her desk and slipped a rubber band around the inch thick folder, tucking it under an arm as she stood. She would drop it off in the typing room on her way to Administration, where the payroll clerks kept a stash of candy bars in a file drawer, made available to hungry staff at a price of fifty cents apiece.

She was about to leave her desk when a disturbance in the direction of Jack's office brought her to attention. There was a thump, like a body hitting a wall, then a woman's scream. Another thump, and a door slamming back against its hinges.

"Oh my G-a-a-a-d!" A pair of high heels clattered down the deserted hall toward Valarie, who stepped through her own office door in time to dodge Patty Kinsemmi, stampeding toward the security office.

"Oh shit," Valarie breathed. She hesitated only a moment. Then she turned toward Jack's office.

She was inside it before she had taken a human step. There, at the speed of thought, where she wanted to be. Jack was facing his window, his back to her, apparently unaware of her presence. More heels were clattering down the hall in their direction. Disoriented by her instant relocation, Valarie slipped behind the heavy wooden door as it opened inward.

"What happened?" It was Karen James, Jack's secretary. Valarie saw the boss turn from the window calmly, his eyes, two black pitch pools. She saw him take her in, without expression, then regard Karen.

"Do you have some business here?"

"Well, no but-- Jack?"

"Then go back to your desk and do what you're paid to do," he said quietly.

"Yes, sir," Karen scowled up at him and left.

"Lock it," he said to Valarie.

She clicked the lock.

"How did you get in here?" he said flatly.

She shook her head slowly at him. Every move he had made until now, everything he'd said, was in slow motion. But now he came around his desk and stood in front of her, moving at what appeared to her to be normal speed. Her speed. Vampire speed.

ARE YOU HUNGRY, JACK?

And his eyes widened at her for an instant. Then he composed his face and answered, YES.

She sighed, closed her eyes and dropped her head.

"Patty knows," he said, quietly. "It's over for me."

Valarie looked up at him. She tried to read his face, to find some sorrow there, some personal remorse. But there was none of those. Resolve, perhaps. But not contrition. Still she shook her head, NOT YET. And disappeared.

Now she was at the end of the hall, near the Security office, watching Patty hurtle her large and very pregnant body toward her. At the sight of Valarie's sudden materialization, Patty screamed, throwing her hands over her mouth, and Valarie hissed, more in surprise than anger, and jumped back like a startled house cat.

Patty looked around wildly, then flung her weight against the ladies room door and disappeared inside.

"Shit, shit, shit," Valarie shoved herself away from the wall and moved toward the ladies' john. And without another thought, she found herself inside a stall with Patty, nose to nose.

Patty opened her mouth to scream for the third time.

"Goddamn it, shut that trap or I'll rip it off you," Valarie growled.

Patty closed her mouth obediently, trembling and sniffling despite her apparent physical advantage over Valarie.

"Wha-what's going on.." she whimpered, her big green eyes filling with tears. "Jack tried to...and you're...I'm going crazy...oh my God..." She sank down to sit on the toilet rim as a herd of high heels clattered into the powder room lounge.

"Patty? Are you okay? Open the door!" It was Karen. Behind her other voices, Donna Deluca, Joanne Harris, Pat McCabe, chimed in. Inside the stall Valarie drew her lips back in a snarl, revealing a pair of long, ivory incisors. And Patty drew back, forcing her large body between the toilet and the plumbing.

"Open up! Come on, Patty, talk to me!" Karen demanded, banging on the stall door.

NO.

"N-no," Patty squeaked, staring into Valarie's diamond hard glare.

I'M BLEEDING.

"I'm bleeding," repeated Patty.

"Oh, shit, a lot?" Karen gasped behind the stall door.

"N-no," Patty continued, taking instruction from the voiceless vampire. "I thought I was miscarrying. It's not bad. It's stopped. I think I'm just spotting. Can somebody take me home?"

And Valarie vanished.

She was back in Jack's office.

The moment she materialized his arms were around her, but there was no passion in his embrace. He clenched her little body against his like a wolverine drowning in a racing river clinging to a low branch.

"It's okay," she said, returning his embrace. "She told them she had thought she was miscarrying. Somebody'll drive her home. She'll be quiet."

He shook his head. "She'll have to die." And then his shoulders heaved and he began to weep.

She shoved him away from herself and struck his face before she knew what she had done.

"For chrissake, Jack, she's pregnant."

"I know that," he answered, his eyes going flat with cruelty. "That's why I wanted her."

For a moment they faced each other, stalemated, he with jaw clenched blinking crimson tears from his depthless black eyes, and she, warily, glaring back a warning. "Look," Jack said at last, "you handle hell your way and I'll handle it mine. But keep in mind I'm dead, my wife is a zombie, I'm an accomplished butcher, and I really don't have a whole lot of compassion to spread around anymore."

"You never did," she countered. "Maybe that's why it happened to you. Maybe that's why you're dead."

He grinned an ugly, angry grin.

"Oh, really? And what's you're excuse, Mother Theresa?" and he chucked her under the chin in a belittling gesture.

Affronted, she moved out of his reach. Then, coolly, she stepped around him and stood at the window.

"I came back once, you know," she said over her shoulder. "I went to Church, confessed my sins, took Holy Communion.... and woke up mortal."

She heard him release an intolerant sigh. "Then I got confused, or something. I started losing it, you know?" She turned to look at him and could see that he did not.

"I missed Old Inlet, Jack. I missed home." She pursed her lips, "I missed my memories, and I missed you, too. You were all I had left of my past. Like a family album after a fire. You knew me when I was a little girl. You know," she gave a sad little shrug, "there's nobody else alive that does? They're all dead. My whole family."

"So what happened when you discovered that poor old Jack Howell meant more to you than a doddering lecher, hm? I'm all ears."

She frowned at him.

"Please," he lifted his hand, gesturing for her to continue.

"I turned back into a vampire."

"Hah!" he threw back his head.

"No, really..."

"Stop it!" His eyes were murderous.

She waited. Finally his expression softened and he stepped toward her.

"You're kidding yourself, Valarie," he said. "You never turned back. You've been dead all along." He set a hand on her shoulder and gave it a shake.

"There's no magic wafer, Valarie, no ritual, no escape hatch. We're both in this forever."

He turned away from her. "There is no God," he said.

Three

"It's happening again," said Valarie to the little priest in the black frock behind the great mahogany desk. The desires are back."

Father Tito nodded pleasantly. "Temptation is always with us," he said.

She cleared her throat, looking down at her hands in her lap. Her nails were long and sharp, and they glistered like mother-of-pearl.

"So what do I do, Father, just keep confessing and eating Communion wafers? Will that bring me back to life?"

"He is the Bread of Life," answered the priest. "'Anyone who eats this bread, shall not suffer death.'"

She sighed, shaking her head. "I'm not sure I believe that any more," she said.

"Then you must pray for faith," said the priest, "and for strength against temptations. God will answer your prayers."

The vampire moaned inwardly. He's talking in circles, she thought. Jack was right. I was just kidding myself. I've been dead all along.

She rose from the red Bergere armchair and picked up her coat.

"Thank you, Father," she said, moving to the door. "I'll do that," she added, knowing full well she would not.

She did not feel the chill outside, but could sense the cold through her nose and mouth, like a wolf. Valarie sighed, shook her head, and walked down the sidewalk to her car. She had driven to Old Inlet to see the little priest, and she had seen him. But now that she was here there seemed no reason to rush home to the desolate loneliness of Pequot Bog.

She stopped in her tracks. Why had she taken the car at all? It was absurd, but her mortal habit of relying on machinery had not lessened with her return to immortality. She still drove, though it was painfully tedious to do so now, just as she used the telephone though she could drive her thoughts into a human head without making a sound. Her senses were keener than they had been during her first death, which was how she had come to think of it, and she could see though the material world with the x-ray vision of a super hero. It did her no good, of course. She could change nothing. All of the benefits of death simply made her a more cunning hunter, lessening her prey's chances with nauseating overkill, like a hunter with a night scope and an assault rifle.

She began walking down Robin's Hill Road toward the center of town. Her cool breath formed no little puffs of condensation in front of her nose, though she wrapped her winter coat more tightly around herself and shivered out of habit. She shoved her hands into her pockets and concentrated on remaining visible.

She was passing the Chowder Pot when she heard a familiar voice within. The Pot, a local hot spot, served haute cuisine and fine wine and Valarie had only been inside on one occasion, when Dean had taken her there to propose. She recalled there was a bar to the right as one entered, behind which was a small, private dining area with a fireplace. A larger dining area to the left was accessible from a door at the opposite end of the bar.

The voice was coming from the little room in the back.

Valarie tapped up the steps to the entrance, pretending to read a menu that had been taped to a window. She peered through the frosted pane, past the bar, to the tables in the back room and saw Jack Howell seated with a woman who was not his wife.

Valarie stepped inside. A row of male heads turned simultaneously in her direction from their seats at the bar. She gave them a flat, dead look and walked past them, to the end of the bar.

"Miss?" said the bartender.

SHERRY. She put the though in his head without opening her mouth.

"Right up," he answered amiably.

Valarie turned and saw that Jack had observed her entrance. Like a panther interrupted in pursuit of a deer he stiffened, his eyes narrowing. She, in turn, lifted one dark brow and curled her lip in an attitude of contest.

When her sherry arrived she picked up the glass by the rim and walked casually to his table.

"Hullo," she said to his companion, a woman in her forties with mannishly short, frosted hair wearing the baggy skirt and sweater ensemble of a social worker. "You must be Mrs. Howell." She set her wine glass down on the lip of the table as she pulled off her coat, exposing a little claret dress that fit her trim figure like a body stocking. "I'm Valarie Valanchuk. I work for your husband." And she extended her hand.

The woman coughed and put one birdlike hand to her throat. She looked at Jack for assistance, but Jack's dark eyes were nailed to Valarie.

"Oh," Valarie gasped, "I'm so sorry, I thought--" she looked from the woman to Jack and back again.

"Go home, Diane," said Jack, still fixing his glare on Valarie. "I'll handle this."

The woman stood up, nearly knocking her chair over as she did so. Then she grabbed her coat and a pocketbook and, squeezing past Valarie, who continued to smile pleasantly at her, escaped toward the bar.

"I could rip you to pieces for that," hissed Jack.

"I doubt it," she answered as she pulled back Diane's chair and seated herself beside him. She leaned over the table to recover her sherry from the other end of it.

"Don't get in my way, you little bitch. I'm stronger than you."

"Oh, how the hell would you know?" Valarie snapped, returning his scowl.

He lowered his voice and smiled. "Perhaps we'll find out some day," he said.

Valarie pursed her lips at him, swallowed a gulp of sherry, and lowered her glass.

"Social worker," she stated the observation as a matter of fact. "Not much innocence there, Jack, you're scraping the barrel on this one."

"Shut up, Valarie," Jack forced a smile over his clenched teeth, noting that his new dinner companion had collected a fan club from the bar.

"Don't be so rude. It doesn't become such a distinguished looking fellow." She flashed him a devilish smile and then turned her attention to the plate before her, left by his previous dinner companion. She picked up a fork and began pushing around what remained of the meal. "What in the hell did she order here?"

"Stop it, people are watching you," Jack hissed, taking the fork from her hand and replacing it on the table cloth.

"They're not watching me, they're watching my dress," she smiled back at him sweetly. Then she sniffed Diane's forgotten drink.

"Wow, heavy hitter. Scotch-and-nothing. Was that a man under that camping ensemble?"

Jack closed his eyes with rage, intent on composing himself before he answered her.

"No matter to you if it was," he breathed.

"But you prefer women," she stated, cocking her head at him. The little motion made her hair pour over her shoulders and she flipped it back irritably.

"I do," he opened his eyes and leered at her.

They regarded each other silently.

"Why did you bring her here?" Valarie asked at last, for genuine concern and curiosity had overcome her. "Any one of your Old Inlet elite friends might walk in and see you together... shortly before her... unfortunate disappearance."

"None of my snob friends would have the guts to say anything if they did. Besides," this last he bent to whisper in her ear, "what makes you think I was going to kill her?"

Valarie stared at him, confused. "Well why else..."

"Why else bother with her?" he lifted one black eyebrow, anticipating her question. "There is more to death than dying, Valarie." He smiled evilly.

206

She shook her head. "I don't get it. You... you have sex with them?" her eyes dropped to his lap before she caught herself and looked away. "With the ones you kill?"

"Don't look so chagrined," he laughed. "I don't normally, no. But they think I will. They beg for it, most of them, and it makes good sport."

He cleared his throat. "What is the point of goodness if there is no God, Valarie? Why not enjoy sin to the fullest?" He took a sip from his glass of port.

She watched him quietly, hearing the ugly words fall from his mouth like clods of earth. Her eyes stung and she blinked away a pink film of tears.

"You don't know that," she said. "You just prefer to believe it. It gives you carte blanche."

"There was never any proof," Jack continued placidly, "of God's existence during my mortal life. We're all supposed to wait for the punch line at the end. Well, now I'm dead as doornails. No punch line. No white light. No clue."

He looked around the restaurant absently. "Certainly no reason to be anything but pleasure-centered from now on."

He returned his black gaze to her, taking her physical presence in from head to toe.

"If you were mortal, I'd take you slowly," he said with a wet growl. "So don't try too hard to turn back now."

That brought Valarie to her feet. She set her glass down, hard, and left him.

Four

It seemed she could be good, and vulnerable, or evil, and indomitable.

She did not cherish weakness.

But evil continued to repulse her.

And her inclinations remained good. She stayed with Dean because he loved her, although she could not return his love. And guilt continued to plague her over her murders, especially the murder of Philip Dumont, which she was reminded of unceasingly. She even considered selling Cecile's great house and moving back to Old Inlet to be rid of it.

She was lonely in Pequot Bog and missed the familiarity of her hometown. More than once she had considered Jack's enormous house, even imagined living in it. Her vampire nature counseled her on those occasions to test the fullness of her powers and take it from him. But her human heart warned her against such greed. And when she thought of the results of her past gluttony, what was left alive in her won the argument.

Then one day she felt the tidal wave of hunger rise up in her again.

It was Sunday and she was downstairs in the oversized chef's kitchen, chopping vegetables for a salad at the wrap-around chrome island and watching her knife slice through the red meat of a tomato, when first the nausea, then a terrible emptiness in her vitals overcame her. She swooned, grabbing for the edge of the sink.

"Oohh," she moaned.

The knife clattered to the floor, bits of tomato seed spattering the hunter green tiles. As she lost her grip she heard a watery sound, like the tide against the dock, lapping in her ears. It took her an instant to recognize the whoosh of her own blood tide, cresting, slapping, rushing against her eardrums.

She sank to the floor, pressing her hands against her temples. Her clothes were soaked with perspiration by the time her body hit the tiles. Hunger enveloped her, like a madness, overwhelming and total. The bloodlust was back in full vigor, and it was crushing her like a piece of ripe red fruit.

She wiped her forehead with her arms and saw the cloth of her sleeve come away bloody, the sight of it terrifying her at first, until she realized it was only her own perspiration, turned to blood, like her tears had after the first death. But something else was different, too. Because this hunger was not a generalized lusting for the red liquor of life, it was specific, and told her without

210

question whose blood called to her. It sang to her not of innocence but of evil. Blood twice stolen for her twice taken soul. Vampire blood.

"No," she wept.

But the hunger was intolerable.

She crawled across the floor, leaving a blood trail as she went. She was weak beyond reason, and she nearly collapsed before she reached the foot of the back stairs. Once there she found it was impossible for her to climb them. Blood tears filled her eyes. The world was crimson.

Andy, tumbling down the staircase in a game of tag with Amos, stopped in his tracks, spat at her and backed up into his brother. Amos hissed, popping up on his toes and arching in the air.

Valarie moaned.

"Help me," she wept to a vision of a hundred old myths of salvation she no longer believed.

"Do you want me?" The voice was gentle and sweet, without gender, and lighthearted, like the tinkling of clay wind chimes in a summer breeze. Valarie lifted her blood filled eyes, panting like a dog, to see the two bloody feet planted beside her, staining the dun-colored carpeting at the bottom of the staircase. The feet were terribly wounded and she had the ridiculous thought, despite her own pain, that it must be agony to stand on them. She raised her eyes to the apparition.

"You came," she murmured in her delirium.

Above the feet hung a robe of woven fabric, once natural but now soaked through with scarlet. Two beautiful, bleeding, long fingered human hands hung from the sleeves of the ensanguined garment. The palms were turned toward her in a gesture of compassion.

"Do you want me?" said the voice, and a choir of a thousand chords lifted heavenward with each word.

As it spoke, the figure knelt and the bloody hands, hands that should have been curling inward to comfort themselves, so wounded were they, reached instead for her, open and merciful.

Valarie looked up into the sapphire eyes of the crimson bird, and fainted.

Five

Jack was hammering the last nails into the lid of his wife's coffin.

He had not made the box. He was hopeless with his hands and would not, even as a supernatural, attempt carpentry. He had ordered the thing from a company in Tennessee, the name of which he had stolen from the desk of a popular Italian undertaker in East Patton.

He had paid a pretty sum for the plain pine coffin, but no questions were asked and he'd had no difficulty using a false name in the purchase. Now he was nearly finished with the most unpleasant part of the task. As he took another nail from the row he clenched in his lips he made a satisfied sound. The coffin had arrived that afternoon, wrapped like a kitchen appliance, (he had to chuckle at the irony). He had no trouble carrying it into the basement. But he waited until dark to call Joan downstairs and order her into it. She had done so without argument, though her doll-like features seemed to cave in, her glass-blue eyes dark with rancor as she climbed into the box. Jack set the lid on over her stare and began the ugly task of sealing her into it forever. He

213

knew that Joan would not rot, but for all intents and purposes, she would disappear. And that was all he really wanted.

He heard Lisa come home from practice at about 6:30 p.m. She called to her mother, then to him, then trotted upstairs. His acute hearing picked up a telephone conversation from her second floor bedroom as he drove home the last of the nails.

All that was left was the disposal of the coffin. Burial above a newly dug grave, (a Mrs. Esther Davis of Cooks Hollow Lane had obligingly died three days ago, and had been interred at the Old Inlet Community Cemetery just this morning) would complete her perfect and eternal concealment.

He could not carry the coffin in the Miata and Joan's Nissan wagon had already been disposed of, having been driven into the Bronx earlier that day by a juvenile offender whom Jack had convinced to relocate after the theft. The boy, who was on probation to Officer Ortiz, was in violation of his probation on another new charge anyway, and the opportunity to escape a stiff prison sentence was not wasted on him. He ditched the car and used the cash (a considerable sum) to abscond to Miami, where his cousin was running a chop shop of his own right out of his mother's garage.

And if all of these benefits were not enough to insure the kid's silence, certainly Jack's demonstration of supernatural snack-time on the boy's accomplice was.

Although there was no vehicle available to him in which to carry the coffin to the cemetery, Jack was not perturbed. He had been noticing his strength and speed increasing for days, and he had no doubt he could carry Joan, without detection, on foot.

"Da-a-ad! There's a woman at the door! She wants to see you!"

Jack heard Lisa's shrill soprano through the floorboards. Cursing, he pulled a plastic tarpaulin over the coffin and had begun ascending the cellar stairs when Lisa opened the basement door to call down to him again.

"Where's your mother?" Jack asked her casually as he reached the landing.

"I don't know. Her car's gone. I guess she's working late again."

"She'd have called and left a message, wouldn't she?" he said over his shoulder, brushing dust from his hands absently as he crossed the kitchen toward the front hall.

"I guess," Lisa considered. Then she followed her father to the front entrance where the woman in black was standing, framed in the doorway like an art-deco silhouette. Delicate and slender, dark eyed and alabaster skinned, she wore a short black cape over what appeared to be a cat suit. A French beret cocked over one glittering brown eye crowned her dark hair, which fell past her

215

shoulders. Her deerskin gloves matched her dove grey boots, upon whose stiletto heels she balanced.

"Valarie," Jack was startled. Of all the visitors his mind could conjure, this one was the least expected and the least desired. "What are you doing here?" He caught the tension in his own voice and softened it, knowing his daughter was watching from the dining room doorway. "Is something wrong?"

"We have to talk," purred the vampire at the front door. "May I come in please?"

Jack looked into his visitor's hypnotic brown eyes and nodded. "Of course, come in." He motioned her into the parlor. Then he looked back at his daughter and added, "This is Lisa, my youngest."

Valarie gave the girl a perfunctory glance and smiled.

GO TO YOUR ROOM, he heard the soundless mental command as she returned her glittering eyes to him.

The girl with the carrot red hair turned and headed down the hall toward the back stairs just as the telephone rang in the kitchen.

"She'll get that in her room," said Jack to Valarie. "Sit down, please. It's probably my wife, she's late home from work and we were just beginning to get worried."

Valarie folded her body into an armchair as Jack settled himself on the across from her.

"How formal," said Valarie, without indicating whether it was the decor of the room or her host's air of propriety to which she

216

referred. Then she smiled and reached across an end table to touch his hand with gloved fingertips.

"You have invited me, my friend, into your home," she said, and a queer chill ran up Jack's spine like the scales of an aria. He gave an involuntary flinch.

Their eyes met, black on black, and held for a long moment.

"You can't be serious." Jack spoke in a clenched whisper.

Valarie's laughter caressed his spine. She stroked the back of his hand playfully.

"Oh, but I am, Jack," she said. Then her face turned to marble as she added, "I'm twice fallen. You can't imagine how hungry I am."

Now it was Jack who laughed. He threw back his head, mocking her with an explosive sound, but stopped abruptly when he realized she had vanished, and that even his supernatural vision had not been able to follow her.

"I hear the dead breathing in your basement."

The words were cooed against his ear on little puffs of air.

Jack jumped. Valarie had moved from the armchair to the sofa, where she rested her body against his, her lips brushing his ear. Now she moved her tongue down the cord of his neck and laid her mouth against the carotid artery. She touched him only with the most unbearable tenderness, like a priest adoring a relic, and Jack felt his blood rush, like a greedy traitor, to meet her lips, his throat flushing with delight at her touch.

217

"What ARE you?" he murmured.

She vanished again, to appear across the room, her arms folded in front of her as she leaned on an elbow at the mantle.

"Perhaps I am your master," she said.

Jack took a breath and forced his features into some semblance of composure. He looked up at the art-deco statue at the fireplace and tried in vain to remember how he had once felt about this creature. But those warm, human feelings were gone. He could see only the vampire now, its sable eyes glittering with hunger, its mouth red and ripe and ravenous, its skin like milky glass. A beautiful beast, deadly and indifferent, waiting to strike, playing with him as if with an injured bird. Occupying itself with the sweet moments before the kill, as so many times he had done, choosing the moment, the method, with the lazy creativity of an accomplished artist. And he detested her, as he had never detested anyone in life or death.

She watched him ponder this revelation from her pose at the mantle.

"You hate me now?" she sounded interested, not hurt.

"I do," he whispered brutally.

She regarded him without emotion for a moment. Then she put a thoughtful finger to her lips and smiled.

"For now," she said.

He glared at her from the sofa. "Forever."

"What an infant you are," she declared. "Innocent even in evil." She gave a little snort. "You thing you're strong, because you've never tested your strength on one of your own kind. But do you know that the farther we fall, the greater our power on earth becomes?"

And she vanished, as if to demonstrate, appearing again in the armchair, where she stretched like a lazy cat before curling her legs beneath her.

"Your great claim to sin is greed, self-indulgence. But who indicts you? Who do you insult when you fall? Only yourself. Only your own infantile vision of good and bad is tarnished with disrespect. You knew no God, answered to no one greater than yourself. Who then, have you betrayed? No one of significance." She lifted her hand at him, pausing, and vanished again.

"But I--!" She was roaring the words into his face, her hands clenching the front of his shirt, shaking him. "I have known Him! I have known Him, and still I despair, still I deny Him!" She let him go, balling up her fists.

"If sin is strength on this earth, then you are only a child, a babe. Your sin is a grain of salt to the ocean of my betrayal!"

She vanished again.

For one instant he thought she might have left him, disappeared for good, gone hunting some other baby vampire in the dark winter night. But then she reappeared in the armchair, her face turned, her chin on the flat of her fist as she gazed out through the parlor windows. She turned her head back toward him so slowly she seemed not to move at all, and as the glittering brown eyes fell on him she blinked once, shedding a single garnet tear.

"So, Jack," she said at last, almost sweetly. "Let's see who's fallen farther from what they might have been to what they are, eh? Let's see who God thinks is more wicked, the selfish and greedy atheist who, just as he believes, will live and die with no more spiritual potential than a plant ... or one of His own, one He counted a friend... who betrayed Him."

Jack watched her silently. After what seemed an eternity, he shook his head, his face hardened to a mask of contempt. "You have no more evidence of God's existence than you ever did," he murmured. "I don't pretend to know what's happened to you, any more than I know what happened to me. But your argument convinces me of nothing. You prove nothing. And you know nothing. None of us," he added, "knows anything."

She gave no answer. Only once more she disappeared, and in that same instant he felt himself lifted up out of his seat and hurled across the room like a sack of clothes, to land before the hearth. Then she was on top of him, pinning him as Laroby had pinned him, with massively superior strength. Only she was not massive, but lithe, a python, all locomotive muscle and bone, surrounding him, suffocating him, crushing him.

She brought her mouth down on his and stopped his breath. He felt his ribs cracking in the power of her embrace. Then she was gone. But as he began to climb to his feet he was hurled across the room, back onto the sofa. He looked up to find her seated in the armchair, her knees under her chin, her arms around her shins, her velvet beret cocked over one eye like a black leprechaun, as if she'd never moved. Her eyes were big with waiting as she watched him right himself and take a deliberate breath.

"You silly man," she said. "You believe in nothing. Not even when you are part of the unbelievable."

Again there seemed an eternity of silence between them, as each regarded the other. Finally Jack cleared his throat and stood up, sliding his hands into his trouser pockets as he did so.

"Do you expect me to believe you can kill me? How can you kill what is already dead?" he demanded.

Valarie sighed.

"Oh, Jack. Listen, there are many ways to die. Like what you did to her," she lifted her chin at a place in the center of the floor, indicating a target beneath. "I can take what little life you still possess, can't I?"

Jack lifted his hands, unabashed by her intimation. "Why? We feast on the innocent."

And Valarie smiled a sad little smile. And for a moment it seemed to Jack that an unearthly tenderness warmed her brown eyes as she looked at him.

221

"To me," she said softly, even affectionately, "you were always quite innocent enough."

She watched him from under the brim of her beret, her eyes sparkling with that eerie fondness, as she rested her chin on her knees.

"What are you waiting for?" he said at last. "Certainly you can feel no mercy for me."

"On the contrary," said sighed the vampire. "I feel great compassion for you. It only makes the hunger worse. My desires invariably outweigh my compassions. So I become more evil each time I betrayal my own goodness."

She stood up and approached him, slowly so that he could see her doing it. "I would spare you if I could," she said, closing the distance between them with immortal patience. "But I am ruled by hunger, just like you." She gave a little chuckle. "Ironic, isn't it? So strong for evil, we're so weak against ourselves." She turned away from him, abruptly, the little trapeze cape fluttering about her as she did so. "We're the weakest of all creatures, we who can't control our appetites."

The sound of footsteps on the stairs interrupted her. Jack looked toward the parlor doorway, his face convulsed with panic.

"Please," he whispered. "Don't hurt my daughter." He reached for Valarie's shoulder and turned her to face him. His fingers bit her. "She has no one but me now."

222

Valarie drew her ears back like an angry cat and flinched away from Jack, her lips curling into a snarl. Yet as the footfalls approached the landing she vanished, and Jack turned to see his daughter entering the room.

"Dad?"

"Yes, Lisa."

"Mom's not home yet?"

"No, honey."

"I called the college. She didn't go in today. I'm scared."

Jack opened his arms as his daughter crossed the carpet.

"Oh, God," he said, embracing her. "What have I done?"

Six

She could have ripped the lid from the coffin with a fingernail, had she been seeking living prey, but the thing in the crate, though animated, was dead, and Valarie could not use her powers of death to save it. So she sliced the top end off the box with a tarnished hacksaw and pulled the zombie out by her stiff, yellowed hair. Then she set it on its feet and slapped the thing across its dead-pan face with all that remained of her vampire strength.

"Fight for your life, damn you! No one has taken anything away from you that you hadn't already thrown away." She shook the platinum doll by its bone shoulders. "Fight for your life! Take it back from him! Take it back!"

But the doll-faced zombie only blinked at her vapidly.

"Aagh," Valarie grunted between clenched teeth. She cracked the thing across its pasty face again. To her disgust, the zombie smiled.

"You're full of crap, you know," sighed Valarie. "This is a farce. You were already dead long before he killed you," she said.

She turned away, looking around as if for a tool with which she might open the dead woman's mind.

224

Then she turned back sharply, and her little trapeze cape danced about her shoulders. She gave the zombie a keen look.

"How did you expect him to live with a dead woman? All those years, all those years he was loving me, what were you doing? Turned into salt like Lot's wife, looking back on the past, on a dead boy." She looked away, clenching her eyes shut. When she looked back at the zombie she saw that it attended her with the typhlotic scrutiny of the blind. "It wasn't Jack's fault your son was killed. He's been living with the same pain you bear. You share it." She shook her head. "Jesus, he's your husband, for Christ's sake, not your enemy..."

The zombie's smile was fading.

"You just don't get it, do you?" Valarie balled up the front of the zombie's shirt in her fist and shook her by it. "You're not locked in tandem like a team of horses! This isn't a contest as to who can make the other suffer more! God," she caught her breath, shoving the dead woman away from her. "If you can't remember how to love him, why don't you just let him go? What in the hell are you doing together, the two of you? There's no life left in either of you. Why do you stay together? Your kids? That's horseshit! It's just easier to hate each other than to let go!"

The zombie's eyes were glittering like beryl marbles. Her skin sagged over her white face like loosened cloth. She watched Valarie with rapt attention and shuffled closer to sniff the scarlet tears that streamed from the vampire's eyes.

Valarie flinched away just as the zombie stuck out its thick, blue tongue to swipe at her bloodstained cheek. Startled, she turned back and peered into its vacuous face.

"Of course!" she said, comprehending the zombie's intentions at last. "You want blood." She stepped back as the zombie pushed forward, flicking her bulbous tongue.

"Alright then," Valarie agreed, keeping the zombie at arm's length. She said, "God likes a sacrificial lamb, doesn't he? Ok. So be it."

She pulled back her lips, bearing the pearly fangs, and raised her own wrist to her mouth to slash across her veins and open them.

The zombie responded immediately. Its bottle-blue eyes flew open, its tongue, protruding from its mouth, flicked back and forth. It gave a squeal and struck at the open vein like a snake. It fastened itself to Valarie's wrist and sucked and sucked, greedy for her life, as Valarie weakened. Still, the vampire allowed the zombie to drink, until, flushed and satisfied, it released her.

Valarie stumbled backward against a beam, panting from weakness. The zombie, newly pink with her blood, put its fingers to its lips and looked about as if it had only just been born.

"Go," panted the vampire. "Take back your life. But don't you even think about hurting him, because I'll come back for you if you do, so help me."

Joan turned to regard the vampire.

"Who are you?" she whispered in a voice raw with disuse. "Don't I know you?"

With the last of her strength Valarie shoved herself from the beam upon which she rested and pulled the heavy plastic tarpaulin back over the opened coffin.

"Who are you?" Joan said again, as her hands flew to her newly warmed and rosy cheeks.

But the vampire only whirled on her, snarling

"Go! Goddamn you, go before I change my mind!"

Then the woman who had been reborn fled up the outside staircase and into the world.

Seven

She was dying.

Not like before. Not to the world of the spirit.

This time she was dying to the world of the flesh.

Valarie stood before her dresser mirror, seeing herself substantiated there. Behind her image, on the Hollywood bed, her husband looked through her to communicate with the reflection of her face in the mirror. "Look at me. I'm completely without substance. I've become totally ineffectual in this world. Nothing is left of my body but the shape of what I once was, reflected in mirrors," she told Dean. "I'm finished."

"But you must be here if I can still see your reflection," said Dean hopefully. "There must be a way out of this. A way to get you back." And then he dropped his face into his hands and sobbed. "Don't leave me, Valarie. I can't stand the idea. Don't you understand? You're part of me."

"Oh, Dean, don't you get it? We live alone, we die alone. I was never a part of you. No one is a part of anybody. We have ourselves. That's all we come in with, that's all we leave with.

228

Ourselves and our histories. Our deeds. All this crap about people being parts of one another, it's infantile, like a baby believing its mother is an extension of itself, because it needs her to survive. Because it needs to believe it has power over this life giver. It's a defense mechanism, a lie we tell ourselves," she said. "Look at me. Look what I've become. Accept it. Our life together is over. You're still in the world. I've been divorced from it."

"Can anyone else see you?" wept Dean. "Is it only me who can't?"

Valarie laughed then, a terrible, defeated laugh. She turned and set a gentle hand upon his shoulder, though she knew he could not feel her touch.

"You," she said, "could never see me. As for everyone else, well, it makes sense, doesn't it? What happens to a person when they die? How long, how many years or decades does it take before their history is forgotten, and they disappear from human memory? Then they may as well have never lived at all." She sighed, turning back to her reflection. "Only those who share your history in some way, can keep you in the world. I guess, those are the only people who are really a part of you." And she knew it was true. She had disappeared from the world. No one would seek her, for the world could not believe what she had become. She was invisible, and to most who had known her, it would soon be as if she had never lived at all.

To most, she suspected, but not to Jack.

Jack Howell stood at the doorway of the steno pool, his fists in the pockets of his topcoat, his face clenched with fury.

"Where the hell is she? Where's Valarie Valanchuk?" he asked Donna Deluca.

"W-w-who?"

"Valarie, Valarie, for God's sake! Valarie Lorraine Rossetti Valanchuk! She hasn't been in all week!"

"Oh," Donna stared at him, "Va-valarie?" She looked at Joanne Harris. "Sh-sh-she quit, didn't she? She was a pret-pretty strange kid, anyway."

Joanne snorted. She was adding a layer of polish to her glamour-length, press on nails. For this Jack, at one time, would have had her head. Now he only stared at her with furious contempt.

"Weird, like...aloof," she offered, without looking up to see his black expression. "Like she thought who-the-hell she was."

"Scary," squeaked the very pregnant Patty Kinsemmi.

Jack went to Administration.

"Why wasn't I told that Valarie Valanchuk was quitting?" he asked Griffin, the Director, who was pouring himself a cup of coffee from the machine in the conference room when Jack appeared.

"Nobody knew," said Griffin, looking up in surprise. "She just disappeared." He turned his body toward the other man with a conspiratorial shrug and said in a near whisper, "We figured it was some kind of woman's problem. You know." He winked. "You have to make exceptions for them sometimes. They want a man's job and a man's pay and then..." He walked across the hall toward his own office, and Jack followed. "Nature catches up to them." He took a seat behind the great, polished expanse of his desk as he continued.

"Just disappeared," he repeated, taking a sip of coffee from his mug and he gestured for Jack to sit down. "No notice. No contact from her. We gave her the week but... well we've taken her off payroll at this point, of course. And let me add," he waved a finger at Jack, "we have no intention of holding her position until she surfaces."

Jack watched the Director of the Suffern County Probation Department wipe his nose on his cuff and turn to his executive phone, which had begun to ring.

"Oh, go to hell, Art," he said as he stood up abruptly to leave.

But Griffin was already bellowing a gruff hello into the phone and waving him off.

"What really happened, Joan? I know as well as you do that you were dead enough to bury."

"I told you. I was robbed. They stole the car..."

"That's what you told Lisa. That's what you told them at the college. That's what you told the police. I'm the one who nailed you in the coffin, Joan. Tell me how you got out."

"Look, that's all behind us now. Let's just pretend-"

"I can't pretend anymore, Joan. You see where pretense has gotten us? Now tell me the truth! How did you get out of that box?" He shook her.

But her blue eyes only regarded him coolly as she shoved herself out of his grasp.

"I told you what happened. I was hijacked. Now, let's just leave it at that, Jack, otherwise--"

"Otherwise what? What for Christ's sake? We separate? I killed you! I took your life! Even if I could believe you could forgive me, I know you would never forget. Hell, I could do it again! It's a testimony of my feelings for you, Joan. Wake up!"

"I'm wide awake, Jack," said Joan. "You can just bet on it. I'm wide awake now."

At night he wandered, sometimes on foot, sometimes in the little black Miata, through the streets of Old Inlet searching. He drove past the Chowder Pot, and down to the Yacht Club. He drove to the end of Beach Neck Lane, and up past the little cottage where she'd once lived.

But Valarie was gone.

232

Then one evening, when he could bear it no longer, he visited the house in Pequot Bog.

"Hey, Jack," Dean opened the ornate oak door to the vampire like a man afflicted, his face betraying a dozen sleepless nights. Under his grey eyes were stamped the tell-tale black half-moons of exhaustion. He wore an ill-fitting burgundy robe and tattered slippers.

Jack pushed past him into the foyer and looked at him unsympathetically.

"Where is she, you silly ass? What have you done with your wife?" His fist shot out and, gripping the taller man by his throat, he shoved him against the door and shook him.

Dean's face contorted with confusion. "What the hell--" he began. But Jack only tightened his grip until Dean's eyes bulged.

"I'll kill you, Goddamn it, do you understand me? Do you want to die?"

Dean's hands came up to pull in vain at Jack's implacable fingers.

"You tell me what you did to her. She's gone two weeks. Disappeared into thin air. No one knows where. No one cares. No one's filed a report. Did you murder her, you pathetic leech? Did you kill her for some moronic, mortal reason?"

He shook Dean again by his neck before releasing him with a thump, against the door.

To his complete surprise, Dean began to weep.

233

"I don't know," he sobbed, drawing a hand over his forehead. "I don't know where she is. She... she just disappeared. I was there... but it didn't matter. There was nothing I could do. She.. she just--" he fought for air, "faded."

Jack regarded him with sudden interest. "What are you saying? You say you saw her," he gripped the other man's arm and pulled him back toward himself, "you saw her fade?"

This time Dean twisted out of his grasp and threw him a malignant look. "What's it to you?" he said, sniffling, his eyes suddenly awake with suspicion.

Jack composed his face. He stepped away from Dean, and into the cavernous interior of the house. And for a moment he forgot his purpose as he took in his surroundings for the first time.

For even in his present state of agitation, it took away his breath.

He saw that the house had deceived him from the outside, its shallow roof line, its short frontal facade, deliberately disguising its depth, hiding its interior capacity. It was in fact not brooding nor dark within, but full of air and light and space, resplendent as a dream in pale sea greens and blues like an enchanted cave. The room in which he stood peaked thirty feet into the air into a cathedralled ceiling. Celadon green walls rose up on either side to meet above his head. Beside him, against one wall, a burnished cherry banister scaled a curving staircase to the second story landing. Across this, and above the foyer, ran a matching railing

234

under a length of narrow, horizontal windows, dressed in pastels to compliment the moonlit clouds beyond. Before him, a row of glass doors, flanked by floor-length windows, overlooked a golden field of frosted hay. Wispy white and azure curtains fell from an elegant cornice to the cherry-wood parquet tiles at his feet.

Jack turned to Dean. He saw the heat of jealous rage in the younger man's eyes and thought, for an instant, of sparing him with a lie. But what would good would it do? Dean had made a mortal's blind decision to believe the worst. That Valarie and he were lovers. And nothing could change that now.

"Everything," he answered him, as he turned and crossed the foyer to the door, leaving Dean to stare with ineffectual rage at his retreating back.

PART FIVE

One

"You see me now as I am made," said the angel, and he folded his magnificent white wings behind his back so that their silver tips swept the ground and crossed behind his heels. Their smooth, feathery shoulders rose a head above his own. His face was the face of David, his hair, a halo of softly shining russet curls. "I am not a dream, nor am I vision. I am as real as you."

"You're too lovely to be real," Valarie answered him. "Besides, I must be dreaming all of this. I'm invisible."

They stood in the field behind the Dumont house. It was early morning, and the frosted day was yellow-gold with newly born sunlight. Valarie could no longer see herself, but the silvery skin of the angel was like a mirror that promised to reveal to her her true nature, if only she might focus the entirety of her will upon it.

236

The angel smiled and the smile lit the sky behind his titian head like heat lightening, or like fireworks on a still summer evening.

"Am I too lovely to be real? But are you not real, Valarie? And are you not loveliness embodied? Nay, I am too lovely not to be the work of the Living One, who knit you in your mother's womb." He pointed to her heart with an elegant finger. "You," he said carefully, "create what you can envision. The Unnamed," he gestured to the sky, "creates the rest."

He gave her a moment to ponder that before he added, "Do you think you could have imagined me?" as he touched his beautiful silver breast.

Then his eyes, which were the deepest sapphire blue, and shot through with copper rays, crinkled at the corners mischievously. But there was no vanity in them.

Valarie could not look at him any longer without feeling the delight of her spirit bubbling up within her in peals of laughter.

"I can't bear to look at you! Why didn't you show yourself to me this way before?"

The specter's ginger brows arched, tenting together in a pretty frown and his melon-colored mouth pursed into a ripe, masculine pout.

"I was with you in your suffering," he said. "Loving you as I do, how could I not bleed when you bled?" He looked positively

237

hurt. The expression, on such a face, made her catch her breath on the beauty of it.

"Oh, please don't!" she gasped. "Don't look so unhappy, I'll die of it!"

So much truth was there in this that she felt her eyes begin to sting with tears. It was as if her heart was tied to his with a puppeteer's string, one that magnified each motion made, the one to the other.

The angel's face softened sympathetically.

"You're not...Him...then, are you," she said.

"I am some of Him," offered the angel, careful not to smile too radiantly.

"Are you...my Guardian then?" The thought had entered her head in a flash so bright she thought she would faint from the explosion of it.

"I am," his smile now widened, uncontrolled, until Valarie had to hide her eyes behind her hands or be blinded by it.

"I am," he said more carefully.

When she peeked through her fingers at him again she saw that his face had stilled.

"How can I bear you?" she whispered, more to herself than to him, "I will never be able to bear your beauty!"

The angel's face saddened. "Nor I yours," he said.

"Are you here to save me, then?" Valarie blurted out the question, not sure herself from what she needed to be saved.

Again the angel gave a cautious, less than blinding smile.

He shook his head, his coppery curls making firecrackers of their own. "You need no saving, daughter. Saved you have already been, by your true nature."

She thought about this a moment.

"It wasn't Communion, after all, was it?"

The angel looked at her patiently. He pressed his fingers together in a little tent and rested them against his apricot lips in contemplation. After a moment, to her surprise, he dropped to one knee before her, his skirt of gold silk skimming the ground. He bowed his fiery head and murmured something indiscernible. When he lifted his long lashes again to regard her, a perfect stillness bathed his face.

He took her hand in both of his.

Her eyes widened as her skin burned deliciously, as if with passion, where he touched her.

"Try to understand," said the angel carefully. "To the Living One, human compassion is the only communion. Without it, there is no God."

Valarie wanted to squeeze her entire being into the hand that he grasped in his own, to flow through it into his veins, to become one with him. But the angel only lifted his brows at her in silent interrogative, waiting for her to acknowledge what he had said and to reply.

"Will I ever be mortal again?" she whispered at last.

He blinked at her, as if surprised by the question.

"Mortal thou hast never been," he answered, rising to his feet and releasing her. For the second time in his presence, Valarie thought she must faint. The agony of losing the touch of him was as bittersweet as his incongruous beauty.

"But... visible?" she managed, taking breath. "Will anyone ever see me again?"

At this the angel lifted his lovely head and chuckled, and the chords that forever played behind his radiant voice danced in a madrigal of heavenly sounds.

"Valarie, the more invisible you are to the world, the more visible to the Living One. Surely you have known this in your heart all along. Why else do you pursue the path you have chosen? It is not an easy one. And no one takes this way involuntarily."

"I think," she nodded thoughtfully, "I am beginning to understand."

The specter smiled.

"Your heart is your teacher," he said, and turning, he unfolded his magnificent, snowy wings and shook them, as if preparing them for flight.

"Wait!" cried Valarie. "Wait, please! Just tell me this, before you go. Who are you? What is your name?"

The angel tilted his head a moment, his sapphire eyes going vacant, as if he listened now to another voice, one still invisible to her. Turning back to her he lifted one great, silken wing and covered her shoulders with it as he bent and whispered in her ear a thing that pierced her like a lance and touched her soul.

"I am your angel, Valarie. I am Valariel," he said, before he disappeared.

Two

"Valariel?"

Valarie was standing in the golden, dew-frosted hay field behind the Dumont house. She was alone now, but she had not awakened from some dream. He had been there, bending like a fiery knight upon one knee, holding her hand so that the heat of his chaste passion for her had burned her also.

And it was passion. Heavenly passion. Passion that the world would ever deny in favor of its own grasping and perverted brand of love. But what did the world know? Valarie had found what she had lost. The world would never truly speak to her again.

As if left there by the angel, particles of light glittered all about her feet, catching in the dawn frost that lay like a blanket of crystals over the quiet field. Valarie looked up and saw the sun, great and gold and wholesome, breach the early morning clouds and bless the azure sky. Her heart was a song bird, fluttering in her breast, singing for joy. Her heart would never break again. It was alive, had always lived, safe and whole, under the fierce, protective wings of her guardian. Dawn had broken at last and her heart sang in her breast like a crimson bird.

Slowly, not wanting to, but knowing that she must, Valarie turned and walked deliberately back to the brooding house. How long had she been invisible to the world? She did not know. She had stepped out of time when she had left the world behind. She would re-enter it for purpose now, not greed for life. For how could she envy what she abounded in? It mattered not what day, what hour it was. Only that she would right what had been wrong. She would retrace her steps. And gently, and without malice, she would return what she could of what she had taken, and reclaim what she could of what she'd given away.

"I want you to have it back, Cecile," she told her friend that evening.

"You know I can't afford it, Valarie," answered Cecile, though she looked about her with obvious longing. "God," she said, "I can't believe that I'd forgotten how I loved this place. Daddy put his heart and soul into it. Did you know he put the parquet down himself? And the cornices, and the banisters, all made by hand, downstairs." She sighed and played with a brown curl. "You really want to sell it?" she murmured, giving Valarie a worried look.

"Not just sell it, Cecile," said Valarie. "Sell it to you."

They had been standing in the foyer of the house in Pequot Bog. Now Valarie turned to gesture her friend in, across the cherrywood parquet and through a row of Japanese pocket doors which opened onto the great room. There she left Cecile to find a seat among the oriental couches while she disappeared, behind a matching pocket door, into the kitchen. When she returned she carried with her a steaming pot of tea on a wicker tray. She set it down on a glass table in the center of the room.

"But Valarie, I can't give you anything for it. I couldn't keep up the mortgage payments before you bought it. So I could hardly take it over again, now, with Daddy gone."

"Cecile, I can't afford what it's cost me either. Please consider what I'm saying. Sell the trailer and give me what you can. I'll hold the mortgage for you, whatever you can afford. I've got to get home, Cecile... and so do you." Valarie handed her friend a cup.

"I can't bring your father back, Cecile," Valarie spoke the words with difficulty, swallowing a hot ball of shame in her throat before continuing. "All I can do is what is humanly possible to give you back what you lost because of me."

"Oh, Val, come on now! You made it possible for us to get out before Mom and I had nothing left to live on! It's not your fault we had to leave the way we did--"

"Part of it is. Let's just say I helped to make it possible for you to give up before you had to. And now I want to make it possible for you to have a second chance. It's yours, Cecile. It always has been. You built it, you and your father and Guy. You stamped it with your character. This isn't me--" she gestured at the magnificent room she sat in. "This is you. It belongs to you."

244

Cecile sighed. "I can't argue with that, but-"

"It's lovely," continued Valarie. "But it's not my loveliness. It's yours. Your vision, your talent. You've got a lot of talent, Cecile. You waste it, hiding in grief. You could do this for a living, you know. You could make other people happy with a gift like this."

"I wouldn't know where to begin," protested Cecile, but her expression lifted at Valarie's suggestion.

Valarie smiled. She took her friend's hand impulsively.

"Sleep on it a while. Don't say no now. The jury isn't in yet. But, think about it, okay?" "To tell you the truth, Valarie, I haven't though of much else since the day I left," Cecile answered.

"If I told you where I'd been or what I'd seen you'd think I'd lost my mind. No one believes in joy," Valarie sighed.

She was leaning on the iron lamp post at the head of her driveway in Pequot Bog. It was dusk and the light sensitive bulb was just turning a dull orange. Valarie kicked a clod of earth from the grass beneath the coach lamp with the toe of her boot. Dean was digging a hole nearby for the new sign he had just finished painting. He was piling the extra dirt up on the lawn, where it would be hardest to remove later. Valarie had asked him to pile it on a drop cloth instead, but he had pointedly ignored her suggestion. "I don't understand why you don't just wait for the Dumonts to take your offer," he said, looking up from his work.

245

"They can't resist it. You're giving the damned place away, for God's sake."

"I'm just putting a fire under their tails, that's all. Cecile has got to realize that she doesn't have forever. None of us does."

Dean slammed the post hole digger into the ground one more time.

"That's it. Deep enough. That's as far as I'm going. Boy, I hate this job."

"You just don't want things to change."

"Well why should I, Valarie?" Dean responded acidly. "I love this place. I always have. I love everything about it." He stared at her as he stood, legs spread, hands clenching the handle of the digger. "If I could afford to I'd buy it from you myself."

She gave him a wary look.

"I wouldn't sell it to you," she reminded him. "This is Cecile's house."

"That didn't seem to bother you six months ago," Dean replied, rocking the handle back and forth to loosen the last shovel full of dirt from the bottom of the new hole.

"Right," Valarie agreed, watching him drop the captured earth on to the grass in yet another spot. "I think you may be catching on to the gist of this thing, Dean."

He let out an exasperated sigh.

"Oh I know, I know. You see the error of your sinful ways and you're going to make it all better now by giving everything you ever owned away. What about me, Valarie? Did you think about that? Where do I fit into your plans?"

Valarie put a hand out and took the handle of the post hole digger with such sudden locomotion that he jumped back.

"You don't," she said, throwing the tool to the ground and looking up at him with dangerous resolve. "You never did. I used you. I never loved you. It's precisely the fact that you could cling to me whether or not I love you that makes loving you impossible to me. That's not the way my heart works. I didn't owe you my love because I enthralled you, Dean. I don't owe you my love now." She shook her head and frowned. "And I'm not doing you any favors carrying on this illusion for you. It's time for you to accept the fact that human hearts are not subject to contractual agreements. It's time for you to grow up, Dean. And I'm going to help you do it. I'm not taking you back to Old Inlet with me. I'm going alone."

Dean's face caved in at her words. "Valarie I--"

"Never mind," she said. "No amount of back peddling on your part is going to change my course, Dean." She looked about her at the dirt strewn lawn and shook her head with an abrupt laugh. "You never did think I knew what I was doing, did you? You're sure as hell not going to start now." She kicked a hill of dirt disgustedly and left him to complete the task he'd started.

Three

Nikolai Larobya was ever hungry.

But like a man who trains his palate to obey his intellect, learning to delight in bitter things, Nikolai Larobya could savor the mundane.

Vapid, tasteless souls teetering ever on the brink of their own destruction, wasteful, yellowing souls with no interior spark, these mediocre lives were food enough for Larobya.

And in the life of Larobya's especial author, the woman, Valarie, there hovered such a soul on such a brink. Dean Valanchuk had never been a godly man. He was a creature bound to the earth upon which he walked with the simple minded self-indulgence that makes all darkness darker. Not the kind of human monster who ravages the world, killing and tormenting human flesh, but the kind of dark and ill-disguised disaster of a man who sucks the life, leech-like, from those around him. Dean Valanchuk was, himself, of little value to the devil. But as a means of sapping life and goodness out of more potent souls, he was a priceless thing indeed.

248

He had isolated Valarie so long from the sources of her vitality, had infected her so thoroughly with the well-meant caution of his own resourceful paranoia, that had there been reward to give in Hell's dark pageantry, he would have been a winner without rival. Dean had a gift for sucking life and spirit from the living. And Larobya believed that gifts like this one should be glorified.

So Nikolai Larobya, awakened once again by human nature from his grave eternal, arose to bring his well of everlasting death to one whose nature had been born to drink from it.

Dean had a plan.

He had often playfully plotted out the "perfect murder" in his mind, when a rival at the office or in his personal arena had threatened the equilibrium of his life. Then he would dwell for hours, and sometimes days, on the details and logistics of the act, the potency and traceability of poisons, the procurement of modus opperandi: a hypodermic needle, a length of piano wire, a certain natural solvent that draws any substance into the body and the circulatory system through simple dermal contact. These thoughts would soothe his fevered soul like a poultice, offering a sense of personal power and control over the unruly and illogical circumstances that often plagued his life.

And now this occasional morbid pastime had become a dark obsession. Now his mind, a mind trained by years of silent and ineffectual plotting, a mind made maddeningly clinical and methodical by paranoia, a mind designed to find solutions where others saw no flaws, had found its calling.

He would remove the rival of his wife's affections forever from her reach. He would do this in such a way as to disguise not only his hand in the murder, but the murder itself. It would appear to be an accident. No one, not even Valarie, would suspect him.

He knew he would have to act fast, before she sold the house in Pequot Bog and made it clear to all the world that she'd returned to Old Inlet to be near the Other, and had separated physically from him. Until then he could achieve what he had planned without detection. For who would suspect him, except Jack himself, and Jack would be no more.

His natural course was to design a toxic substance, something not inherently deadly but capable of instantaneous death upon the proper application of events.

He thought of the simple, nearly undetectable alternative of air, injected into an artery by hypodermic needle, inducing embolism and heart failure. Surely, a man in his mid-fifties, however fit, dropping dead of heart attack at work, would cause no one suspicion, least of all men of a similar profession. But where and how to do the job, and the awful necessity it required for physical confrontation (for Dean was a man who loathed a confrontation), these elements of this method discouraged him from considering this alternative too seriously.

He mulled over the various homemade poisons he had researched. Arsenic out of insecticide or rat poison, cyanide extracted from peach or apricot pits, strychnine from rodenticide, toxic doses of iron sulfate, or paint pigment procured from an art supply store having toxic levels of one or another heavy metal as a base. The list was endless. There was even the possibility of infecting food with botulism bacteria which might be harvested from an open can of fish or other meat. But all required the victim to ingest some bit of food or liquid, and being sure that Jack would eat or drink a tainted morsel, once prepared, was something that Dean couldn't be. For what if he consumed a part and not all of the required dose? The medical examiner would test the rest, especially if Jack did not succumb, or lingered.

No, these dreams of victory were sweet, but unrealistic. Neither voluntary ingestion nor injection would be safe enough.

That left inhalants.

For example, a simple bottle of bleach, another of ammonia. Left on the floor in the back of Jack's car, in such a way as to look as if they'd just been purchased, but out of Jack's immediate range of vision, and somehow opened and arranged so that the simple act of pulling out of a driveway would tip them and cause their marriage.

Could it cause death? In the little airspace of a closed Miata, Dean bet that it would. Of course he would have to be careful not to leave fingerprints, and other traces of his identity. But those things could be ironed out. A few other groceries and cleaning items, together with the ingredients of death, left in a biodegradable plastic bag behind the driver's seat, would give the appearance that Jack had simply done some shopping before the terrible accident had occurred.

Or perhaps they would accuse his wife? No matter.

As long as he acted before the affair was made public by Valarie's insane return to Old Inlet, he would never be considered a suspect.

Four

In his grief, Jack recognized the magnitude of his affections for her. Now the world was a long winter night, braced for hardship, and his house, his great, rambling hotel of a house, was a chamber of loneliness and alienation.

The office was a torment of hours, devoted to petty details, insignificant and vain, a treadmill of inconsequential trivia. He longed to be free of it, yet when he left at night and drove home to Old Inlet in the little Miata, he could think only of Valarie, sitting beside him in it at the dock, a hungry little vampire with greedy mouth and pain-bright eyes, fighting her nature to spare him.

How you must have loved me, he thought, to fight so hard against yourself to save me. What kind of love is that? I've never known it. I had thought love was a needful, wanting thing. But you denied yourself for me.

He, himself, killed less often, the thrill of evil having naturally diminished in the wake of his loss. He began enjoying his hunger, deliberately wooing it, sparing victims as Valarie had spared him. Drawing close, crossing the magnificent threshold of a human embrace, tasting the heartbeat on their lips, without succumbing to

253

his bloodlust. It was a kind of self-annihilation. And yet it kept his mortal part alive.

He learned that mercy was difficult to camouflage, even to the innocent. His spared victims, male and female, sought him out. They called his house, courted his friendship, some fell in love with him, tried to seduce him with their bromidic human passion. He was kind, but unresponsive. In her memory always, he practiced humanity in spite of his vampire nature.

In this way, he began to weaken. The black and predatory glint that had for so long haunted his dark eyes now faded. His skin, too, lost its vampire luster, as humanity aged it. Blood began to lose its sorcery over him. He drank gin and ate bread and fish and fruit. But even these things he did in moderation and without enjoyment. He remained slim, and, if not inhumanly strong, then at least athletic, fit. He jogged in the evenings, down to the Wyandott's crumbling beach hotel at the end of Beach Neck Lane, sometimes through the village and down to the Old Inlet Yacht Club, or over to the golf course. Now and then he ran up North Beach Neck to jog past Valarie's little cottage, which had been mysteriously vacated by its new owners and was once again for sale.

His marriage endured with superficial civility. Joan would not release him, and indeed, he had no desire to cause his children grief with a divorce that could not bring him joy. It was of no consequence to him that he and Joan continued to rattle about together in the enormous house where they had once shared the experience of parenthood. Joan's presence in his life was not significant enough to affect him. He doubted that her absence would do more.

He slept little, but when he did, he occupied a bedroom on the opposite side of the house from hers. It had, in fact, been Kevin's room, long culled of any reminder of his occupation. Jack slept there but he did not let the room's young ghost torment his heart over sorrow he had learned, long ago, how to survive.

There was a new ghost to be haunted by. A sweeter torment.

Spring came, at last, the first crocuses pushing up their bright green heads through soil that Valarie's hands had once turned in the beds all around his house. He managed his own gardening now, preferring to dig and turn the pungent earth he owned, than to trod over fairways someone other than George Lorraine now tended.

He saw Dean Valanchuk at an occasional meeting in the Suffern office, but the younger man ignored him, or treated him with almost comic, and begrudged respect. Clearly there was no point in his asking Dean if Valarie had ever reappeared. He could not give an honest answer.

Then one Monday morning in May a remarkable thing occurred. Staring out his office window during a case review with Harry Culhane, one of Stan Gould's field officers, Jack saw a bright red civic pulling into the office parking lot. Out from it, on a pair of long, black clad, athletic legs, appeared a vision he had lost all hope of ever witnessing again. For Valarie, lovely as ever in her typically outrageous beatnik attire, was advancing toward the Suffern Office lobby doors.

Jack squinted, blinked, and finally leaned completely over the sill to stare in disbelief at the creature crossing the grass toward the building which he occupied. All interest in Harry's entertaining account of his cases lost, he came to his attention only after Culhane, who'd by now moved to see what fascinated him at the window, whistled in his ear.

"I don't believe it!" said Harry, sliding his beefy hands into his trouser pockets. "It's Valanchuk's wife!" What a set on that one! It's two months since she disappeared. What does she think, Griffin's gonna hand her her job back? Jeez!"

"Oh, shut up, Harry," Jack grumbled under a grin he could not camouflage with a curt reply. "You don't know why she disappeared or what she's been through. Show a little compassion."

Harry looked at his boss in dumb surprise. He opened his mouth to speak, then shut it again abruptly. The two men looked at one another as a silent understanding passed between them. Then Harry's ruddy face broke into a puckish grin and he stepped back to let Jack pass.

"Yeah, she's gonna need some help in there, if she's here for her job," he considered, turning to clear his cases off Gould's desk. "This stuff can wait til Stan gets back on Monday. Maybe you ought to go ... put a word in for her with Art."

Jack gave Harry a measured look. Then he nodded, fighting to keep a straight face. "That might be a good idea," he concurred casually. But he clapped the big man on his shoulder before he headed out the door and down the hall towards Administration.

Jack stopped in his tracks when he reached the hall outside Art Griffin's office and saw that the Director's door was already closed in conference. He made a quick perusal of the hallway and, satisfied that no one would observe him, walked quietly to the door and paused outside. Through it, it was not difficult to hear Art's solicitous banter.

"Weh-hell, Valarie. This is quite unexpected. How, eh... is everything working out? Things back to normal now? I'm sure Dean's told you how we all felt terrible about what happened. What a shock. These things can certainly come at the most unlikely times and under the most unusual circumstances."

"I can't explain my absence, sir," he heard Valarie's reply. "It was inexcusable, I know. I'm not here for my job, I'm here to make what best amends I can. I left you short-handed and without warning. I never meant to. This ...thing wasn't planned--"

"Well of course not. No one has a crystal ball in these matters. No one knows what the next day may bring. Hell, you're young yet. Wait! Life has a way of throwing you curves, Valarie, take it from an old timer."

"I'm finding that out, sir."

"Well now, after all, Howell did put in for an extended leave of absence for you. I understand you kept him informed and let him in on the...er...circumstances... of your whereabouts and so on."

"My--?"

"Family is an important consideration, Valarie. No one can fault a person for rushing to the aid of a family member in need--"

"Sir?"

"I know if my brother was in any kind of trouble, I'd drop whatever I was doing and go to bat for him myself. Everyone has crisis' in their life at one time or another. Lord knows I've had my share, what with Martha and her illness. How is your brother? I understand they've got him in a psychiatric hospital now? Hell of a thing, manic-depression. And to happen at his age. What is he? Early forties? Awful for his wife... kids...you have nieces and nephews? Of course, you were helping her out with them weren't you."

"Y--"

"Look. Let me give it a little thought. We may have something for you... Howell had suggested Leo's spot in County

Court Liaison. Thought a young woman might be a welcomed change for the judges out there. 'Stead of Leo's old sourpuss. Maybe he's got something. You do..." he paused, "present quite well. I always said so."

"You mean Mr. How--"

"Let me bat it around. Leo retires in July. You'll return to your old slot until we can get you for a formal interview, of course. Got to go by procedure--"

Outside in the hall, Jack smiled to himself and shook his dark head.

"Thank you," he whispered to the empty hallway. Then he stepped out of Griffin's line of vision as the door opened and Valarie backed out of the director's office, her face a wedding of confusion and relief.

"Next Monday, then. I'll be here. Thank you, Mr. Griffin." And she edged out of the office, shut the door behind her, and leaning her little bottom against it, she closed her eyes and sighed.

"He generally keeps it open when he's not in conference," Jack startled her with the whispered comment.

"Oh!" She gasped, backing away from him, her eyes big as walnuts.

He smiled, content to stand there in the hallway and examine her while she recovered her guard. Under her little trapeze cape he could see she was slighter than she'd been. Her hip bones pressed the fabric of her skirt, below which off-black tights defined a dancer's legs. Even her face was narrower, her cheekbones huge above her heart shaped chin line. Her cheeks were slightly sunken, her eyes, overwhelming under the black brim of her beret.

"I've missed you," he said simply. And then, "You look like you could use some lunch. When did you last eat?"

"God knows," she murmured. She was staring at him with a most peculiar expression.

"Then let me take you out for some," he said, and took her arm. Her muscles jumped under his fingers but she walked obediently out through the lobby and into the parking field, at his side.

"Are..." she said at last when he opened the door of the Miata for her, "you hungry, Jack?" The look on her face was pitiful, but Jack couldn't resist tormenting her just a little longer.

He gave her a dangerous look as he pushed her into the car.

"Starved," he announced, and shut her in.

When he got in on the other side she swallowed and said to the dashboard, "I don't have a brother."

Jack lifted his brows at her and chuckled. He slid the key into the ignition and revved the engine. "Well who in hell cares if you do?" he asked.

She stared at him nervously.

"Well, Art, for one. Art thinks I have one."

Jack took his eyes off her to back out of his space, throwing his arm over the back of her seat as he did so.

"Cheer up. I'm sure they'll never have occasion to meet." Then he turned back to her and gave her a gentle look. "It's okay, Valarie, it's all taken care of. Trust me."

He pulled out of the parking lot and on to the narrow two lane road that led out of the complex.

Valarie played with her fingers in her lap. Peripherally, he could see that her lips were still pursed in consternation. He patted her knee and had to bite his own lip to keep his face straight when she flinched.

"Any particular reason you're so jumpy?" he asked.

She looked over at him. He felt her eyes drop to his mouth.

"I was just wondering..."

"M-m-m?"

"Well," she swallowed again. "Nothing."

He let it pass.

"So where have you been anyway, or should I ask," he said after a moment.

She sighed, pushing a length of shiny chestnut hair behind an ear.

"You don't want to answer that?"

She licked her lips. He was pulling out onto the highway, into southbound traffic.

"Where are you taking me, Jack," she sounded resigned.

261

"I told you. To lunch. To the Chowder Pot."

There was a moment's silence.

"You're just taking me to lunch," she repeated, as if trying to convince herself.

"Mmmm-hm," he agreed.

She looked out of her window, smoothing her skirt unconsciously over her lap. After a bit she began to fidget with her hands again, picking at her cuticles.

"You were kind of mad at me last time we saw one another--" she started. "I've been wondering how things--" she plunged on, "worked out for you and... and Mrs. Howell."

"Oh, Mrs. Howell. You're wondering about Mrs. Howell. I see. How thoughtful of you, Valarie."

"Well--"

"Mrs. Howell is just dandy. Right as rain. A picture of health. We are talking about physical health, aren't we? Because if we're not, if we're discussing her mental life, I'm afraid I'd have to say she's somewhere between a rattlesnake and a pit bull."

He laid a hand on her knee again and watched, out of the corner of his eye, the muscles along her jaw clench involuntarily.

"Thanks to you, Valarie. Thanks to my meddling angel of mercy."

Valarie made a little noise in her throat and looked down miserably at the hand that rested squarely on her knee.

262

They drove on for some time in silence. When they reached Old Inlet village Jack pulled down Robin's Hill Lane and parked behind the restaurant. Then he jumped out to open Valarie's door. As he came around to let her out he saw she was sitting quite still, looking out at the rear of the old hotel-turned-eatery.

"We're at the Chowder Pot," she observed as he opened her door for her and offered her his hand.

"Apparently," he conceded, watching her lift her legs out of the little cockpit and set her heels on the gravel. She took his hand with some reluctance, and smiled at him nervously when he pulled her to her feet. For a moment he corralled her in the margin left between his body and the car. He took a moment just to look down at her, and to soak in the luxury of her presence. Then he took her elbow and led her to the door.

Inside the bartender nodded to Jack and gave Valarie an interested perusal.

"Maybe this wasn't such a good idea," Valarie whispered as Jack pulled out a chair for her at a table near the fireplace.

"Why is that?" he questioned, seating himself.

"Jesus, everybody knows you here, Jack. Mrs. Howell ... your wife...might not like hearing about her husband taking another woman out to lunch."

He gave her a black look.

"You're just full of concern for our Mrs. Howell today, aren't you? Order something." He nodded at the luncheon menu left at her place setting.

"I'm not very hungry," she concluded after looking at the menu a moment.

"Valarie," Jack leaned over to her, putting down his own menu. "Be a good girl and eat. You look like something out of Oliver Twist."

She gave him a helpless look, her eyes huge and guileless.

"I tried eating chicken the other night. I kept imagining I could feel its little birdie footies running around in my mouth. When I bit into it, I thought I heard it scream."

"Dead chickens don't scream, Valarie."

"This one did."

"Good God," he shook his head, losing patience. "So eat pasta."

"Ok," she put her menu down, decided.

When the food came, Valarie took a bite, chewed and swallowed it without relish, and put her fork down beside her plate. Then she stared sadly at Jack's flounder.

"Something wrong with your fettuccini?" he nodded at her meal.

Valarie lifted her eyes from his plate.

"What, is my fish screaming now?"

"It's just that...," she frowned, trying to find her words. "I spent my whole life eating and eating and eating. Consuming, like a human pac-woman. Filling my body, while my soul starved. Stuffing myself with the lives I took. Jesus, that's not living, Jack. We're not here to consume one another. It's a violation, don't you see? We're all here together on this earth, each of us hidden within a flesh prison of one kind or another. Every creature, every race and breed. All conscious, all sentient. And there's such sweetness within the souls of all living things, if only we look for it, rather than lusting for the salt of their bodies on our tongues. We shouldn't be butchering one another. We should be opening one another up like... like Christmas presents on a snowy morning."

She looked at him helplessly. "I've got so many presents left to open, Jack." Her voice was soft, a plea.

He studied her beautiful face, lost himself in it momentarily.

"Valarie," he said at last. "For God's sake, look at me. Are you blind? I'm not going to hurt you." He cleared the lump in his throat and looked down, taking his napkin from his lap and crushing it beside his plate.

She was silent.

"You're not?"

"That's what I said."

She watched him motion to their waiter for the check.

"I'm moving back to Old Inlet, Jack."

"You're what?"

"I want to come home. I," she looked up and managed a little smile as the waiter cleared their table. "I don't know why I'm telling you..."

When they were outside he asked her, "Did you know the cottage is for sale?"

"My house?"

"Mmm-hm."

He opened the passenger door for her.

"I can't go back there," she watched him slide in beside her. " I couldn't afford it now."

Jack raised an eyebrow as he turned the ignition.

"Something wrong between you and Dean?"

"That's an understatement."

He took a deep breath, expelled it slowly. Then he remembered himself.

"I'm sorry," he offered.

"Don't be. I'm just righting something that was wrong from the start."

He said nothing to this, only put the Miata in gear and pulled out onto Robin's Hill Road.

At the corner of Main, he made a left.

"Where are you taking me now?" Valarie looked at him, suddenly bewildered.

"I want to show you something." He continued west to Beach Neck, then turned south, toward his own house.

"You have my complete attention," she said huskily.

Five

Dean had seen his wife leave the Sharon office with Jack Howell at lunchtime.

He'd followed her there, had been sitting in his Cherokee waiting for his suspicions to be confirmed, when the two of them left the office, Jack leading Valarie by the arm, and got into Jack's car.

Dean had gone to his work station in Riverdale as usual. But that day he knew his wife was going to the Sharon office to talk to Griffin about her unexplained absence. And that knowledge was enough to prime the pump of his obsession to find out, for sure, if there was anything going on overtly between them.

Now he knew that there was.

Dean followed Jack's Miata out of the Sharon office parking lot with all the instincts of a criminal. He knew that Jack, with twenty years in the Department, would be aware of a tail. Anyone who'd been a field officer as long as he had would. No, they weren't glorified by the media, like cops, but P.O.'s nevertheless carried guns, made arrests, tracked absconders, and faced dangerous situations on a regular basis. Over the years more than one cop had told Dean that he preferred his own job, where one was not dealing with convicted criminals consistently, but with a more reliable cross-section of society. In a volatile situation, P.O.'s might act like social workers, using their words, rather than their weapons, to overcome an opponent. But on the road, on the street, they tended to think like cops. They knew what was happening around them, just in case.

So Dean followed a quarter mile and several cars behind Jack, guessing his next move, to the Chowder Pot. Then he waited. He saw Jack take Valarie's hand and lead her into the restaurant, saw him lean over her, too close, as she got out of the little car, saw the look in his face as he gazed down at her. He watched them enter the restaurant and waited for them to come out.

Then he tailed them to the corner of South Beach Neck Lane, where he had no choice but to let them go. That road was a dead end, private and narrow, and his observation of their little afternoon rendezvous would be evident if he followed them.

He continued on Main Street instead. Half a mile down the road he made a two-point turn and parked on the opposite shoulder. He waited five long minutes. Then he pulled out into traffic, east on Main, and turned south onto South Beach Neck.

By the time he passed Jack's house his heart was fluttering in his throat like the wings of a sick bird. His chest was one massive knot of tension, his stomach burning with the acid of suspicion.

269

He nearly ran off the road and into a tree craning his neck to look for the black Miata down the long drive.

But it wasn't there.

In fact the only car in the driveway was a brand new Electra, license plate JMH-1.

There was only one explanation. Jack had seen the wife's car in his driveway and changed his plans to bring Valarie home for a little afternoon tete-a-tete. He'd driven past, with typical Howell nonchalance, to park down at the end of the lane.

The picture of Jack Howell riding his wife in the little Miata exploded in Dean's head like a bouncing-betty.

"A-a-a-a-g-h-!!" he hit the steering wheel with his fist. His heart pounding, the muscles in his chest clenched in a knot of desperate fury, he jammed on the brakes, nearly putting himself through his own windshield.

"Fucking bastard!" He panted like a winded animal. "I'll tear your fucking head off, you son-of-a-bitching cock-sucking fuck!!!"

Dean closed his eyes and fought the tears threatening behind his burning lids. DON'T FALL APART NOW, YOU IDIOT, he heard a voice inside his head instruct him.

EASY DOES IT. SLOW AND EASY WINS THE RACE, AS THEY SAY. BREATH NORMALLY. COUNT TO TEN. THAT'S IT. IT WILL DO NO GOOD TO HAVE A HEART ATTACK BEFORE YOU HAVE A CHANCE TO KILL THE SON-OF-A-BITCH, NOW, WILL IT?

"No," he panted. "No it won't." He looked up, baring his teeth unconsciously as he looked down the road toward the beach. "Fine. So now you die, you shithead. I get to go second."

And in a hole not far from him, a fiend with emerald eyes and porcelain skin rejoiced and came to life.

"That's my boy," he smiled, a grin splitting his handsome face from ear to ear.

Six

At the end of Beach Neck Lane the black Miata was parked on a sandy shoulder beside the unkempt privet hedge surrounding the old Wyandott Hotel. Its two occupants, after crossing a hay field that had once been a carefully manicured lawn, now stood on an open porch which ran the full length of the building and faced the beach. The taller figure, a man in his early fifties, in dark slacks, yellow shirt and bright tie, slipped his hands into his pockets and watched while the other, a feminine silhouette in black beret and hip-length cape, tried the handle of the rotting screen door.

"You have the keys?"

The man nodded.

She looked at his pockets expectantly as he fumbled in them for the right key chain.

"I don't believe this," she said. "Do you know my mother used to take me here when I was a little girl?"

"You're kidding," he laughed as he began to pick through a fistful of keys.

"She and my Aunt Renee were hired to clean the place out after it was closed down. I don't know why. It never reopened.

272

But Mom came down here every day for a month with Aunt Renee. They'd bring me and my cousins along, and Holly and Joey and I would play all day long in these big dark empty rooms. We found all kinds of things to would play with cards and cork coasters with pictures of race horses on the backs. And those plastic swizzle sticks that came in different colors, with the names of liquors stamped on them. We'd collect those. Most of the time Holly would confiscate mine or make me trade her for the rare ones. I was only three or four and she was a lot older."

As he listened to her reminisce, Jack had been picking though the bunch of keys, looking for the mate to the lock on the storm door. Now he pulled one from the bunch and tried it, struck pay dirt, and opened the warped wood and screen contraption. Inside they crossed a veranda to a second entrance. This was protected from the weather by a heavy outer door, closed with a simple hook and eye. Behind it, a frame door required a second key. It took Jack only a moment to find it on his key ring next to the first.

Inside was an elongated lobby with a narrow horseshoe bar running the length of one wall. Behind it a row of black-mottled mirrors, draped with silver cob-webs, reflected the pine paneling opposite. A turned staircase at the end of the bar split the first floor in two. Beyond it, to the right, was a dining area. To the left, a wide hallway led to the polished oak floor of a ballroom.

"Wow."

"You like it."

She turned to him in amazement.

"How long have you owned it? It's like stepping back a half century, into the twenties."

He led her past the bar and into the ballroom.

"It was an investment I made... many years ago. But I've never been able to let it go. Never needed to. It's ... got sentimental value, I suppose."

"I don't understand."

He chuckled, more to himself than to her. After a moment he turned to face her.

"That wasn't the last time you set foot on this property, was it, Valarie, as a little girl with your mother and aunt and your nasty little cousins?"

Valarie cocked her head at him, remembering.

"Well, ... oh!" she laughed, raising a hand to cover her mouth. "Oh, God, I used to come here with Paul!"

"Paul?"

Her cheeks had flushed.

"Oh, I don't want to tell you about that."

"A boyfriend?"

She gave him a sheepish look and turned from him, then walked to a stack of furniture covered by a canvas drop cloth on the far side of the room.

"Tell me."

Valarie turned back to him with an embarrassed smile.

274

"Well, I wasn't supposed to be seeing him, you see. He was a hippy. My father hated him. I had to sneak around to see him my whole junior year. That summer, Paul and I met down here a lot."

She bent to peek under a corner of the drop cloth.

"Until one night my father gave me this funny look at the dinner table. He didn't say anything right away. I was clearing the table when he turned to my mother and said he never realized how well he could see the old Wyandott place from the fairways, clear across the canal. I looked up from the dishes, and he was staring right at me with this ... sad look. I'd been down here with Paul that afternoon. Boy was I was mortified. It was the last time we came here."

Jack allowed himself a smile.

"Your Dad wasn't the only one who saw you down here with your young man that summer," he confided.

She gave him a defeated sigh.

"Oh, boy."

He nodded, and crossed the room to stand beside her. "I'd come upon you quite innocently one day. Back then I was working in the Riverdale office. Once in a while I'd drive down to the bay and park for a few minutes after work. Steal a moment of peace and quiet before going home to my own kids. One day I looked across this--" he gestured back toward the porch, "golden hay field... and there you were, the two of you. You and the boy in the field jacket. George Lorraine's lovely little girl, right there on the brink of her womanhood, not knowing enough about life yet not to celebrate it. You were... so enchanting, the two of you. I thought of the painting, The Sailor and the Mermaid. The fleeting sadness of it. You seemed to have fallen from heaven ... to ... to decorate the beach at the end of my street... you with this sheet of shining hair cascading over your shoulders, covering him with it when you bent to kiss him."

He sighed, a deep, painful sigh. "I felt like someone had just pulled my guts out of me though my throat. I felt a hundred years old. I thought, 'I wonder if George feels like this to. I wonder if he's cutting fairways today for the tournament and sees his beautiful daughter from the course, frolicking like a colt with this boy in a ... a golden hay field by the sea.'"

She didn't answer. She was looking straight up at him, now, her lips slightly parted. Light filtering in from the high, dirty, ballroom windows played about in her hair and in her eyes.

Jack took her by the hand and shook it lightly.

"Stop that," he chided, and he bopped her on the nose with a fingertip. "You're giving me the wrong ideas."

But he only set his hand against the curve of her back to turn her toward to the dining room.

Seven

"You fucking bastard. You old prick," Dean seethed. He had pulled up behind the Miata in his Cherokee, and now he was rummaging under his seat for his Colt revolver. Being a supervisor he had had no need to carry a weapon on the job for many years, but he had continued to carry it in his civilian life, just as a precaution, in case some criminal tried to rob him, or rape his wife.

Now, as far as he was concerned, both of those unlikely eventualities were in progress.

TAKE IT EASY, MY BOY, TAKE IT EASY. NO USE THROWING THE BABY OUT WITH THE BATH WATER. IT'S HOWELL YOU WANT, ISN'T IT? NOT 25 TO LIFE.

"Right," thought Dean. That interior voice was making too much sense to ignore. There was no point in carrying this thing out like some imbecile who couldn't think ahead to the next minute. He was not a man given to spontaneous action. Indeed, he knew it of himself that he was often meticulous to a fault in his preparations for life's challenges. His plodding, exacting nature denied him certain pleasures, true, but he was not one who delighted in surprises. Rather, the perfect execution of a well-made plan was his greatest joy.

Dean shoved the Colt back under his seat just as he heard the screen door slap shut against its hinges through his open passenger window. He could not see them through the privet, but imagined Jack taking one last, lovesick look at his wife before they headed across the hay field to the car.

Dean put the Cherokee in reverse, then made a quick U-turn and drove, with exaggerated calm, back up toward the main road and the highway.

"That was odd," remarked Valarie as Jack came up behind her to open her door.

"What was odd, sweetheart?" The word was out of his mouth before he realized it. It made them both smile foolishly at one another.

"A car just came down here and turned right around and left. Didn't you hear it?"

"So? People do it all the time."

She dropped the subject.

"My father used to call me that."

She let him pull the passenger door open for her, then gave him an impulsive peck on the cheek before getting inside.

"What was that for?"

"Just thanks."

"Thanks for what? For bringing you here? I haven't even told you why yet."

"Well, thanks for that too," she said.

He looked at her and frowned.

"How did you know I was going to offer you the place?"

"It's obvious," she said simply.

"You're a little cocky, aren't you? Maybe I brought you here to dine on your sweet little neck. That's what you thought in the restaurant, isn't it?"

"You're not a vampire anymore."

"You want to bet?"

"I don't have to bet, you're as soft as butter, old man. You reek of humanity."

He walked around to the other side and let himself into the driver's seat.

"Valarie," he sat quietly when they were inside, his hand in his lap with the ignition key between his thumb and index finger.

"What?"

He took a deep breath.

"I want you to have this place."

"What?"

"I want you to have it. I think I've always wanted you to have it."

279

"Oh, right. Good idea, Jack. How the hell are you going to explain that to Mrs. H-"

"Damn it if you bring that woman's name up again I'll... throw you in the bay, so help me. Now just listen for a minute."

She waited for him to continue.

"I'm listening."

"Valarie, Joan doesn't know about this. She... we ... well as you probably know, we aren't getting along too well lately. Haven't been for some time. I have made investments in certain properties over the years, investments which she has not been privy to. Nor is she entitled to a share in them under the law as long as I'm alive, as they were purchased with money acquired before our union. Unfortunately, everything I own will go to her when I expire. This house... is an exception."

"I love that kind of talk. I just love it. How do you know you're going first? You got inside information? Hey, I've talked to people at the top and let me tell you, Jack, they're pretty tight lipped about that sort of thing."

"What I'm trying to tell you is that I'd like to leave it to you."

"Oh."

"I'd like you to stay here, if you mean to move back to Old Inlet. And when I'm gone...I'd like it to be yours."

There was a moment of uncomfortable silence. Then Jack looked over to Valarie and saw that her head was bowed, her face hidden from him by a curtain of shining hair.

280

She brought her sleeve up, passed it across her eyes and sniffled.

Jack's heart gave a thump.

"Valarie?"

He lifted her chin with a finger and her beret fell into the back seat.

"It's okay," he whispered, gathering her into his arms. "It's okay."

She crumpled the shoulders of his shirt in her fists and hugged him tight, sniffling against his neck.

"I told you, you weren't a vampire anymore," she murmured.

Eight

On the second day of June Valarie moved her things back to Old Inlet, to the old hotel on the bay at the end of Beach Neck Lane.

With her she took her grandmother's mahogany secretary, her father's maple dresser, and an assortment of kitchen paraphernalia she and Claude had collected during their brief marriage. Both of the gas stoves in the kitchen of the old hotel still worked. So did the Frigidaire, and a surprising number of smaller appliances (an ancient Mix Master, a Waring Blender, an eight-slot toaster) responded to a bit of loving care, a new cord or plug, or at worst a complete overhaul at Point Appliance and Hardware. The enormous cooler behind the pantry, with its floor-to-ceiling cabinets, remained inoperable. But at Jack's offer to hire a mechanic to fix it Valarie only laughed.

"What on earth would I do with more refrigeration? So far I've got a pint of Amaretto Coffeemate and a bottle of ketchup in the Frigidaire. I'm not exactly hurting for cold storage space."

All over the inn there were treasures to be resurrected. In the lounge she found a camel-backed sofa, covered in coarse brown

282

fabric, hiding under a painter's drop cloth. In the ballroom, shoved in a corner under a sheet, was a wing-backed armchair, a hassock, two tray tables and a floor lamp. In one of the rooms upstairs she discovered an armoire and a chest of drawers. In another she found an ancient, iron, double bed. These she hauled up to the top floor, to the brightest and largest guest room in the inn, and made that her bedchamber.

From the basement she carried up a yellowing Formica dinette with chrome legs and pull-out extensions, and three chrome legged chairs of the same ilk. She re-upholstered the chairs in apple-red Naugahyde and arranged the set together in a corner of the dining room, nearest the French doors, overlooking the edge of the canal. Later she clipped some wild roses from a rotting trellis behind the house, placed them in a long-necked vase she'd found in the pantry, and set them on a white linen cloth in the center of the dinette table. To Jack she referred to the spot as her breakfast nook, though it looked more an oasis, floating in a corner of the sand-colored marble tiles in the enormous L-shaped room. The rest of her things she left to Dean, who had been invited by Cecile to stay at the house in Pequot Bog, at least until Cecile and her mother were settled in and he had found a suitable alternative. This solution seemed agreeable to all but especially to Mrs. Dumont, who saw in Dean a touch of her late husband's meticulous nature, and welcomed his company.

In the evenings that summer, having no other source of entertainment, Valarie sat on the steps of the hotel's veranda, listening to the tide lap the beach and watching purple clouds streak across a crimson sun. Now and then a motor boat thundered across the bay toward Old Inlet Dock and sometimes a silent sailboat, a sunfish or a catamaran, would peak the horizon. On Sunday afternoons the Old Inlet Yacht Club hosted the summer races, and with her ideal vantage point at the end of Beach Neck Lane, Valarie shared the best view in the village with only the Lavin's, who lived across the street on the other side of the shingle. On those days Valarie would climb to the catwalk on the third floor and watch from the railing as the graceful ballet of boats made their slow progress, tacking back and forth across the bay to the finish line. Jack's visits were always arranged around his social and family obligations. He did not dote on her nor hover over her, although it seemed to Valarie that he was keeping a closer eye on her since it had become town gossip that the greens keeper's daughter had left her husband suddenly and moved into the old Wyandott alone. She knew he deliberately parked the Miata under the port-cochere at the rear of the hotel when he made his visits to avoid a scandal, and that he drove out of town to purchase the bottle of wine, the fruit and cheese and delicacies that he brought with him. He always arrived late in the evening, letting himself in with his own key to find her curled up with one of the cats in the ballroom, basking in the overabundance of time and space that surrounded her, at peace at last with solitude.

And she would share a few hours of that abundance with him, talking quietly or watching an old movie on the little television he'd bought her as a housewarming present. In unspoken agreement, they never discussed why or when he must go, nor when he would come again. But sometimes he fell asleep on the sofa, Amos perched on one arm and Andy curled behind the crook of his knees. When that happened Valarie would turn the T.V. off and watch him just a little while, reminded of her father's darkly handsome face as he slumbered, open-mouthed, in his favorite recliner, until common sense told her it was time to wake him. Then she would turn the T.V. back on, raising the volume until he stirred.

"Time to go home," she would smile, taking Amos' big body up in her arms and snapping the floor lamp on to illuminate the dark room.

And Jack would clear his throat and rise.

"I must have dozed."

"Yeah, me too," she would agree for his sake.

And Jack would sigh, slip on his shoes, give her a tepid kiss good-by and find his way out. It was a peaceful enough arrangement. If her life was not happy, it was at least reliably vacant. And if her friendship with Jack was not passionate, it was at least loving. To Valarie, it seemed she was home at last.

285

To Jack, it seemed as if all of his aching desires, all of his hungers, had fallen asleep at last, enchanted perhaps by his nearness to Valarie. But one evening everything changed when, returning to the port-cochere for the car, he had the unmistakable clairvoyance that someone was watching him.

Now Jack had known for some time that Dean had been following his every move. He had known that the car Valarie had heard turning around at the end of the lane that first day was Dean's Cherokee, for he had been standing on the veranda and could see above her head over the hedges. Indeed he had seen the Cherokee pulling out of the Suffern office parking lot behind him an hour earlier, and knew even then that Dean would follow him at a distance to the Chowder Pot. In the first weeks of Valarie's arrival Jack had spied the Cherokee a dozen times, either tailing him from work, or hiding behind the privet at the edge of the lane, after Jack had pulled his car under the carport. In fact he had suspected that Dean might go so far as to harass Valarie, or even harm her and for that reason he had hired his own tail, a retired Suffern County cop, to keep an eye on Dean.

But this evening it was not Dean's paranoia that he sensed in the warm summer air as he approached the carport. This evening it was something worse. For something inhuman was watching him tonight. Something he had never stopped believing in. Something that had been silent for a very long time, but would not be stilled forever.

Jack waited until he was in his car and had closed his door. Then he turned on the ignition and whispered to the darkness, "Why are you here?"

As if called by the incantation of his question, the demon appeared beside him instantly, his terrifying dimensions compressed into the passenger side of the little car. One great cloaked arm draped over Jack's headrest as his mouth breathed the cool vapors of death into Jack's face.

"Why?" grinned Laroby as Jack choked back a scream. "Oh, Jack," he chortled. "Do not ask me rhetorical questions. Better to ask, why are YOU here, my little gelding! That is the question! Let us put our heads together and see if we can figure it out, shall we?"

And he palmed Jack's head and pressed it to his own as if to meld their minds.

"You disgusting freak, let me alone!" Jack spat through grit teeth as he shoved the beast away. "Get out of my life, Laroby, I'm finished with your kind!"

"How noble," said the vampire, straightening himself as best he could without putting his head through the roof. "Drive."

"Drive yourself, you bastard."

Laroby looked abashed. "Not very grateful are you, Jack? Would you prefer we go back inside?"

Jack gripped the wheel and clenched his teeth. But in the end he pulled out of the driveway and parked on the road.

"I won't take you back to my house," he said. "I'll never let you in my house again."

"Fair enough, Jack," purred the vampire. "We'll go to my place."

With that, a five-iron slammed into Jack's chest and took his breath. He felt himself pulled indelicately over the console and out of the car, then hoisted into the air, before he blacked out. When he came to he was hanging upside down from Laroby's shoulder, smothering on the velvety blackness of the demon's cloak as the fiend carried him through the wrought iron gates of the Old Inlet Community Cemetery. He opened his mouth to scream but was given no time to do so. Like a bag of dried bones he was tossed to the ground at the foot of an open grave. Clutching his bruised abdomen he spat a mouthful of dirt from his teeth.

"Up, up!" ordered his captor. "On your feet, now! Let's have it out, shall we? Man to man!"

Jack rolled over onto his back and looked up at the vampire, who stood like a pirate above him, his cloak sailing about his silhouette, his arms crossed over his chest. The black rectangular pit of the new grave yawned between them.

"Do you mean to put me in it?" Jack choked.

"It shall be filled," advised the vampire. "See to it it is not your cor'se that fills it."

"What in God's name do you want?" Jack screamed, rising to his feet. "How can you do this? I didn't invite you--"

"Oh, pleeezzze!" the vampire rolled his eyes.

"You think I want her don't you? You think I want to get her into bed. You think that's all I think of her. Well you're wrong. You're dead wrong. I wouldn't do anything to hurt that girl."

"Never kid a kidder!" chuckled the vampire. "I am the architect of your fantasies, you fop. I know exactly what you want to do to her and how you'd like to go about doing it."

"Get in," he ordered, and he grabbed Jack by the back of his neck and dropped him unceremoniously into the hole, then hopped nimbly down to sit at the edge, his long legs dangling into the pit above Jack's head.

"And, now you mention it, what is all this pious chivalry about, hmmm? Since when does a bit of playful fornication hurt anyone? What are you protecting her from, Jack, and who are you kidding? That little wench is as hot as a poker! You saw it in her when she was still a child, didn't you? Or will you give me a line of clap-trap about Mermaids and Sailors and 'the fleeting sadness of it' all? Oh, do spare me. No, you wouldn't exactly be deflowering her, if you took a little of that heat for yourself, now would you, Jack?"

He kicked his heels against the wall of the freshly dug pit playfully, then threw back his dark mane of hair and howled with laughter.

The pain in Jack's chest could only partly be explained by the blow he'd taken earlier.

"Just tell me what you want from me," he panted. "What do I do to be rid of you?"

"Of me? Of me? Would your life be worth living without me, you gutless, sexless, sanctimonious fraud? You don't want to be rid of me you want to be rid of Him!!!" And he pointed heavenward. "I'm the one who thinks up the entertainment around here!"

He watched Jack take this in, then he arranged his face into a pleasant and conspiratorial smile and slapped his knees.

"Now. Let us be honest with one another, shall we? You have desires for that woman. Normal, honest desires. It's why you bought the hotel and installed her in it. To be your private concubine. It's why you've been obsessed with her since she was a child. You just lost your nerve when she disappeared. You assumed the man upstairs was punishing you for being what he made you. An animal. A virile, healthy, animal. Not the feeble old fool I see before me, who has somehow forgotten where he put his parts. Be what He made you, Jack. Stop being a hypocrite. The great I AM doesn't like hypocrites. Do it."

He thought about that a moment and added, "Just Do It," with a smug smile, lifting his shoulders in a shrug.

Jack pushed himself to his feet and looked about in the moonlight for a foothold on the sheer dirt walls that surrounded him, but there were none to find. He was covered with damp earth, his nose and eyes filled with dirt, his tongue and teeth caked with grit. The walls of the grave seemed to be leaning over him, closing in about him. He had the hideous feeling that he had been in this hole, this very hole, before somehow. He looked up into the demon's emerald eyes and saw the horrific vision of his own burial reflected in them.

"Help me out, Laroby," he begged. "Help me out of this grave and I'll do whatever you want. Only promise me, promise me it isn't...mine."

"Not very pleasant, is it? Maybe you should have thought of this while you were playing dead with that woman all summer, eh? You're going to be reclining in a hole very much like this one for a long, long time, Jack. Better live while you have the chance. Don't throw it away for some pious misconception about good and evil. You're an animal. That's what He made you. Go ahead and act like one. Have your day in the sun before the sun goes down on you forever."

He leapt easily into the grave and pulled Jack out behind him.

"You were a delight to me, once, Jack. A true delight. You broke my heart when you turned away." He thumped his chest with his fist dramatically, looking skyward.

"Figlio mio," he sighed and bowed his head. "Ah, but all is not lost. A man can lose his soul in many ways. 'Les jeux sont fait,' as the croupier says. The wagers are placed, and the wheel is about to be spun. You may still be mine, Jackie my boy." He clapped Jack on the back, snapped his cape like a circus ringmaster, and disappeared.

Nine

Jack stood at the edge of the open grave in the moonlight shivering. His clothes were damp with mud from the bottom of the hole, and his first thought was to clean himself off. He could not be seen walking home this way, and it was a long walk from the cemetery to his house. He looked around for a faucet, made an educated guess, and found one on the edge of the gravel roadway circling the cemetery. It was only a foot of pipe sticking up out of the ground with a spigot at the top, meant for filling visitor's flowerpots but Jack sighed with relief when he turned on the valve and cold water sputtered into the metal drip pan under the nozzle. He cupped his hands under the stream and splashed his face, washing the grit from his eyes. Then he knelt and let the water run into his mouth and washed the grave dirt from his teeth. His clothes were still filthy but there was nothing to be done about that. He shut the spigot off, and without a backward look, started home.

After a ten minute walk he had reached the corner of South Beach Neck and Main. As he started down his street he saw a pair of headlights moving slowly up the lane.

"Oh, wonderful. A neighbor. Just the thing."

Jack was about to duck behind a hedge when the vehicle passed under a street light.

"Whitney?"

He stepped back out into the street and the dark blue Taurus pulled up alongside of him. A familiar baritone greeted him from within.

"I thought it was you. Jesus, Jack, you look like you fell in the shitter."

"Whitney, what in hell are you doing down here. I hired you to look after Valanchuk, not spy on me."

"That's what I'm doing," the big man leaned over to push the passenger door open. "Get in."

Jack hesitated, looking down at his soiled clothing.

"No thanks, Whitney, I'll walk."

"What the hell happened to you anyway?" Whitney's dark face, illuminated by the cabin light, betrayed his amusement.

"Would you please forget it and tell me why you're down here?"

"I told you. He's here. Down the end of the street, pokin' around in your car."

"WHAT?"

Jack looked down the lane in time to see another set of headlights moving up the road toward them.

"That might be him." He hopped into Whitney's Taurus and slammed the door shut. "Sorry about your car," he mumbled.

"It'll wash," Whitney pulled back on to the roadway and drove casually past the oncoming car.

"That's him," he agreed.

"What the hell was he doing in my car?" Jack wondered.

"Looked like he was putting something in the back seat."

When they reached Jack's Miata Whitney pulled up across the street from it and killed the ignition. Then he grabbed a flashlight from the floor and caught Jack's arm.

"You just stay put a minute," he gave Jack a stern look and hopped out of the car.

He crossed the lane and shone the light into the cab of the Miata, first the driver's window, then the rear, leaning over the little car but not putting his substantial weight on it. Then he got down on his hands and knees and checked under the engine.

When he came back he had a strange look on his face.

"You been doing some shopping?"

"What?"

"There's a bag full of stuff behind your seat, looks like cleaning fluid."

"There was nothing in my car. He put it there. Does it look dangerous?"

"Depends how crazy he is. If he's cooked enough he might have booby-trapped it."

"That's pretty far-fetched."

"So's leaving a bag of bottles in somebody's back seat."

"What should I do?"

"Go home. That's what you're paying me for, so you can sleep. I know a fella over in the bomb unit, owes me a favor. I'll get him out of bed. Have him come down and make sure the car's safe before we move anything."

"Whitney?"

"Yeah, boss."

"Keep this to yourself, okay?"

"Jerry's cool. Don't worry about him."

"Alright. "But no one else." Jack slipped him the keys to the Miata and walked home.

Ten

"Dad?"

"What is it, Lisa."

"Who's that woman at the Wyandott? The one that came the night Mom was car-jacked. Who is she?"

"Why, Lisa. Why do you ask?"

"A man stopped me today, on the way home from the bus. In one of those Jeep Cherokee's. He said he worked with you. He said he knew I was your daughter. He wanted to know if you'd moved out yet. If you were living with her over there. He said she was his wife."

"Lise, for God's sake, how old were you when I first told you not to talk to strangers, two? Three?"

"Dad, what's going on? Are you seeing that woman? Are you moving in with her? Are you and Mom getting a divorce? Is she that guy's wife?"

"We haven't established who HE is yet, have we. You stop and talk to some Bozo in a van."

"A Jeep. He was driving a Jeep."

"Lisa, don't talk to strange men in Jeeps. Just run to the nearest house and scream fire."

"Dad--"

"The issue is closed."

He was losing his patience with Dean Valanchuk. He had never liked the man, had always thought him an egotistical ass. It didn't help matters when he married Valarie, just like that. Just dropped his neurotic, overweight wife like a hot potato and snatched up Valarie, lovely Valarie, as if he deserved to have her.

To be perfectly honest, he had no use for the man at all.

The incident with the car had been one thing. It was almost too juvenile to take seriously. Had Dean really believed that his stupid idea would work? Had he really thought that the bottles of bleach and ammonia would tip and their contents mingle, like in some second rate mystery novel, right on cue, when Jack turned into his driveway? When the fellow from the bomb unit had opened the car the smell of ammonia had nearly knocked him over. Had Dean really expect Jack to ignore a smell like that and get into his car and drive it? Had he lost all touch with reality? Even if Jack had somehow ignored the smell, tipped over the bottles, and choked on the gas, didn't Dean think the police would be just a tad suspicious? Two open bottles of cleaning fluid behind his seat, just waiting to make the headlines?

298

And now he had included Lisa in his paranoid fantasies. Now he had crossed a line.

Jack was not going to sit idly by and tolerate that.

He knew his daughter well enough to know that she would never speak to the man in the Jeep again. He knew also that she would not mention the incident to her mother. Lisa, unlike any of his other children, was cut from the same cloth as he. She was a Howell, not a Mullen. She would not ask him about Valarie a second time. She would make her own assumptions, one of them being the truth, that her stodgy, steady, predictable father was human after all, and was in love with a woman who was not her mother. Perhaps she would assume that he was having an affair, that the mysterious beauty who had moved into the old hotel had stolen his heart, that he was going through some kind of mid-life crisis. But she would respect his secret, knowing with unacquired wisdom that she might one day chose the same path, and therefore could not condemn him for taking it. Mullens judged and railed. Howells lived and let live.

He would always, even if everyone else abandoned him, be able to count on Lisa, because her love for him, like his for her, was unconditional.

Jack visited Dean in the Riverdale Office the day after Lisa asked about his relationship with Valarie.

"I have two points to make to you, Dean, and I intend to be brief so listen closely. Number one. I am not sleeping with your wife. I have not had that pleasure. Though I must say that if I had, it would be none of your business since she is legally separated from you and has filed for a divorce."

"Number two. If you ever go near my daughter again, if you so much as drive past my daughter unexpectedly in a strange town, I will have you suspended from the Department, I will have you brought up on every criminal charge I can think of, and I will see to it that you never work in Suffern County again. You know I can do it. I will."

"Oh and by the way," he added, "I'm having you tailed. And I already have enough evidence to have you arrested for attempted murder. Don't piss me off, Dean. It's going to be a long drop before you hit the pavement."

He saw what he was looking for when he turned to give Dean one last look, one piercing, dead black glare, before he left. He saw hatred, oh yes, and a measure of surprise, but he also saw trepidation. It was this last he wanted, because it signaled the onslaught of reason. And reason had been something Dean had been operating without for too many months.

"Get some rest, Dean. Take a vacation. Get out of town for a while. Get hold of yourself. You're losing control. You're starting to think you're invulnerable and that's a dangerous illusion. You're not the only human being with a temper. You've got far fewer resources at your disposal than I. I'll destroy you if you come near my family again. I'll make it my life's work."

Dean had not said a word throughout this discourse. He sat behind his desk with his long legs stretched out before him, his hands in his lap, listening with the grudging regard of a bad dog to its master. His eyes never left Jack's face. Finally he spoke.

"You don't know what it's like, losing someone you built your whole life around. You blue-blooded prick, you stepped in shit the day you were born."

Jack expelled a resigned sigh. He had said what he had come to say. He turned to leave as Dean's hand shot out across his desk and caught his forearm.

"Is she in love with you?" he whispered.

Jack looked down at the pale hand that held him. He wanted to wrench his arm away and slap the son-of-bitch. Instead he grit his teeth and waited. But Dean was nothing if not tenacious. His grip only tightened.

"For Christ's sake, Dean. What does it matter? The point is, she doesn't love you. You can hunt her like an animal, you can watch her every move, you can poison every rival. She still isn't going to feel more than pity for you. Accept it."

Dean's grip loosened and slipped from Jack's forearm.

"I know that," he said quietly. "I just can't stand the thought of you having her. Can't you understand that?"

At this Jack gave an unexpected and humorless chuckle. He thought of the first time he'd heard Valarie's lovely French name butchered over the intercom with the unhappy suffix, Valanchuk. How he had hated Dean for that! The girl, the child he had adored all those years, his Valarie, married to this Slavic bastard. He shook his head.

"Yes," he answered. "Yes, I can." He left Dean to consider this.

That night he left the Miata at his house and jogged down to the Wyandott in shorts and sneakers. He let himself in and called through the house for her, tripping over the cats in the dark. But the place was empty. He trotted up the stairs to the second floor, then the third. She was not in her bedchamber, although her bed was unmade and appeared recently occupied. He pushed aside the floor length sheers that billowed at the open balcony doors and walked out to lean over the balustrade and scan the lawn, the shoreline. The shingle was a length of white ribbon sparkling in the clear moonlight. Beach grass and phragmites waved in the breeze across his line of vision, making it difficult to see the shore.

"Valarie!" he called, but the wind whipped the name off his tongue and lifted it over the roof behind his head. No one on the beach would hear him tonight, no matter how he shouted.

"Valarie."

He spoke the word to himself. The wind snatched it away from him like a jealous lover.

Andy jumped to the railing beside him and yowled up at him, his yellow eyes wide and glittering. Jack flinched, then batted the cat off the rail.

He peered out over the silvery lawn and into the blackened shadows down at the shoreline. Some intolerably sad melody was playing in the wind and in the rafters above his head. He felt a hot chill pour through his bowels like an emotional scald and he shuddered.

Then he saw it. A white shape lifting out of the breakers, bobbing toward the beach. He squinted, blinked. The figure was soaked in moonlight. It shimmered like a ghost.

Jack stepped away from the railing, stumbling once more over Andy before losing his balance momentarily and landing with a thump against the narrow end of a French door.

"Jesus." He kicked at the cat. Andy shrieked and scampered away. He had a thought of leaving quietly, as if he'd never come, padding down the stairs and out the door under the port-cochere like a burglar. The ghostly figure on the beach disturbed him, and he was not inclined to confront it. But when he reached the lobby he found himself drawn toward the veranda. He stepped out into the night and looked down at the shoreline from the top of the steps.

Perhaps it had been an illusion. His imagination. Or perhaps the specter was hidden now in the tall reeds bordering the lawn.

Then he heard the singing again, lifting across the lawn toward him in the moonlight. A soft, girlish alto riding the bay wind over the damp lawn. The same sad melody he had heard from the balcony. Like an angel weeping.

He felt the weight of his years pressing down on him as he descended the rotting porch stairs to follow that sound. A puff of salt air lifted his hair back over his scalp. A young girl's fingers. He hesitated, and crossed the dew-slick lawn to the shoal. At the edge of the reed grass he found the narrow path that led to the beach. He picked his way through, imagining the ticks and sand fleas accumulating in his socks. The path opened up suddenly onto a short strip of sand, choked with seaweed, and Jack looked about for the white silhouette he'd spotted from the catwalk.

"Hey, Jack."

The soft voice behind him startled him enough to make him jump, though it was she he had been searching for. He turned and lost his breath, struck dumb by the sight of her.

Her hair was a tangle of wet satin against her neck and shoulders. The short silk nightshirt, sheer as gauze, clung to the sculpture of her body, the sepia circles of her nipples peaking the fabric on either side of the open button front. Her skin was dark honey against the shimmering whiteness of the shirt. Moonlight reflected in the particles of salt and sand that coated the taut drum

304

of her belly. In her left hand she held the neck of a half-empty wine bottle against her thigh. Her eyes were cloudy with intoxication. "Whats'a matter? You look like you saw a ghost."

She took another step toward him and stumbled into his chest. He grabbed her instinctively, holding her away from himself by her shoulders. His effort caused the last few buttons of her shirt to give way.

His eyes dropped helplessly. The delicately striated pectorals along her breast bone, glimmering with droplets of salt water, begged to be tasted. The shadow of her sex darkened the hollow under her belly.

He shook her instead.

"What are you doing out here half naked? You want to be attacked by some animal? Button that up, Valarie, and get in the house."

But she only giggled, lifting the wine bottle to her lips to take another swallow. Half of it ran down her chin to course down the valley between her breasts.

"C'mon, lighten up, Jack. There's nobody down here but us vampires." She offered him the bottle. "I'm going back in. Hold this for me."

He took the bottle from her obligingly and let her go, assuming she meant to return to the house. When he realized she was headed for the water he came after her, grabbing her arm roughly so that she spun around and landed against him with a soft thump. His shirt took the wet imprint of her shape and he moaned.

"Aw, come on, come in with me. Don't be such an old geezer." She tugged his shirt.

"Valarie, please. You're drunk, sweetheart. Let me take you back to the house and put you to bed."

She pulled out of his grasp and frowned, her mouth a piece of soft, sienna fruit. "You don't own me."

She started for the water, then turned abruptly back to him.

"And you're not my father either," she considered, snatching the bottle from him. "So what if I'm drunk. I'm bored. I'm lonely. I wanna have some fun."

She started back toward the water. This time, when he caught her arm, she slipped out of his hands and fell down on the sand on her bottom. That made her tumble over with uncontrollable laughter. She laughed until she lost her breath and choked.

"Valarie, for God's sake," he begged. He sank to one knee beside her, gathering her against himself. Even as he did it he knew it was a mistake. She wrapped her arms around him and the little nightshirt fell open further so that her sand-jeweled breast pressed his shirt. He grit his teeth and began to rise with her to his feet.

"M-m-m-m-m," she nuzzled his neck, murmuring against his ear.

"Let's play," she cooed, and lifting herself up on her feet unexpectedly she shoved her weight into him, expertly knocking him down into the sand underneath her.

Now he was on his back and she was straddling his middle on her knees, nothing but his shirt between her sex and his skin.

She leaned her elbows against his chest and kissed his mouth, salt and sea water tickling his tongue. She made a satisfied little sound and lifted her bottom off his belly enough so that she could slip her hand down to tug at the button of his shorts.

He snared her wrists in his hands and shook her a second time.

"Valarie, for God's sake don't do this. You don't mean it, honey. You're drunk--"

But she had already twisted one wrist out of his fingers and slipped her hand under his waistband, finding him easily, capturing the length of him in her hand. Now she leaned over to tug his shirt up and away from his stomach with her teeth.

He froze.

He was split in two. Though his heart was breaking in his breast, his body, the betrayer, had already reacted with violent readiness to her caress. For a moment he lay beneath her, stunned, caught under the lean-to of her soft thighs, a deep moan of defeat echoing in his throat.

The moonlight caught in her bay hair and shimmered playfully.

She lifted away the shirt and sat on him so that the silken heat of her sex scalded the bare flesh of his abdomen. With agonizing accuracy she pushed herself down on him until she had forced the waistband of his shorts back and could feel his body heat answering hers.

"M-m-m-n-n, you feel nice," she whispered, trailing kisses over the stubble on his chin and down his jaw to his ear as she reached behind her to undo his shorts.

"Jesus. God." With superhuman effort he snatched her wrists up into his hands once more before she reached her mark. She tried to twist from his grasp again but this time he held her firmly, his fingers easily encircling her narrow bones.

"Lemme go," she begged, tugging vainly against his strength. He had pinned her hands behind her.

"Will you behave?"

She frowned down at him miserably.

"Oh, okay," she conceded, pouting.

He released her.

"Where's my bottle? Did you drop it?" She looked around in the sand. "Oh, m-a-a-a-n," To his surprise she got off him abruptly and went to find it.

"Valarie." He arose with less agility. She had wandered down the beach to the water, in search of the wine bottle.

He was not going to make the same mistake twice.

"I'm going. If you won't come inside--"

"Wait, wait, I'm coming. I'm just looking for the bottle--"

"Leave it."

Valarie came up beside him. "Fine."

He looked down at her, puzzled.

"What's the matter now," he asked her as they started through the reeds. You're mad at me?"

"S'okay."

"Valarie, I'm not made of steel," he said, stopping her to give a gentle look of reproach.

"Yes you are," she pouted.

"Come on, you don't really want that from me."

They had reached the lawn.

"Oh, you read minds, too?"

"What's that supposed to mean?"

"It means you don't."

On the porch she stopped to button her shirt. He was holding the screen door open for her.

"That doesn't really help," he murmured.

She finished buttoning it and stalked past him into the house. He stared after her and sighed, watching her bottom twitch under the wet nightshirt.

He followed her into the kitchen where she had found another bottle of wine in the Frigidaire.

"You're going to make yourself sick."

"Too late." She walked past him back into the lounge where she clattered around under the bar for a glass.

"Was Dean very... attentive to you, Valarie?"

She shot him a queer look over the bar.

"Are you kidding?"

He cleared his throat.

"Valarie, beside being two decades your senior, I'm married."

She had found a goblet and was pouring the wine into it. Now she looked up from her task, a sudden, unhappy recognition in her eyes. She bit her lip.

"Yeah." She looked down at the glass and murmured, "I'm sorry," soberly.

"S'okay," he stared at her quietly.

She bent under the bar to find another glass.

"You want some?"

"No, no." He waved his hand, annoyed at her quick recovery. "I'm trying to make a point here. Will you please forget the wine and listen to me?"

She blinked at his sharp tone. Obediently, she set down the bottle and the second glass and came around the bar.

She stood under his chin, looking straight up into his face, all of her earlier playfulness gone. This was not the vixen on the beach. This was a child, scolded and guilty, waiting for punishment to be doled out by an angry parent.

It was more tempting to him, that innocence, than all of her earlier invitation. He took a breath and looked down into her face, into the root-beer-brown eyes, and whispered her name. Without thinking he caught her up in his arms and pressed his face into her wet hair. "What am I going to do with you, Valarie?"

She smelled of seaweed and salt. Under the wet nightshirt her skin was freezing.

"Jesus, you're going to catch your death."

"Too late," she mumbled, pushing herself away and starting for the staircase, snatching the goblet off the bar as she passed it. At the foot she turned around and gave him a sudden, serious look. She sat down abruptly on the bottom step, holding her wine glass between her palms and rolling it absently, like a piece of dough. When she looked up, her gaze drifted past him, out through the lobby windows to the dark porch.

"Don't you ever get hungry anymore, Jack?" she asked quietly.

"What do you think?" he answered.

She looked straight at him.

"I think you're on a starvation diet." She set the glass down onto the hardwood floor and clasped her hands together.

"The alternative is pretty grim," he replied.

She looked down at her untouched wine.

"I'm sorry if I scared you, Jack. You're right. I was bad to do that to you. I'm sorry."

"I can't believe I'm having this conversation." Jack shook his head, sliding his fingers though his hair.

"I did. I scared you."

He looked around him in the dark as if for a prompter.

"This is crazy," he whispered.

"I came back to set things straight and I'm just screwing everything up. One way or another, I keep making mistakes. I can't seem to get it right."

"It's not you," he said. "There's nothing wrong with you. You have no malice in you. It's intention that matters. Yours are always pure."

Valarie's lips were trembling.

"But I'm getting hungry again, Jack," she whimpered, and rising to her feet, she turned and started quickly up the stairs.

As if on cue, Amos and Andy galloped across the lounge and bolted up the staircase behind her.

PART SIX

One

In early August, Patrick John Howell flew home to Old Inlet to spend a few weeks with his family before returning to Johns Hopkins for his final year of medical school.

Lisa had informed her older brother in her last clandestine call that their mother had been sober for a week in anticipation of his arrival, that she had been downright civil to their father, and that she had been catering shamelessly to Lisa's every whim. Mom would not hear of him taking a limo from the airport, so in the end both parents had agreed to call a truce and endure each other's company long enough to pick him up, together, in the Electra.

Lisa had kept her brother well informed during his spring semester, and none of this new information should have caused him much anxiety. They both new, after all, how heavily their mother had been drinking since Kevin's death and that their parents were barely speaking. But it had almost seemed to Lisa that her brother's brief visit might end without her having to tell him about the woman at the Wyandott. And then, on his last evening, he opened the subject himself.

"So what's with the babe down at the Wyandott Hotel? That place has been closed up since we were kids. Kenny Weiss says she just moved in out of the blue this summer."

Patrick had waited until his parents had gone to bed to give her bedroom door a perfunctory knock and let himself in. Now he stood in the shallow light of her night stand lamp, leaning against the knob, the easy grin on his face indicating to her that nothing she might say could affect his casual attitude on the matter.

"Better not let Dad hear you call her that," she had said just as casually. She thought better of it almost immediately.

But it was too late. The flip comment was all she had to say to turn her brainy brother into a bloodhound on the trail of a fox. Patrick was the suspicious one in the family, often teased by their father for not having followed a more obvious career path in law. It was well known that no secret was safe for long once his curiosity had been piqued.

"I see." He rubbed his chin, considering. "So that's why they haven't mentioned it."

"That's why who hasn't mentioned what?" she shot back.

"Dad and Mom. It's the town gossip. Everybody's talking." He dropped onto her bed and grabbed a pillow. "So Dad's got an interest in this lady, hmm?"

"Patrick, don't start assuming things," Lisa rolled her eyes at him. "You always do this. You always make mountains out of mole hills. Just like Mom."

But it was clear he wasn't going anywhere until he was satisfied that he knew everything she knew.

"How should I know?" she said at last.

"Jesus, Lise, you live here, don't you? When did they start sleeping in separate bedrooms?"

"A few months ago."

"You don't think that's a little odd, kiddo?"

"She's been drinking a lot," Lisa offered in her father's defense.

"Maybe so. But you know something about that Wyandott woman you're not telling me." He crushed the pillow under his head of jet black hair and stretched himself out on her bed. Lisa groaned.

"Come on, Patrick, I wanna go to bed. Get out of here."

"Sure. As soon as you tell me about Dad's girlfriend."

"I didn't say she was his girlfriend! God!"

But Patrick only fixed her with his best unruffled stare. He had his mother's periwinkle blue eyes, his father's jet lashes, and some unknown predecessor's dogged determination. He smiled and his features softened, a dimple clefting his chin. His sister giggled. Her brother was hard to stay mad at.

315

"Come on Lise, I'm not gonna tell Mom. Is that it? Mom doesn't know? Shit."

Lisa sighed. "Ok. I think he's seeing her, but I'm not sure." She paused. "I think her husband works with him," she added.

Patrick got up from the bed and walked to the door.

"You're not going to tell anyone I told you, are you? Please, Patrick?" Lisa pleaded.

"Mum's the word," he made a zipping gesture across his lips and winked.

****

Shutting the door of his sisters room behind him, Patrick Howell slumped against the frame for a moment and sighed heavily. His stomach was full of knives.

How could his father do this? Hadn't his mother been through enough?

MORE THAN ENOUGH, came the reply.

And on its heels, an idea sprang to life.

He pushed himself from the door and padded down the stairs to the kitchen. He had an errand to run before he left for Baltimore in the morning.

Two

Patrick swiped the keys to his father's sports car from the rack behind the kitchen door and stepped out quietly into the evening. It was raining lightly, the kind of soft, murmuring rain that typified Old Inlet summer nights. Realizing he would need a jacket, he leaned back inside the dark kitchen and grabbed his father's windbreaker off its peg near the key rack. Then, drawing the black jacket over his head like a poncho, he closed the kitchen door softly behind him and jogged across the gravel drive to the car.

When he pulled out onto the street there was nothing else on the road, only a silver Grand Am parked on the shoulder a few houses down, in front of the Tuthill's place. Preoccupied with the task ahead of him he drove past the Grand Am heading south, toward the old Wyandott Hotel. When he reached the end of Beach Neck Lane he pulled the Miata to the side of the road against the Lavin's property and cut the engine. Across the street, on the third floor of the hotel, an orange light burned in a south window. Patrick considered. He would have preferred to hide the car behind the building, under the port-cochere. But driving his father's car up to the hotel at this time of night might do more harm than good. In a neighborhood as old and well established as his, everyone knew everyone else's business. Patrick didn't want the affair getting back to his mother because of his own blundering.

He slipped the black windbreaker back over his head and jumped out of the little car to jog across the street, the makeshift umbrella tented over his head against the rain. Finding no bell at the servant's entry he walked around to the veranda and banged on the frame of the screen door for several minutes until he saw a light come on downstairs.

A silhouette cut the light in two as the inner door opened and the mistress of the house stood in the outline of the doorway, hesitating for a moment before crossing the porch to the screen door.

Patrick was not ready for the woman he saw.

She was young, her face too innocent and unlined to be his father's mistress. Her hair was a sheet of satin falling straight over her shoulders in a chestnut cascade, untouched by bleach, unclenched by noxious chemicals. Her eyes were soft as a doe's. A doe startled by gunshots in a quiet wood. She did, in fact, looked startled, as if she beheld a ghost, and not the handsome, gentile young man she must see before her now.

"I'm Patrick Howell," he said after a moment of hesitation. "May I come in? It's very important that I speak with you in regards to my father."

She flinched at his name, her almond eyes widening to circles. Still she did not speak.

"May I come in, please?" he repeated. "I haven't got much time and I intend to say what I've got to say to you before I leave."

"I'm sorry, yes. Of course."

She stepped away from the door, raking her fingers through that silky rope of dark hair. Patrick had the sudden, foreign thought that it would be interesting to know what it felt like to touch it. He frowned at his own perversity and stepped past her into the house as she moved out of his way.

"I... you look so much like.." stammered the woman.

"Yes," Patrick finished her thought for her. "I am aware of your...intimacy... with my father." He drew his brows together and tried to look mature. He succeeded only in shocking the woman further.

She put a hand over her mouth, her eyes enormous, and stammered, "Oh."

Valarie had never in her life been quite so sure that she was finally witnessing an apparition. The young man at her porch door was the specter of her late husband, Claude Rossetti.

His striking features, his thick black head of hair, his pale complexion and bottle-blue eyes, even the handsome cleft in his chin, all bore, in sum, an uncanny resemblance to Claude.

This experience, shocking as it might be, did not frighten Valarie. On the contrary it filled her heart with a sickening joy.

But then the boy identified himself and her mind sank into a mire of all too familiar grief.

Patrick Howell? Jack's son? Not Claude?

Not Claude.

She stared at the ghost of her dead husband and felt her body begin its delayed reaction to shock. She pulled her robe around herself and fought to conceal the violence of it from the intruder. Still, her body trembled as if with hypothermia. The fingers of her throat closed, threatening to choke her.

"Might we sit down somewhere?" Patrick was studying her with intense interest, his bright eyes taking in her features, her movements. He was like a big cat watching a bird, all focus, all intent.

Valarie stepped back from the door and murmured, "Of course." Then she forced herself to turn her back on the beautiful apparition a second time, and led the way across the lounge to the ballroom.

There she stopped and raised her hand to offer him the sofa.

"Please," he gestured to the armchair, indicating she should sit first.

Valarie sank to the edge of the cushion.

"I understand you're having an affair with my father," Patrick said suddenly, still standing.

She blinked up at him. The mouth that accused her was Claude's mouth. Thin lipped, precise. She looked down the length of his body. He was tall. Taller than his father. Claude's height.

She shook her head softly, "No, no. There's been no affair."

"Am I correct in assuming my father works with your husband?" Patrick continued, undaunted.

It took her a moment for her to realize he was speaking of Dean. She nodded in the affirmative.

"That's pretty risky, isn't it Mrs.--"

"Rossetti," she answered instinctively. Then catching her error she frowned and shook her head, lifting a hand to her cheek, "no, no,..." but he cut her off again.

"Well, Mrs. Rossetti, don't you think Mr. Rossetti would be rather upset to discover this ... liaison?"

Valarie's brows knotted up into a little bundle.

"No, no. You don't understand, Patrick," she began again.

"Don't I, Mrs. Rossetti? I think I do. I think you've found yourself a sugar daddy in my father. I think you prefer my father's gifts of old money to your husband's paycheck. You're separated, is that correct? Does your husband know, Mrs. Rossetti? Is he aware of the set up? Or is he still supporting you as well?"

"I work," she responded, confused by his logic. "No one is supporting--"

"Spare me." He stepped closer, forcing her to look up at him from the chair at an uncomfortable angle.

321

"I want you to stay away from my father," he said, lowering his voice, and his resemblance to Jack became more apparent. "My family has been through enough. Are you aware that my brother was killed in a car accident several years ago? Do you know what that did to my mother?"

Valarie shrank against the back of the armchair as Patrick leaned over her.

"I... I'm so sorry," she whispered.

"Enough is enough," said Patrick. He closed the distance between their faces.

"Patrick, your father and I never--"

"Never what? Never slept together? Do you think I really give a damn, Mrs. Rossetti, what he does with his dick? It's my mother I'm concerned for. The whole town is talking. If it gets back to my mother that he's seeing you... I don't know what she'll do. But I'm not going to sit by and let it happen. I want you out of here. Packed and gone. I'm on a plane to Baltimore in the morning. But I have friends, Mrs. Rossetti, in the neighborhood. See to it I hear of your departure within the week. Or we start playing hardball."

He leaned on the arms of the chair, corralling her, waiting for her answer.

Valarie turned her face from him and swallowed.

"I don't want that," she whispered. "I don't want to hurt you, Patrick. I never wanted to hurt you, or your family."

322

"Then do as I say, Mrs. Rossetti."

"Very well," she nodded. "I'll pack tonight, I swear it."

Satisfied with her easy surrender, Patrick straightened.

"See to it," he said.

It was the last thing he said before he died.

Three

The explosion shook the rafters of the old Wyandott Hotel.

Seconds later, after a call to the police, Valarie was the first person at the scene.

When she saw the black Miata, its canvas top torn off, its contents, a twisting bloody shape that continued to move and moan although it was-- it must be-- dead, Valarie knew it was Jack. Horrified by her own helplessness as she watched the grotesque vision writhe in agony in the cab of the little car, she began to back away from it, her own screams piercing the night, drowning out those of the victim.

"NOOOOOOO! Not Jack, not Jack, not JACK--" she cried, yet she could not approach the suffering apparition, so hideous it was in the throes of death. Instead she froze as the monstrosity of her own guilt paralyzed her. For she knew, even as she watched him die, that it was because of her that he was dying.

Just then a pair of large hands grabbed her and pulled her back as a second explosion rocked the beach.

Valarie felt herself thrown to the ground under a body much bigger than her own.

"NOOOOOOOOO!" she howled.

Dean turned her around to face him, but she only cried out Jack's name again and again, balling up her fists and pounding on his chest with the strength of the insane.

Dean sighed. Then he lifted her into his arms and carried her back to the Hotel, forcing her face into his shoulder to muffle her cries.

"Jack?"

"What is it, Whitney?"

"There's been an accident--"

"Oh my God. Not Valarie?"

"No Jack. It's... your son. It's Patrick. He must have taken the Miata tonight after you went to bed. Took it down to the woman's place... It was booby-trapped, Jack."

"Is he ... did he survive, Whitney?"

There was a terrible silence.

"I'm sorry, Jack."

He had been careful this time. So careful! Instructed by evil, he had planned every move, every moment.

From a Soldier of Fortune magazine he had procured a manual on booby trapping, sold "for information purposes only." Once he had memorized the information and built the bomb, a simple pipe-bomb that exploded when fired by the ignition, he destroyed the magazine in the paper shredder at the Sharon office and packed the device in a guitar case which he then installed under a blanket in the rear of the Cherokee.

That night he waited for the Dumonts to go up to bed. Then he crept downstairs to the kitchen, lifted Cecile's keys from the key rack by the side door, and transferred the guitar case into Cecile's silver Grand Am.

When he pulled out into the cul de sac at 10:30 p.m. he hunched down in his seat and pulled the hood of his sweatshirt over his head, ever exercising the greatest caution, although Cecile's tinted windows were sufficient camouflage, especially on a rainy night.

By the time he arrived at the hotel he had convinced himself that he had, indeed, designed a foolproof plan. After planting the bomb, he would simply return to Pequot Bog with the rest of his equipment and the guitar case in Cecile's car. Then he would return the guitar case to the cellar where he kept his guitar and amplifier, return his tools to their proper places, wipe down the car, and go to bed. The only person who would suspect him would be dead. He was even beginning to believe he could convince Valarie to come back to him once Jack was gone.

But when he reached his destination and saw his mark pull out of the Howell driveway and turn south, toward the beach, his heart began to race so violently he nearly turned back.

It was that voice in his head, ridiculing him, egging him on, that finally gave him the courage to do what he had to do, and set him to it.

It was not long afterward that his plan began to fall apart. He had waited for the Miata to disappear down the road before he pulled off the shoulder and made a u-turn to head back toward the highway, then west to Half Acre Drive, which ran parallel to Beach Neck on the opposite side of the golf course. He drove to the end of Half Acre and parked the Grand Am by the bay. Then he walked along the deserted beach behind the course, carrying his paraphernalia in the guitar case, until he came up behind the hotel.

Peering out over the lawn into the ballroom, he could just make out a man with black hair standing in the thin light of the electric chandelier. He wasted no more time. He crossed the remaining distance to the Miata and set to work.

He had only just completed his task, and had trotted back up the beach into the reed grass behind the hotel, when his thoughts were interrupted. WHY NOT WATCH?

"Why not indeed," he thought smugly.

He could still see the shape of the Miata outlined against the glow of the streetlamps at the end of Beach Neck. He had intended to leave immediately. But he had no sooner turned back than a figure darted out from the privet hedge surrounding the Wyandott and crossed the street to the Miata.

327

The problem was, he knew something was wrong the minute he saw the figure, holding a jacket over its head against the rain, sprint to the car.

Because it didn't move like a man in his 50's, and it had left the Wyandott far too early.

Dean could not be sure, of course. But the movements, the youthful energy of the sprinter shocked him, sent a ripple of cold fear through his guts, made his throat open as he fought back a scream-- STOP! DON'T TOUCH IT!

Why was Jack, it if was Jack, leaving the love nest so early in the evening? Had they had a spat? Dean had watched his car on many a night, and never did Jack leave before two or three in the morning. It wasn't yet midnight. Yes. Something was fearfully wrong.

The next event completely unnerved Dean, who was by now too fascinated by the possibility that the figure sprinting to the Miata was not Jack, to move. Trussed up in the ropes of his own confusion, paralyzed by the fascinating concept that he hadn't thought of everything, Dean watched the explosion, saw the roof of the Miata fly in slow motion shreds outward from the vehicle, saw the little car cant to one side as a tire blew out, heard the horrible gong of doom that was the concussion, tolling over the empty bay in the stillness of the black night.

And then, as fear and self-preservation kicked in and he moved to make his escape, he saw the second figure, small and feminine, rushing toward the pipe-bombed car.

"Oh, Jesus! Valarie, no!"

Did he imagine a second explosion? Could he be sure the gas tank had ignited, or was a fire burning toward the gas line even as she stood, two yards from the smoking hulk, her hands in her hair, her voice a human howl of helpless desperation?

Dean ran toward her, covering the distance between them in a flash on his long legs, darting behind the privet so as not to be seen in the glare of the streetlights, and pulling her to safety as the second explosion indeed rocked the ground and lit the sky over the bay.

Dean instinctively hit the dirt and rolled protectively over Valarie's body in the hay behind the privet.

As the roar of the flames receded he looked down at the little package he was holding in his arms and sighed with relief.

"Valarie," he squeezed her against himself, tucking her head under his chin. "It's alright. It's going to be alright, honey."

But she was still sobbing, still repeating her incantation, "not Jack, not Jack," as he brought her to her feet and carried her into the hotel.

Four

The red strobe lights of the police units lit up the black sky above the bay at the end of Beach Neck Lane.

Three police cars, the Crime Scene van, and Whitney's Taurus were strewn about the shoulders of the dead end when Jack arrived in the Electra. Whitney's great dark shape materialized from a group of plainclothes milling about the Miata, and came toward Jack as he approached.

"Jack," Whitney, deliberately blocking Jack's view of the scene with his body, grabbed his friend by the arm and turned him back toward the car with brute force.

"You shouldn't have come down here. They're going to want you up at the Medical Examiner's office to identify him."

"Jesus Christ, Whitney, you were supposed to be watching him."

"I was, Jack, the Cherokee never moved out of the driveway tonight. I watched him leave work, followed him home. I'm a sitting duck in that cul de sac, had to keep an eye out for the Cherokee up at the other end of the street. All I can figure is he

330

snuck out of the house some by other means. Or had someone else plant the explosive."

"It was him. It was Valanchuk." Jack's eyes were glittering with an unholy light in the red glow of the police flashers. "Find him before I do, Whitney," he whispered through clenched teeth, "or you won't find him at all."

Then he yanked himself free of the big man's grip and started across the road toward the Wyandott.

"Leave it alone, Jack. Let the police handle it," Whitney called to his retreating back. But Jack had disappeared into the dark behind the privet hedge.

Valarie knew she had to get away.

This knowledge had come to her, as if by instruction, as she gradually realized that it was not Jack who had been killed in the booby-trapped car.

Dean had vanished after bringing her into the house. He had told her that he'd only come by to talk things over when he felt the first explosion shake the beach. Crazy luck. And a good thing, too, because she might have been injured in the second blast if he hadn't been there to pull her to safety. He would go back down to the scene now to find out what had happened to Jack. He'd come back and let her know what he'd learned.

After he left, Valarie's wits slowly began to return to her. Curled on the edge of the sofa in a trembling bundle, rocking back and forth like an autistic child, she had begun somehow to think clearly.

How could it be Jack? Jack hadn't visited her tonight, Patrick had. He had obviously taken the Miata without his father's consent, probably after his parents had gone to bed. But whoever rigged the Miata to explode hadn't known that. Whoever had set the bomb had intended to kill Jack. Instead, it was Patrick's mutilated body, moving and moaning in slow motion agony in the shelled car, not Jack's. Patrick, that mass of blood and torn flesh beneath the black head of hair.

Jack's son.

Jack's child.

And just as swiftly, on the feet of demons, came the comprehension that Jack would kill her for this. She was to blame. She was the reason Patrick had taken the car, to come to talk to her. She was the reason Patrick had been struck down.

Because of her, Jack's son was dead.

And he would kill her for that. Not as a man kills. But as a vampire. Lust and murder, inextricably married into one furious weapon. One hellish beast.

It was what he had wanted all along. And now he had his excuse.

Cold terror chased her grief and shock away, and set up shop in her bowels.

She must leave it, everything, the hotel, her job, her things, all of it. It didn't matter. She must pack a few articles of clothing, something to get her to the next town, the next county, the next state.

Vermont. She'd always wanted to live there. Somewhere cold and hostile. Somewhere he wouldn't think to follow her. Because if he ever found her...

He would tear her apart.

Struggling with her terror, terror that lulled her, paralyzed her like a siren's song, turning her to salt like the sight of Sodom, she willed her body off the couch and up the stairs to her bedchamber. There she pulled a small trunk from her closet and began to fill it with clean clothing. When she was finished she tossed off her robe and pulled on a pair of blue jeans, a man-tailored shirt and a pair of boots. Then she grabbed her leather jacket and slipped it over her shoulders as she hauled the bag down to the second floor landing.

The sound of the screen door slamming on its hinges stopped her in her tracks.

Dean?

Dean was back to tell her... Patrick wasn't dead! He was going to be alright! The police had gotten to him in time!

Valarie rushed down the lower staircase to the lobby.

"Dean!"

But the man whose silhouette blocked the doorway to the porch was not Dean.

A black shape, inhuman in its stillness, loomed in the red strobe light reflecting off the bay. Loomed and waited. Like a dark wolf who waits in shadow for a deer.

"Jack."

Valarie's bag dropped to the floor with a thud.

"Where are you going, Valarie?"

His voice was soft, almost kind. It raked up her spine like a shard of glass, splitting her nerves.

He began to advance toward her and the Tiffany lamp over the bar illuminated his face as he moved into its range.

His eyes were pitch. Shark infested. The frigid black depths of the ocean glimmered in them. His mouth, never generous, was a purple cut across his lower face. His skin was luminous, sleek. Waxen.

"Even now you call for your accomplice?" he murmured. "Where is he, Valarie? Tell me where he is and I'll only torture you a little while before I kill you. Don't tell me, and I'll take all of eternity."

Valarie, backing away from him as he advanced, tripped on the bottom of the staircase. She came down hard on the edge of the third stair and pain shot down her legs. She whimpered and turned to scramble to her feet.

But he was too fast for her. Instantly he caught her by her hair. He brought her up by it, slamming the "s" of her back against the banister as he drew her to her feet. He leaned over her, his eyes inhumanly black. His cold, dry breath brushed her cheek.

"I can tear you limb from limb, I can dislocate every bone in your body, before you die. I can keep you alive, Valarie, to die again and again."

He snatched her right wrist and slammed it against the rail, then caught her forefinger and with one thumb bent it backward. Valarie opened her mouth to scream but her mouth was stopped by the gag of his teeth and tongue. She felt a raw, hot explosion of pain shoot up her arm and elbow, heard the complex miracle of her hand bones snap in an eerie staccato riff as she collapsed against the wall of his body.

He began to drag her up the stairs by her hair, heedless of the bruises he inflicted as her body struck each one in its unconscious ascent. He was in no hurry. Better still if she should awaken enroute to the bedchamber.

On the third floor landing she began to moan. He picked her up, hefting her over his shoulder like a sack of bread, carried her across her bedroom and into her bath, where he dropped her carelessly on the tile.

"How many deaths will you endure for me?" he murmured to her as she came to. He was drawing water into the porcelain sink, his fist still tangled in her hair, and now he drew her up onto her feet again and pushed her against it, holding the narrow of her middle between his body and the rim.

"Jaa-Jack--" she gasped, her head drawn back by the rein of his fingers in her hair.

"Don't." He pushed her face toward the filling basin. Wide awake now she began to struggle, clawing with her good hand, shoving back from the little pool of death he had created for her.

"N-A-A, N-n-n-"

"Cats hate water, don't they? Let's start with drowning, then."

He shoved her face into the water, holding her easily, one fist wading in the river of brunette silk at her nape.

Within two minutes she had stopped her wild struggling. He lifted her unconscious face from the water.

"Too easy," he mused. "Wake up."

He lowered her to the floor, expertly applying pressure to her chest with one knee and blowing air into her lungs with rhythmic indifference. Presently she convulsed, spitting up a little water and coughing. Her eyes flew open as she gasped great draughts of air and began to hyperventilate.

He slapped his hand over her nose and mouth blocking her airways.

"Not so fast." He yanked her to her feet and shoved her before him back into her bedroom.

She landed on her face on the unmade white lace bedspread.

His eyes slid from her gasping body to the balcony doors and lit with interest, like a wolf who has wounded the fawn and now smells the doe coming back for it. He walked across the hardwood floor and pushed the curtains aside. The red strobes were still pulsing over the bay.

"So he comes of his own accord," he considered to himself, turning back to the bed.

Valarie was still gulping air, raised to her elbows on the coverlet.

"Take off that jacket," he ordered. She lifted her head, focused her eyes on him, and let out a howl of fear. She shoved herself off the mattress and darted for the doorway.

But he was too quick. He grabbed her by the collar of her jacket and yanked her toward himself. As she struggled away from him, he tore it from her back. Then he circled her throat with one hand and pulled her body against his.

"Isn't this what you wanted?" he hissed in her ear as he ripped the front of her white shirt apart, exposing her breast.

"I can hurt you in ways you never dreamed of," he snarled, but the sound of footfalls on the stairs drew his attention away from his victim.

"Leave her alone, you fuck, she had nothing to do with it!"

Dean was standing in the bedroom doorway, his silver Colt Special in his right hand.

"Let her go," he repeated.

337

But Jack only smiled, his viperous grin dead-white and humorless, cutting his handsome face in two.

"Now watch me destroy what you love best, Dean."

He stroked his hand down the narrow lane of Valarie's ribs for Dean's benefit and cupped one white breast indifferently in his palm.

"Leave her the fuck alone!" Dean aimed the barrel of the Colt at Jack's head, but Jack was holding Valarie up and against himself, making the shot a risky one.

Valarie whimpered.

Dean took a step forward.

And Jack vanished.

Instantly Dean's right arm was snapped apart like a chicken wing as unseen jaws caught his forearm and bicep and broke the elbow inward. Dean howled in agony but his scream was cut in two by a blow to his torso. He fell back against the door frame in a heap, clutching his shattered rib cage. Bloody vomit stained the front of his sweatshirt.

When Jack materialized again he was a dark shape at the open balcony doorway, his glittering eyes fixed on Valarie, who had backed into the wall beside the bed.

"I never touched her," he spoke in a deep whisper to Dean. "But now-"

He took a step toward her. She turned toward the wall and pressed herself into it, her eyes clenched shut.

338

Dean's eyes followed Jack as he moved toward his wife.

"That's right, Dean. Watch. I want you to watch." He spun Valarie around to face him and in with the same movement he cracked her, back-handed, across her face. She yelped and fell back against the wall, her head slamming into it. Her body began to slide into a crouch but he pulled her back to her feet by her hair and pinned her, so that the flat of his hand splayed across the caramel satin of her abdomen under the shredded white shirt.

Dean watched helplessly as Jack slid his hand over his wife's belly and unfastened the waistband of her jeans. She twisted away and he lifted his fist again and struck her, bloodying her mouth. Then he continued to slide his fingers down under the denim of her jeans until he had cupped her sex in his hand.

He stroked her roughly and she flinched.

"Don't you want me, Valarie?" he whispered against her mouth, tilting her chin with his free hand so that she had to look into the pitch nightmare of his eyes.

He splayed his fingers, opening her, and she cried out. When he moved his fingers inside her again it was to hurt her. She bared her teeth and snapped at his free hand.

He snarled, slammed her head back against the wall and covered her mouth with his again. Her body arched involuntarily, keening, as his fingers bruised her womb.

"Fucking bastard," panted Dean, falling forward on the floor to struggle toward his wife.

339

He found the Colt lying beside him and raised it with his good arm.

But there was no time to fire a shot.

In the blinking of an eye Jack had his throat.

"Enough. Imagine the rest on your way down."

And he hauled Dean out onto the catwalk and pitched him unceremoniously over the balustrade.

Valarie was on her feet the instant Jack released her. She flew across the bedchamber to the stairs, oblivious to her husband's death in the face of her fear of the vampire. She raced down the staircase to the lobby and hurtled across the tiles to the porch door.

Where she struck the unyielding barrier of his body.

"Time to die," Jack hissed, and clapped his hand over her nose and mouth as he pushed her to the floor.

It took less than a minute to suffocate her this time. When she was still he began forcing air back into her lungs again, rhythmically pumping life he did not have into her lifeless body. When she came to he turned her on her belly and tied her wrists with the tails of her shirt.

"No more games."

He ordered her onto her feet and up the stairs.

"Get on your back," he said when they were back in her bedchamber.

She dropped to a sit at the edge of the bed and looked up at him quietly, her defiance gone.

"On your back," he repeated, and she took a shuddering breath and leaned back as best she could on her bound arms.

"Give me your throat."

She tilted her chin up, her eyes downcast.

"More."

She sobbed once, then let her head fall back for him so that her throat was a curve of delicate muscle, arched toward him. Her hair folded into a shiny russet ribbon on the white linen coverlet beneath her head.

He set one knee beside her hip, leaning over her like a wild dog, to scent the blood heat along the column of her throat and down the indent of her breastbone.

Then he raised himself up on his hands to take one last look at her living face.

One last, before he bared his throbbing fangs and sank them into her surrender.

Instantly his mouth was filled with a sweetness he had never known. Euphoria flooded him, coursed through his veins. He sank down on her, mindless, intoxicated. His heartbeat filling his senses, embracing hers. He fell with her body clutched against his to his knees, and drank, and drank, until the rapture climaxed with her expiration and his soul fell back, without her, into the fruition of eternal darkness.

There was no ecstasy, only horror, for Valarie in the poisoned vampire bite. The initial shock of his hot mouth, the sting of his incisors, was nothing compared to her terror as he emptied her life into the vessel of his dead body.

A sickening panic filled her as his heartbeat overtook hers, like a lion bringing down a deer. It pursued its target at a gallop, heavy with corporeal strength, indifferent with want. She heard her own heartbeat fade under the throbbing dominance of his, felt her life ebb, saw the passive clarity of heaven beckon on white wings of light as she fell into unconsciousness.

An eternity of echoes, flashes of experience, her father's laughter, her fingers in Claude's insanely thick black hair, all spinning under the soft halo of shock that was her death. And underneath, the drum beat of the vampire's heart, beating her further into unconsciousness, casting her out of the garden of her humanity.

And up and up into another landscape, a new territory, her being fled, bounding away from the vacuum of his jaws, leaping ahead of the drumbeat of his heart, until it broke some surface, like a dolphin exploding above blue waters, leaping into the brilliance of a new Eden.

Valarie was free.

Epilogue

Jack was lounging on the camel backed sofa in the ballroom, watching a remake of "Dracula" on Homebox and sipping a gin and tonic.

The police had finally left the hotel after three hours of questioning and crime scene analysis. It was clear enough to them what had happened to Dean when they saw the man's body lying in a twisted heap on the steps to the veranda, his neck and right arm and rib cage broken (pulverized was a better term) by the fall. The man had simply lost what was left of his mind and suicided after he discovered that it hadn't been Jack, after all, who had been killed by his pipe-bomb, and that the jig was up.

Jack explained that he had come to see Valarie, (yes, he had been having an affair with her) and had instead discovered Dean putting together a satchel of her clothes in the bedroom on the third floor. When he confronted him, Dean pulled out the Colt. There was a struggle, during which somehow Jack had been able to wrestle the revolver away from the bigger man.

"What are you doing? What have you done with Valarie?" Jack remembered asking him.

"I'm taking her away from you. You'll never see her again," he had answered.

That was when Jack aimed the gun at Dean's head.

"Tell me where she is," he had said.

All this time Dean had been backing out of the bedroom onto the balcony. Now he looked over the rail and then back at Jack.

"You'll never have her, you bastard," he had said. And then he jumped.

"Of course, you won't find handprints on the rail," Jack had added. "or on her bag. He still had those gloves on, the ones he used when he booby-trapped my car. We have boxes of them at the office. The officer's use them when they handle On-Trak urine samples. He wouldn't have had any trouble rigging the bomb with them on, they're paper thin. I guess you must have found them on the body."

Valarie's absence puzzled the police more than anything else. They found the satchel where Jack had said it would be, upstairs, half packed and open, on the unmade bed. They had searched the hotel, every crack, every crevice of it, even checked the cooler, which was working now, and the ice machine behind the pantry. But they didn't find her. Nor had they found any evidence to contradict Jack's story.

Now they were gone. Even Whitney, who had hung back and had given Jack a strange, almost spooked look before he finally turned and left him in the lobby

****

Jack had to smile.

The police would not find Valarie's body.

Because Valarie was in the canal.

She wouldn't have begun to rot yet. He'd stuffed her in a few plastic lawn and leaf bags and filled them with ice from the machine. It was fortunate that he had had it fixed, over Valarie's protests, only last week. He was beginning to find it interesting how evil always seemed to be in league with itself, safeguarding itself even when the mind did not comprehend the significance of certain events and urges until after they had become part of a solution.

Jack put down his empty glass, clicking the ice in the bottom against the sides abstractly, and chuckled a little to himself as he rose from the sofa and walked toward the servant's entrance behind the kitchen. It was time to collect his little package from its watery hiding place.

He slipped out of the house and crossed the gravel to the edge of the canal. It took a few minutes to find the bag, which he had hidden behind a ridge of reeds and was visible only as a ruffle of black plastic above the waterline. That ruffle was the top of the bag, the only part that might let the murky brown water in to taint its contents.

But luck, as ever, was on his side. The bag had not leaked, nor had the tied end become submerged. He pulled it out indifferently and dragged it back to the house. In the cooler he opened it. Valarie was blue, but otherwise in rather good shape. Rigor was beginning to set in to the facial muscles, giving her cheeks a pulled expression, but the rest of her body was still limp.

Jack laid her out on a metal counter and pushed the cuff of his left sleeve up to his elbow. Then he grinned a jackal's grin and lifted his upper lip, exposing his two gleaming incisors.

With a single elegant motion he slashed his palm, dead center, and a lozenge of red appeared.

His black eyes raked down the length of Valarie's body.

He thought of her in his absolute service and he had to grin again.

What a lovely little zombie she would be.

The End

ABOUT THE AUTHOR

Susan Shepherd is a retired law enforcement officer who has spent most of her career interviewing criminals and writing reports for the Court. She lives on the North Fork of Long Island, New York with her husband, three horses and four cats.

www.ingramcontent.com/pod-product-compliance
Lightning Source LLC
Chambersburg PA
CBHW061926170626
46813CB00006B/2317